MURDER AT THE PARIS FASHION HOUSE

NANCY WARREN

Storm

This is a work of fiction. Names, characters, business, events and incidents are the products of the author's imagination. Any resemblance to actual persons, living or dead, or actual events is purely coincidental.

Copyright © Nancy Warren, 2020, 2024

The moral right of the author has been asserted.

Previously published in 2020 as *Death of a Flapper* by Ambleside Publishing.

All rights reserved. No part of this book may be reproduced or used in any manner without the prior written permission of the copyright owner.

To request permissions, contact the publisher at rights@stormpublishing.co

Ebook ISBN: 978-1-80508-109-8
Paperback ISBN: 978-1-80508-111-1

Cover design: Emily Courdelle
Cover images: Shutterstock

Published by Storm Publishing.
For further information, visit:
www.stormpublishing.co

ALSO BY NANCY WARREN

An Abigail Dixon Mystery

Death at Darrington Manor

Vampire Knitting Club

Tangles and Treason
The Vampire Knitting Club
Stitches and Witches
Crochet and Cauldrons
Stockings and Spells
Purls and Potions
Fair Isle and Fortunes
Lace and Lies
Bobbles and Broomsticks
Popcorn and Poltergeists
Garters and Gargoyles
Diamonds and Daggers
Herringbones and Hexes
Ribbing and Runes
Mosaics and Magic
Cat's Paws and Curses

Vampire Knitting Club: Cornwall

The Vampire Knitting Club: Cornwall

The Great Witches Baking Show

The Great Witches Baking Show
Baker's Coven
A Rolling Scone
A Bundt Instrument
Blood, Sweat and Tiers
Crumbs and Misdemeanors
A Cream of Passion
Cakes and Pains
Whisk and Reward
Gingerdead House

Village Flower Shop

Peony Dreadful
Karma Camellia
Highway to Hellebore
Luck of the Iris

Vampire Book Club

Crossing the Lines
The Vampire Book Club
Chapter and Curse
A Spelling Mistake
A Poisonous Review
In Want of a Knife

Toni Diamond Mysteries

Frosted Shadow
Ultimate Concealer
Midnight Shimmer

A Diamond Choker For Christmas

The Almost Wives Club

The Almost Wives Club: Kate
Secondhand Bride
Bridesmaid for Hire
The Wedding Flight
If the Dress Fits

Take a Chance

Chance Encounter
Kiss a Girl in the Rain
Iris in Bloom
Blueprint for a Kiss
Every Rose
Love to Go
The Sheriff's Sweet Surrender
The Daisy Game

"It was in Paris that the fashions were made, and it is always in the great moments when everything changes that fashions are important, because they make something go up in the air or go down or go around that has nothing to do with anything. Paris is the real thing in abstraction."

Gertrude Stein, Paris, France

ONE
PARIS

February 5, 1925

Abigail Dixon strode along Rue de l'Opera, headed for her new job as a reporter with the *Chicago International Post*. On either side of her, tall, ornate townhouses ribboned with lacy black balconies led up the avenue to the Opera Garnier, a fantasy of carved arches, green domed roof and statues that gleamed gold in the cold, gray light.

The streets echoed with the noise and chaos of electric trams, automobiles, buses and bicycles all in a hurry. She passed a boulangerie and through the steamed windows spied a line of customers chatting while they waited for the pleasure of a long baton of bread. The door opened and out came a man in a cap, a baguette under his arm. The yeasty scent of bread mixed with the familiar acrid smell of coal fires.

Paris! She'd think she was dreaming, except that in her dreams, she was never this cold. Her breath came in icy gasps and emerged in white puffs, but she hadn't been tempted to ride the great lozenge-shaped buses. There was too much to see, and she had too much energy to sit still. On her walk, she'd caught glimpses of the Eiffel Tower, the tallest structure in the world, a reminder that both her life and career were on their way up.

She walked so quickly, she nearly passed her destination. The front page of today's newspaper was pasted to the window. She skimmed the headlines: "Exposition of Paris Will Be Keen Magnet." "Boudoir Bandit Gets $20000." "Al Capone Takes Over Chicago Bootlegging."

She stopped a gentleman walking by in a black overcoat and homburg and pointed to the front page. "Pretty soon you'll see my byline on that paper. Watch for me. Abigail Dixon."

The man stared down his long nose at her. "*Les Americaines, mon Dieu!*" His French contempt was so thick, he sounded like he had pommes frites stuffed up his nose, wine fumes in his lungs, and tiny escargots rattling in his windpipe.

Undaunted, she pulled open the heavy glass and brass door and entered the newspaper building. She assured a suspicious young man at the front desk that she was neither a hysterical young woman looking to tell her story to the press, nor a radical with a bomb hidden in her handbag. She was a journalist with an appointment. She presented the letter of introduction from Charles Abernathy, her editor in Chicago for the past two years, addressed to Mr. Walter Strutt, managing editor of their sister paper in Paris.

She followed him up a flight of stairs and into a newsroom whose barely controlled mayhem looked and smelled so familiar, she felt she'd been transported back to Chicago.

The noise hit her first. The rhythmic clatter of typewriters, the sound of voices speaking urgently into telephones, the column printer grumbling out an article from Reuters all seemed to say, *hurry, hurry, hurry.* Abby's pulse picked up the rhythm. She longed to sit at one of the desks and get to work.

She smelled cigarette smoke, stronger than the tobacco they smoked at home, the smoldering coal in the marble fireplace at one end of the room and, as a top note, the acrid smell of deadline-induced sweat.

The room was rectangular, with high ceilings and long, elegant windows at odds with the jumble of desks, leaning stacks of newspapers, and the six men at work on phones, typewriters or with pencil and paper. There was a single woman in the room, a black telephone receiver wedged between her shoulder and her ear as she scribbled notes.

Once, this must have been the townhouse of a rich aristo, perhaps one of those who lost their heads in the revolution. Instead of housing rich dukes and duchesses wearing silks and dancing the quadrille, the room now hosted a slovenly crew of American reporters.

Her excitement dimmed when she faced her new editor. Walter Strutt did not rise when she reached his desk. He was lean, his skin so tight that when he sucked in smoke, she was uncomfortably reminded of the shape of his skull. He was so thin and gray, she suspected he had gastric trouble.

He squinted at her through his smoke with no hint of warmth or welcome. She leaned across his desk with her hand outstretched anyway, because she had manners even if he had none. "I'm Abigail Dixon. I'm so pleased to meet you." She thought for a second he'd ignore the friendly gesture. In the end, he squeezed her hand briefly and let go. Somewhat deflated, she sat down on the hard, wooden chair facing his paper-strewn desk.

He didn't say a word, just picked up Uncle Charles's letter and glanced at it as though her arrival was a surprise, though she knew she was expected.

"What are your interests, Miss Dixon?" he asked, finally. If he was any less enthusiastic, they'd be nailing the lid on his coffin. "The latest hairstyles? Fashion?" He took in her gray tweed skirt and straw-colored woolen sweater, the long brown hair she'd worn in the same simple updo since she was sixteen. "Perhaps pets? Cooking?"

"Pets? Cooking?" She shook her head so hard the pins threatened to fly out of her hair. "I want to write hard news. Especially as it affects women." She leaned forward. "The French Union for Women's Suffrage is organizing a march. I want to talk to women on the street, cover the demonstration. I've already spoken to the organizers." Pretty darn good, since she'd only been in Paris for five days.

A young reporter knocked into the back of her chair as he ran past. He glanced at the huge clock on the wall, swore, then sat at one of the desks without stopping to remove his jacket or hat. He flipped open his notepad, then bashed typewriter keys with the index and middle fingers of each hand. It sounded like he was lining up words and shooting them down with a Gatling gun.

The editor lit another cigarette. "Miss Dixon, I appreciate your enthusiasm." His tone reminded her of the bank manager's when he'd explained about the family money being all gone—patronizing and as though he couldn't wait for the interview to be over.

"Everybody calls me Abby."

"Well, Abby, first, the women's suffrage vote won't pass because the Senate will block it." He sounded so certain, when the vote wouldn't be held for weeks yet. She checked the urge to ask him sweetly where he kept his crystal ball.

"But that's just wrong. American and British women have had the vote for five years. We should—"

He held up a hand, stopping the flow of her words. "Second, our paper caters to the expat community and to the folks back home. You're here to write for the women's pages. Tell the girls about the latest hairstyles and the Paris fashions. We have seasoned newsmen for the hard stuff."

The seasoned newsman who'd just arrived got stuck for a

word and knocked his fist against the back of his head so his hat wobbled back and forth.

The Paris office was much smaller than that of its parent broadsheet, but she'd believed that meant more opportunity.

She held her teeth tight together to stop the rush of words from storming the barricade. When the hasty words had retreated, she unclenched her teeth. Nellie Bly would never have let herself be treated like this. She invoked the spirit of her heroine. "Mr. Strutt, I was top of my class at the University of Missouri's journalism program. In Chicago, I wrote extensively about how the expanding city is threatening farmland."

She drew a tear sheet from her bag and laid it on top of a mound of newspapers and what looked like the remains of an old sandwich. It was her only front-page story, and she was proud of her work.

The editor barely gave the page a glance. "Look, Abby, I'm going to level with you. The only reason you're here is because Abernathy assigned you to me. Says you've had a bad time back in Chicago and you need a change. I got a dozen reporters with more experience. You take the assignments I give you, turn your copy in on time, fact-checked, spelled right, and we'll get on fine. Understood?"

She snatched back her article and pushed it into her bag so fast, the precious page creased. Heat rushed up the back of her neck and prickled at her hairline. "Charles Abernathy told me this was a promotion."

Walter Strutt squinted against the smoke as he took another drag on his cigarette. Even the sharp exhale sounded like an insult. "Sure, it's a promotion. You're in Paris. The pay is two hundred and fifty francs a month." He saw her trying to do the conversion in her head and said, "That's fifty dollars."

"Oh." The same salary she'd been earning in Chicago. Fifty a month didn't go far back home. She'd heard the dollars would stretch much further here. She certainly hoped so.

He looked her up and down. "You're what, twenty-three?"

"Twenty-five."

"You're young. Enjoy everything Paris has to offer. Just stay out of trouble."

She wanted to tell Mr. Strutt to find another girl for his women's pages, but she'd traveled across the Atlantic in third class and, after paying for her first month's rent, had less than a hundred dollars to her name. She needed this job.

He pushed a paper toward her with fingers mottled by nicotine and ink. "You heard of Paul Joubert? The couturier?"

"No." She wasn't entirely sure what a couturier was.

"He runs a fashion house. All the girls rave about him. You've got an appointment to interview him Monday, get the new trends. Remember, you're writing for the dames who live here but can't afford designer clothes, as well as the girls back home. Housewives and factory girls who dream of seeing Paris. You want them willing to spend two cents to read about the new hairstyles and what the society ladies are wearing, so make sure you gush."

She took the page with a silent nod. Fashion was for silly women with more money than sense. She was interested in the plight of those who worked in sweatshops ruining their eyesight sewing, not in the rich women who wore the results of their labor.

She'd write a second piece exposing the working conditions of the factory girls. She'd show Walter Strutt she could write hard news, then he'd have to give her more interesting assignments.

"Come in after you've been to *Maison Joubert*." He glanced around. "We'll find you someplace to sit." Then he turned and raised his voice. "Ruth, come on over here."

The only other woman stopped typing and rolled her head on her neck, then rose. Her black hair was threaded with gray and was set in tight waves around a pale face. Her eyes looked tired, and most of her lipstick had worn off.

"Ruth keeps up with the who's who of Paris. Who's arriving on what ship, where they're staying, who they're entertaining. Who's back from the Riviera. Ruth will feed you stories she can't handle herself. Right, Ru?"

"Sure." She looked Abby up and down and didn't seem impressed with what she saw.

"You hand your first story to me, and after that, you'll give your pieces to Ruth. When she's done, you'll give the finished copy to Emmett." He waved toward a heavyset man with food stains down the front of his shirt. Emmett was striking a pencil through copy as though it were a butcher's knife carving up a carcass. "Understood?"

"Yes."

One of the three phones on his desk began to ring. "You give her the spiel, Ru. You know the one." And he made a shooing motion, dismissing her, as he picked up the receiver. "Walter Strutt." He grabbed a pencil and pulled a pad of paper close. "Yeah, Johnny. What ya got for me?"

Abby stood up and introduced herself once more. Ruth said, "So, Abernathy's your uncle." Her expression was as flat as the prairies.

She'd worked so hard to prove herself in Chicago. Now she'd have to start all over again. "We're not related. He and my father were friends." She thought about telling Ruth about the degree and her front-page article and decided to hold her breath for something useful. Like howling into a gale.

Ruth said, as though reciting a list of rules, "There are thirty-five thousand Americans in Paris. Almost as many British. That's our readership. If a tidal wave washes away Japan on the same day that an American hostess serves oysters Rockefeller at her daughter's engagement party, the oysters will lead. Got it?"

Abby nodded, trying not to sag with the weight of her disappointment. "Oysters Rockefeller. Let Japan sink. Got it."

The older woman looked at her and lowered her voice. "If you've come to Paris to find a husband, you'd have been better to stay at home. Half the French soldiers in the Great War were killed or maimed. Of the ones who came back, well, if they aren't broken in body, they are in spirit." She glanced around the room. "And the boys from back home aren't exactly the catches of the century." As though on cue, Emmett, the copy editor, emitted a loud, rumbling burp.

How many times must she tell them that she wanted to be a reporter? She wasn't a socialite with marriage on her mind. She wanted a career. She'd hoped the only other woman might understand, but Ruth seemed as contemptuous of Abby as the editor had been.

Paris was reputed to be forward-thinking and progressive, but from what she'd seen so far, their attitude toward women was from the dark ages. Pretty ironic for a place calling itself the City of Light.

TWO

When she emerged back onto the street, it was still bitterly cold. Abby debated taking the Metro, but she'd seen so little of Paris that she decided she could stay warm if she walked briskly enough. Her irritation was hot under her skin, and that helped.

She found her way to the Louvre. Another day she'd lose herself inside, but today she needed to move and continued through the gardens.

At the Pont des Arts, the smell of roasting chestnuts drew her and she bought a paper cone from a street vendor, cupping their warmth in her hands as she crossed the ornate metal bridge over the Seine. The trees were bare and skeletal, but still the view brought some of her optimism back. On the right bank was the Louvre, and on the left was the Institut de France, according to her guidebook, though that seemed a dull name for the lovely, domed building.

Upstream, Notre Dame overlooked the city, a saintly mother in prayer. There could not be a more elegant city in the world. She paused to look over the edge of the bridge and saw two fishermen sitting silently in a shallow-bottomed boat, their lines draped into the gray water. Ice laced the river's edges. For a moment she pictured her father teaching her to fish, her mother telling their cook to prepare the trout she'd caught, back in the happy times.

She finished the chestnuts and walked on toward the Jardin du Luxembourg. The guidebook promised that it was a place of calmness, good for quiet contemplation, which seemed an excellent destination for one who felt decidedly uncalm. Besides, it was on her way home.

She deliberately chose smaller streets to get a feel of the neighborhood. The Latin Quarter was where expats with more ambition than money settled. People like her. She stepped aside as a group of uniformed schoolchildren clomped past in their wooden shoes. A horse-drawn cart rumbled by on the cobbled street as two women shouted good-naturedly across the road to each other. A man in a cloth cap and wool overcoat swung past on wooden crutches. His left trouser leg was pinned up where he'd lost his leg at the knee.

She found herself on Boulevard Saint-Michel. As she headed for the park, she noticed the stone walls were pockmarked. She stopped and dipped her finger into one of the holes.

"If you're thinking they're bullet holes, you're right," a man's voice said from behind her.

Startled, she turned. The man had spoken to her in English. American, in fact.

He was about her own age, mid-twenties, with a boyish, round face, a luxurious mustache and intense dark eyes. He wore an ancient sweater, a threadbare jacket, and his hat perched on his head as though looking around for a better place to land. "How did you know I spoke English?" she asked.

"You walk like an American. Take long strides and look like you know where you're going."

If only that were true. She wasn't certain whether she

should be flattered or offended. "How do Parisian women walk?"

His eyes crinkled when he smiled. "To be admired."

She might be fresh off the boat, but she hadn't been born yesterday. "And you're absolutely positive these are bullet holes?"

"Yes, ma'am. I deal in facts. I'm a newspaperman."

Now her interest picked up. "Really? So am I."

He held out a hand. "Ernest Hemingway. And I should say I *was* a journalist. Toronto *Star*. Now, I write stories."

"Abigail Dixon. Were you here during the war?"

"Drove an ambulance for the Red Cross. But you can trust me. These are bullet holes."

"I believe you." She smiled at him, deciding she liked him.

"Thought I knew most of the pencil pushers, but I haven't seen you around. You new in town?"

"Yes. I'll be writing for the *Chicago International Post*."

"What's your beat?"

"The women's pages."

He must have heard her chagrin, for he said, "You have to start somewhere." Then he motioned to one of the cafés. "I'm usually at Les Deux Magots this time of day. Or Le Dome, Le Select or La Rotonde. If you feel like shooting the breeze after a hard day at the typewriter, you'll usually find me and some other newsmen. Be glad to introduce you around."

"Thank you."

He tipped his hat to her. "Be seeing you."

And then he walked past her. She studied his gait, but she couldn't see that he had an American walk any more than he had a British walk or a Hungarian one.

She turned back to the bullet-marked wall, thinking of what Ruth had said. She wasn't here to find a husband. She was here to start her life again after a very different kind of tragedy back home.

She looked longingly at the green-awninged café where Mr. Hemingway had gone but thought she'd wait until she'd worked a day or two before meeting her fellow scribes.

The Luxembourg Gardens were too large to be tackled today, and she was too cold. She headed home.

She pushed open the heavy black door of the fourth-floor walk-up on Rue d'Erable, a tiny twisting side street off Boulevard Saint-Michel. After a fortifying deep breath, she started up the first spiral of bare wooden stairs. She was sharing an apartment on the top floor with Vivian O'Connell, a friend of a reporter she'd worked with in Chicago.

So far, Vivian seemed to be an easygoing, if somewhat brainless, roommate, and the rent was cheap. Her bedroom contained a single bed with a black wrought-iron frame and a small wooden crucifix on the plaster wall above it. A heavy armoire completed the supplied furnishings. She'd bought an old table at a street market and lugged it up the stairs. On it sat her Underwood typewriter, a sheet of yellow paper already in the roller, awaiting a hot news story.

Hopefully hot enough to dispel some of the cold. Condensation froze on the inside of the windowpane. The apartment boasted three fireplaces with marble mantels, but the cost of coal was too high to keep fires burning during the daytime. She tucked her woolen scarf more tightly around her neck. The interview today hadn't gone as she'd hoped, but she refused to be disheartened. An inspirational quote from her heroine Nellie Bly was pinned to her wall: *Energy rightly applied and directed will accomplish anything.*

She and Vivian had their own bedrooms and shared a tiny kitchen, an even tinier bathroom, and a faded but rather beautiful main room with floor-to-ceiling windows that looked out over the street. She walked over and stared out the window.

So many people coming and going on the street below. How

many news stories out there, waiting for her to write them? Real stories. She simply had to make Walter Strutt see things her way.

* * *

Abby was attempting to make a very small fire act like a much bigger blaze when her roommate came in, huffing as usual from the climb to their apartment.

Vivian was a petite, curvy blonde, while Abby was a tall, lanky and athletic brunette. Viv had come to Paris for a year to recover from a romantic disappointment and had never gone home. She worked in a *parfumerie* and always smelled of flowers and spice.

"I had the most divine day," she said, slipping off her gloves but leaving on her navy cloche hat, matching woolen coat and even her boots as she crouched beside Abby's puny fire. "A man walked by the shop window three times, looking in at me each time, and then he finally got up the courage to come in. He was dressed very nicely and bought a bottle of our best perfume." She dipped her head coquettishly. "He sprayed it on my wrist so he could smell it. He was very charming."

"Let's hope his wife's wrist smells like yours."

Vivian opened her innocent blue eyes wide. "It's not for his wife, silly. It's for his mother."

"Sure it is." She hadn't known Viv for long, but still, she felt she had her roommate's measure. "And when are you going out with him?"

She dimpled. "Tomorrow evening. It's a good thing I bought that new hat." Unlike Abby, Vivian had every intention of finding a marriageable man in Paris. Preferably American and rich. She held her hands to the fire and looked over at Abby. "Why so glum?"

"My editor's not interested in my women's suffrage story. He's sending me to Paul Joubert, couturier, for some tedious fashion piece."

Viv let out a squeak. "Paul Joubert? There is no justice in this world. I and every other woman in Paris would give absolutely anything to step inside those hallowed halls and see the new Joubert collection."

"I would happily send you in my place."

"When is your interview?"

"Monday."

"Monday!" Vivian looked horrified. "But that only gives you a few days to get ready. What are you going to wear?"

She wrinkled her nose. "Who cares what I wear? I'm not a model. I'm a reporter. And I can't afford a new dress."

Vivian pulled off her hat, automatically smoothing her blond bobbed hair. "Abby! You can't turn up at a couture house looking like one of those displaced refugees."

"I can't afford new clothes."

Vivian shook her head. "I would lend you something, but you're so tall, I don't think I have anything that would fit."

"Nonsense. I'll be fine."

Vivian clicked her tongue against her teeth and stood. "Let's have a look at your wardrobe."

Since she'd filled half of her steamer trunk with her typewriter, the books she couldn't part with, and a few family photos, Abby hadn't brought many clothes to Paris. Her meager wardrobe didn't fill the armoire in her room, as black as though it were mourning the contents. Vivian looked critically at each piece and finally chose a navy dress with a sailor collar and a pleated skirt. "I suppose you don't have navy shoes?"

"Only my black T-straps."

"Make sure you polish them. And wear some lipstick."

"Gertrude Stein says that in Paris one can afford paintings or clothes."

Vivian looked at her with her guileless blue eyes. "And Vivian O'Connell says that in Paris one can either look at a work of art in a museum or dress well and *be* a work of art."

THREE

Rue du Faubourg Saint-Honoré was one of the most fashionable streets in Paris. In the chilly afternoon, the discreet brass plaques whispered the names of the top designers in the world: Vionnet, Lanvin, Poiret.

A couple of automobiles passed Abby as she strode along. One pulled over, and from the back emerged two women. Both wore fur coats against the chill, and one carried a tiny white dog. Everything about them, from their hats to their patterned shoes, proclaimed wealth.

She found the address for Paul Joubert and rang the bell. An elegant woman wearing a simple black gown and pearls opened the door. "*Oui, madam?*" She looked Abby up and down, and her fine French nostrils flared slightly.

Abby suddenly became conscious that her coat was from Sears and had cost $16.49 back in Chicago. A lot of money on her reporter's pay. She suspected one glove from the house of Joubert would cost more than that. "*Je suis ici a voir* Monsieur Joubert," she said in her schoolgirl French.

"And what is your name?" The woman replied in English. So much for Abby's schoolgirl French. Or maybe it was her wardrobe that gave her away as an American. She might as well have wrapped herself in the Stars and Stripes.

"My name is Abigail Dixon."

The woman glanced at her with sharp suspicion. "*Impossible*. Madame Dixon is already here."

Abby pulled herself to her full height of five feet, ten inches and gazed down at the much shorter woman. One did not become a top reporter by being brushed off so easily. "Obviously, I am not inside. I am standing here in the cold. My name is Abigail Dixon, and I am a reporter for the *Chicago International Post.*" She showed the woman the invitation that Walter Strutt had given her. "I have an appointment."

"A moment." The woman in black shut the door, leaving Abby standing outside. A minute later, the door opened, and an extremely stylish man stepped out onto the sidewalk to greet her. His manner could not have been more different.

He was almost her height, dressed in a black suit open to display a waistcoat that looked like an Impressionist painting. His spats were so white, he must never walk outside. His hair was black and oiled and his mustache a work of art. Dark blue eyes twinkled above a beak of a nose and a strong chin with a dimple in its center. He put out his long white hands and clasped her shoulders. "Miss Dixon. It is a pleasure to meet you."

And then he shocked her by kissing her on one cheek and then the other. He pulled away and grinned in an entirely charming way. "I see you are not quite used to our Gallic ways. One must accustom oneself. Please, come inside. I hope you enjoy to see my new collection, and I am at hand to answer any of your questions—or indeed, to take you on a tour of my atelier."

Here was the master himself, and not by the flick of an eye did he seem to notice her wardrobe, much less judge it. She liked him immediately and swept in on his arm past the disapproving woman in black. Her host indicated a wide stairway that curved up into the sacred firmament of fashion. Would that be enough gush for Walter Strutt?

"We have a few very special ladies in the salon, where I will show you samples of my new collection."

She followed him up a set of wide stairs to a marble-floored landing. Several corridors headed discreetly off this foyer, and double glass doors stood open, revealing a grand salon. Here the special few could view models languidly floating up and down the room looking as though wearing exquisite clothing was rather a bore.

Abby paused at the doorway and gazed about her.

The white walls had to be twenty feet high and were patterned in gilt molding. Huge, gold-framed mirrors hung on two walls, and where she imagined paintings might once have hung, large photographs of models wearing Paul Joubert creations stared down their chic noses at her.

Couches and chairs in gold and blue silk and velvet provided plenty of seating while marble-topped tables gave the ladies a place to put their tiny cups of coffee or crystal glasses of champagne.

Two models were in the room circulating. One wore a silk gown the color of a pumpkin with a drop waist and a matching coat. The other model displayed a gown that gleamed like the coat of one of Abby's favorite chestnut horses back home.

"You will find you are not the only American here today, Miss Dixon. And you are an experienced fashion journalist?"

She wasn't going to lie to him. "No. I really know nothing about fashion." As though that weren't obvious from her clothing.

He gestured with one arm, like the maître d' in a fancy restaurant, about to lead her to the best table in the house. "Then I have much to teach you. Come, enter my world."

She took a step inside. Four female customers were already

assembled. Two of the women clearly knew each other and chattered in rapid French as the model wearing orange turned, posing in front of them.

It looked to Abby as though the two Frenchwomen could have circled the room themselves and been mistaken for models. They looked fashionably gaunt. One wore a suit in pale green trimmed with fur, the other a drop-waist dress in palest yellow. Silk hose shone on their narrow calves, and both wore shoes with pointed toes. Soon she would know the terminology for all of these details, she realized with irritation.

As she turned to look at the other pair of customers, she stopped dead as she caught sight of a blond woman who had embraced the flapper look. She had a round face, big childlike blue eyes and a cupid's-bow mouth painted oxblood red. A long string of pearls hung from her neck onto a blue drop-waist with a beaded fringe. A mink stole adorned her shoulders. The woman was regarding the model posed in front of her with an expression bored enough to match that of the mannequin.

An awful tightness began in Abby's chest, as though fists were squeezing her lungs so she couldn't draw breath. *No.* It couldn't be Lillian. Not here. Not today. But it was. Lillian Dixon was the other American. Abby's only instinct was to escape before the blonde turned her head and recognized her.

Abby rapidly backed out of the doorway and grabbed *Monsieur's* arm. "Since I know nothing of fashion, could I possibly see your atelier first?" She spoke fast, feeling as though air were rushing in her ears. "I would so love to see how each of these wonderful garments is constructed so I can more completely understand the process."

He paused for a moment, clearly surprised by her request. Shot a quick glance into the room and back at her face, which felt hot. Then his urbane manner reasserted itself. "But of course, Miss Dixon. Please, follow me."

She hoped he'd assume her odd behavior was due to her

dowdy wardrobe when compared with those fashionable women. Why had she not pressed the woman at the front door who'd claimed Madame Dixon was already there? What kind of reporter didn't check her facts?

She tried to pull her wits together as she climbed up one more set of stairs. She couldn't afford to make a mess of her first assignment. No matter the provocation.

"This way, please." Abby felt as though she were entering yet another world. The elegance and tranquility of the display rooms was nowhere to be seen up here. This was a workshop. Rows of tables filled a long room, and seamstresses sat elbow to elbow at the tables. It reminded her of the dining room at her college, but instead of trays of food, each woman had a garment or piece of a garment in front of her. They were lit with gray light from the overhead skylights as well as large, electric lights.

The clatter of black sewing machines and a hum of chatter filled the air until a plump woman wearing a white smock rushed forward.

"*Monsieur!*"

Instantly, the chatter ceased. Even the machines stopped for a moment before the seamstresses continued with their work.

"Miss Dixon, allow me to present to you our *première,* Madame Ginette Bernard. The *première* is, as the name suggests, the number one in the atelier."

The *première* shook her head and blushed. She was about fifty, with iron-gray hair in no sort of style, her face devoid of makeup. Under the smock, she appeared to be wearing a shapeless black dress. "*Non, non, non!*" she protested. And then she spoke a sentence in rapid French of which Abby only understood the word *Monsieur*.

He chuckled. "She says I am the number one and she only keeps the girls in order. But she does a great deal more. *Alors,* it all begins in my mind, with a sketch, yes?"

Understanding he was about to explain his process, Abby

dragged her reporter's notebook from her bag along with a sharpened pencil, realizing that she needed to get her mind on her work. She flipped open the pad to a fresh page and nodded.

"Then my design goes to the patternmaker, who turns it into a proper pattern." He led her forward to where a woman was cutting white muslin around a paper pattern pinned to it. The scissors sliced through the fabric so quickly and easily, they must be razor-sharp.

"This is Hélène. She has been with me almost as long as Madame Bernard."

The woman bobbed and smiled and he translated. Then she bobbed and smiled again. She was a soft-faced woman of perhaps forty-five, with red hair pinned away from her face. She wore a gray skirt under her smock. These women might work with high-end fashion all day, but they all dressed plainly. Abby fit in much better up here with the working girls.

"We make each garment in muslin first so I can see the finished dress on a model and make adjustments. Once I am happy, then we work with the real fabrics."

He glanced, ever so subtly, at his gold pocket watch. "And now, if you'll excuse me, Miss Dixon, I must go downstairs and greet my other guests. I will have Suzanne explain you the rest. She speaks English. Better than me. Come down to the main salon whenever you are ready."

"Thank you so much, *Monsieur*."

Suzanne was about her age and the most glamorous woman in the atelier apart from the models and customers. She wore her black hair in a fashionable bob. Her eyes were heavily made up and her lips painted a vivid red. Under her white smock, she wore black trousers.

"I'm so pleased to meet you," she said. Her accent was British.

"You're English."

The woman smiled. "Half English. I grew up in France, was

sent to school in England and came back here to work. Someday I want to open my own couture house in London, and there is no better teacher than Paul Joubert."

Suzanne showed her the various stages of garment construction, and the sheer amount of hand-stitching was staggering. Tables of women and, now she noticed, a few men stitched crystals onto silk or bugle beads onto taffeta.

In one corner, a woman with enormous arms wielded an iron.

Suzanne was clearly more than happy to take a break from her own duties to show a visitor around. She earned a couple of sharp glances from the *première*, but nothing was said.

She led Abby out of the large workroom and down a hallway where their shoes tapped against the wooden parquet flooring. "In here we keep the fabrics. It's like a cave of treasure." She opened the door, and Abby caught her breath. Rainbows of silk reached from floor to ceiling. An entire wall was given to black fabrics from velvet to taffeta. Another wall was woolens. Her fingers itched to touch and play like a child.

"Isn't it simply amazing? During the war, the couture houses shut their doors, of course. There was no fabric. And even if there were, everyone was too poor to buy fashion. But now, we import silks from Persia and these wonderful wools from Yorkshire. I could—"

"Suzanne?" an urgent voice called and then spoke to her in French from outside the door.

"*J'arrive.*" She turned to Abby. "They need me to get the length right on a hem. It is my particular gown, you see. Stay in here and enjoy. Over there we keep samples of beads and special threads. I'll be as quick as I can."

Abby felt like a particularly plain dormouse as she walked among the gleaming bolts of cloth. A bulging scrapbook sat on a table. She opened it and discovered pencil sketches of gowns in long, elegant lines, and pinned to each page were fabric samples and tiny pieces of embroidery or beading. As her imagination fired, she could feel the luxurious silk against her skin, the hemline brushing her calves.

She imagined herself in the kind of dress she'd seen in Vivian's *Vogue* magazines, or on Lillian Gish or Louise Brooks in film. For just a moment, she was swept away in fantasy, wearing one of those designs, her hair a sleek bob, a cocktail in one hand, and three men fighting for the honor of lighting her cigarette.

She was yanked back to reality when she heard the yelling.

FOUR

Abby ran back to the atelier, toward the sound of angry voices, and found the red-headed seamstress, Hélène, shouting and waving her arms around, then poking the air toward another seamstress who suddenly rose and began yelling back equally passionately. In their loose, black smocks, they looked like squabbling crows.

Abby vowed to work doubly hard on her French lessons. It was too frustrating not being able to catch more than one word in ten.

Most of the other workers continued on with their tasks as though shouting matches in the middle of the atelier were not unusual.

Suzanne stepped over to where she stood and whispered, "Hélène is very protective of her scissors. And sometimes people borrow them when they shouldn't."

"Scissors? She's this upset about a pair of scissors? What would happen if someone borrowed her husband?"

"Already happened. And they didn't give him back."

"Ah." Now the fury made sense.

The arguing continued, and a few others joined in, obviously taking sides in the dispute. It might have escalated had not the *première* stood.

"*Silence!*"

Immediately the hubbub died down and all the seamstresses got back to work. Now all heads were down, and the only sound was of the machines whirring.

Except for the woman who'd lost her scissors. She rose and began to search for them, muttering under her breath.

"No doubt she left them in one of the dress fitting rooms," Suzanne said. "Come on, we'll continue the tour there."

Suzanne led the way down the stairs and explained, "When we custom-design a gown, it may take several fittings before the garment is perfect."

"Demanding customers?" Abby guessed.

"Yes. But also Paul Joubert. He says every woman who wears one of his creations is an ambassador for the House of Joubert. He takes his work very seriously."

Abby sensed a whiff of discontent and asked, "Is he a difficult taskmaster?"

"Oh, yes. But, as he says, 'to achieve perfection, one must be a perfectionist.'" That sounded like the sort of line "the girls back home" might enjoy reading with their morning coffee, so Abby paused to add it to the notes she'd been making.

They reached the lower floor and, instead of turning toward the display room, Suzanne led her down another hallway. "These are our fitting rooms. As you can see, they are completely equipped for alterations on the spot." She opened one of the doors. "I'd better check them all in case someone left Hélène's scissors down here. We're not supposed to borrow each other's tools, but sometimes if you're in a hurry..."

She shrugged. She might be half English, but that shrug was all French. Suzanne disappeared inside the fitting room. Abby was about to follow her when her attention was caught by the last room at the end of the corridor. The door was open, and a tail of mink snaked out like a beckoning finger.

She knew the owner of that mink.

Abby stood undecided for a second or two. She could hear the low tones of Paul Joubert, no doubt explaining his designs to the privileged clients in his salon.

Abby had panicked when she'd first seen Lillian, but now that she was over her initial shock, it was time to find out what that woman was doing in Paris. There were some things she wanted to say to Lillian.

She strode purposefully down the corridor.

Abby could feel how hard she was clutching her pencil and notepad and forced herself to relax.

As she reached for the fitting room door, she found her hands were shaking. She'd come to Paris to get away from Lillian and everything she'd caused, but the ugly past had followed her. Perhaps this horrible coincidence was a good thing. It was time to confront the woman who'd caused her so much pain.

She opened the door fully and then froze in place as she took in the horror before her. She didn't cry out or scream. She just stood there, as though her brain had stopped functioning.

"Abby?" Suzanne's voice seemed to come from far away.

"I think I found Hélène's scissors," she said in a high, tight voice she did not recognize as her own. The scissors had been plunged into Lillian's neck. She lay sprawled on the floor, one arm stretched out as though reaching for something. Blood soaked the front of her dress and the surrounding carpet. Her blue china-doll eyes stared blankly.

Abby walked quickly forward and dropped to her knees. "Lillian?"

Her hands were shaking as she felt for the pulse in Lillian's wrist. There was no pulse. The skin felt smooth and cool. "She's dead."

She heard a scream behind her. Suzanne was backing away, looking ready to scream again.

Abby rose and turned to her. "Get *Monsieur*. Immediately."

Suzanne's back bumped into the wall, and she nodded, so pale her lips were vivid.

What else? "Call the police. And make sure no one leaves this building."

* * *

Abby had imagined she'd get to know the police in Paris as a journalist. She'd never anticipated being interviewed because she'd discovered a murder victim.

Her queasiness had passed, but she knew she'd see that twisted face and the staring dead eyes during many a night to come.

Monsieur Joubert had taken charge immediately. Suzanne had run to find him. Abby had remained with Lillian. Somehow, she didn't want to leave her alone. Not like that.

"The police?" she asked when Monsieur Joubert came into the fitting room, where she was still kneeling beside the dead woman.

He muttered a few words in low French. "They are coming."

"She's dead." She was proud of how calm she sounded.

"Yes. And you must come with me."

"But, I'm a reporter. No. I need to stay." Her mind was whirling. She felt sick, sad and angry all at once. Surely, she should stay until the police came.

"And do what, Miss Dixon?"

She'd have argued but sudden illness made her comply. She'd be less than popular with the police if she polluted her first crime scene. Oh, she'd seen photographs. No one could work for a newspaper in Chicago, or even read one and not be familiar with the sight of violent death. But no matter how graphic the picture, it couldn't come close to being at the scene. It wasn't only the smell, but the tiny details that she knew would be etched on her mind forever. The expression of surprise in the open eyes. The feeling of violence and fear that hung in that small room like the steam from the irons upstairs.

He'd ushered Abby into an office containing a table and chairs. She had no idea whether the room was used for meetings or for cutting cloth. Perhaps both. She was happy to be quiet and alone. A nervous woman brought her coffee. Otherwise she saw no one. She heard the commotion in the corridors, though, and imagined police, the coroner, a photographer.

Abby was scribbling in her reporter's notebook when a tall man walked in. He wore his hair brushed fashionably back off his high forehead. Everything about him was large, from his build to his boxer's nose and uncompromising chin. His eyes were gray and seemed to see right through her. He wore a brown tweed suit with a woolen waistcoat and a black tie. Like her, he carried a notebook. "Mademoiselle Dixon?"

She rose. "Yes. I'm Abigail Dixon."

"I am Inspector Henri Deschamps."

"How do you do?" She held out her hand as though this were a social call. She had no idea what the etiquette was in a case like this.

"Better than you, I think." He clasped her hand briefly and then settled in a chair across from her and motioned for her to resume her seat. He set his notebook down so their two notebooks lined up vertically. His nearly touched hers.

A second police officer came in but wasn't introduced. He was a younger man and also carried a notebook, which he immediately flipped open.

Inspector Deschamps looked at her, and she forced herself not to fidget. He said, "Tell me what happened."

"What happened?" She shrugged helplessly. She could still

smell the butcher shop scent of that fitting room, still see the sticky red oozing down Lillian's throat and into the bodice of her dress.

Still see those eyes. Oh, those eyes. Open, with that innocent gaze that had so belied the woman Lillian Dixon had been. And the scissors. She blinked as though the gleam of those sharp, silver shears had blinded her. "A woman was murdered." Her voice emerged too sharp, too shrill. Nausea tickled her throat. She swallowed hard.

"And you discovered the body?" His English was excellent, and he spoke it with a slight British accent.

Of course, he already knew she'd discovered the body. Surely, *Monsieur* had told him. She nodded, repressing a shiver.

"Did you touch the deceased?" He spoke equably, no judgment in his tone, merely a request for information. However, those clear gray eyes were sharp.

She licked her lips and tasted salt from the sweat that prickled her upper lip. She'd never considered that she'd done a monumentally stupid thing until this moment. "I checked her pulse to see if she was alive."

He nodded. "Show me, on your own body, how you checked her pulse."

She took her index and forefinger and pressed them to her wrist. Her pulse skipped with nervous speed.

He watched her. "And there was a pulse?"

"No. She was dead."

He was so still, only his eyes moving. His stillness made her aware that she was tapping the toe of one shoe against the other. Probably trying to talk her feet into getting up and running. "You have blood on your dress."

She glanced down and shuddered. There was a smudge of rusty-brown at her knee, another stain on the hem of her skirt. She wanted to jump up, to tear off her clothes, to scrub her skin in the hottest water and harshest soap she could find. "I must have...there was a great deal of blood."

"You and the victim share a surname, I see." His smile was quite charming and oddly disconcerting in the middle of this interview. "But perhaps it is like *Martin* here in France. Many people share the surname and have no knowledge of each other."

Oh, how she wished that were true in her case. If only Lillian had never come into their lives. Never lured her father away from their mother with her innocent beauty and fragility, both of which were as false as her heart. "We were related in a way. She was my father's second wife."

He nodded. "Your stepmother?"

"Yes." Though she hated that term. No one could have been less motherly than Lillian or less like her true mother. He continued to gaze at her, but she refused to be rattled into saying more. The young officer shifted his feet and tapped his pen on his notepad before Inspector Deschamps finally spoke again.

"Both Monsieur Joubert and the other ladies who were in the salon believe you and Madame Dixon did not speak together in their presence. In fact, *Monsieur* tells me that when he would have taken you into the room where Madame Dixon was, you asked to see the atelier."

"That is true."

"You preferred to avoid your stepmother, perhaps?"

"Yes."

"And you don't seem overwhelmed with grief at her death."

A feeling very much like panic began to beat in her chest. "I am in shock, Inspector."

He dipped his head as though acknowledging the reasonableness of her comment. "And when this shock wears off? Will you mourn your father's second wife?"

She would not lie. That had been Lillian's way; it wouldn't

be hers. She shook her head. "That woman destroyed my family and caused my father's early death. My mother never recovered from the shock. It quite literally broke her heart. I will not mourn the woman who took so much from me."

"Some people might consider you have a strong motive for murder." Still in the same conversational tone.

She breathed in and out so fast she grew dizzy. "I didn't like her, but I did not murder that woman."

It was so quiet inside this room that she could hear a car drive past on the street down below. The inspector's eyes were like a deliberating jury, and she wasn't sure she wanted to hear the verdict.

"When did you last see Lillian Dixon alive? Before today?"

She thought back, rattled and dimly suspecting he was deliberately trying to rattle her. "At my father's funeral." Abby pictured the dismal day, gray and drizzling, the crowd of mourners. That awful black box lowered into the ground. Lillian, playing at being a widow, dabbing a lace handkerchief to her dry eyes. "That was in November of last year. November fifteenth, 1924."

Once more, he nodded. "My condolences. He was an elderly man, your father? His death was expected?"

She swallowed, her pain still raw. "He was fifty-two years old. Lillian had announced her intention to divorce him. He took a shotgun out and suffered a fatal accident. Lillian then played the bereaved widow." She experienced the familiar burning in her chest, the grief mingled with disgust at the woman's greed and insensitivity. Reginald Dixon's grave was still a raw oblong of fresh dirt when she'd taken all of her husband's remaining money from the bank and disappeared.

She hadn't left enough to pay the outstanding bill for his burial.

"How long have you been in Paris, mademoiselle?"

She was startled at the sudden change in subject. "Um."

She tried to think, but her mind felt fuzzy. "Eight—no. Nine days."

"Did you know Madame Dixon was also in Paris?"

"No. Of course not. I was assigned to come to Paris and cover stories for the *Chicago International Post*, my employer."

"It's interesting, is it not? That you should turn up at the same couture house where Madame Dixon was shopping."

"A horrible coincidence."

He looked at her as though she'd somehow disappointed him. "I am a policeman, Miss Dixon. I do not like coincidence. I do not like it at all."

FIVE

She was still reeling from finding Lillian dead. Now she heard a note in the inspector's tone that struck like a knife through her fuddled thoughts. She stared into those thoughtful gray eyes. They weren't cold or condemning. It was as though he'd seen everything people at their worst could do to each other and accepted that his job was to find justice. Did he think she'd killed Lillian?

She'd think so in his place. She opened her notebook and turned it to face him. "I tried to write down what I know—knew about Lillian Dixon. I'm afraid it's not much."

He glanced down at her scribbled notes and back to her face. "Why don't you tell me about her? Who is her next of kin, for instance?"

"I don't know." Somewhere Lillian must have parents, family, people who cared about her. How little she knew of her father's second wife. How little she'd cared to know. "Lillian said she came from Boston. She met my father playing golf." She swallowed. She needed to stay calm and not let this clear-eyed policeman see how much even talking about Lillian and her father made her insides burn.

The young officer took notes, but Inspector Deschamps watched her. "She said she came from Boston?"

Oh, he was good. "Yes. I don't think she did." How to explain what had only been a suspicion? "She didn't seem to know anyone in Boston. I suspected she chose it as it sounded so respectable."

"And she met your father playing golf, you said."

"Yes. He was passionate about the sport. They were introduced at his club."

"What was her maiden name?"

"She was a widow. Her name was Musgrave. Lillian Musgrave. I have no idea what her maiden name was."

"You never met any family? Friends?"

"No. Frankly, I rarely saw my father after he married Lillian. My mother was ill, and Lillian was not interested in a stepdaughter nearly her own age." Her gaze dropped to her notes, which blurred as she fought foolish tears. Perhaps if she'd seen her father, in spite of Lillian, he would still be alive. She'd been hurt, angry, helpless as her mother faded and died. Now she'd lost them both.

"Is there anything else you can tell us about Lillian Dixon?"

"She celebrated her birthday in July." She smiled slightly. "But I don't know the year. A woman like Lillian never reveals her age."

When Abby left the atelier, it was dark outside, damp and cold. She shivered, not only from the chill. The inspector had offered to have her driven home, but she'd refused. The thought of driving in a police automobile made her feel ill all over again. She turned her steps toward the Rue de l'Opera and began to walk, dragging in great lungfuls of air, but still, she smelled death.

A glance at her mother's gold watch pinned to her lapel told her it was nearly six. But Abby was familiar with newsrooms. They rarely slept. She walked to the *Post* building, and bracing herself with one more deep, steadying breath, she walked in.

How different she was from the woman who'd so cheerfully arrived for her first assignment only a few days ago.

She stood there blindly. The clatter and smell, the people busy at desks and phones all seemed like so many characters in a motion picture. She took a step forward, determined to keep her professionalism about her, at least until she got home.

Walter Strutt glanced up from the phone, saw her, and said, "Call you back." He replaced the receiver and stood for the first time since she'd met him.

"Abby," he said, coming around the desk. "How are you holding up?"

"You heard then?" At least she wouldn't have to explain the last few hours to him.

"Yeah, course I heard. I've got friends in the police who let me know when anything good happens." He quickly shook his head and cleared his throat with noisy embarrassment. "Not that this is good, obviously."

But she knew what he meant. The juicy murder of an American woman in Paris? That would sell papers and lots of them.

She remembered when Charles Abernathy had told her that her father was dead. The feeling was similar, as though she couldn't take in the truth. Even now, with Lillian's blood on her skirt, she half thought she'd dreamed the last few hours. She blinked until Walter Strutt's face sharpened into focus. "They took my passport. And my notebook." She wasn't sure which was the more serious loss.

She looked around and became aware that every reporter and staffer in the room was staring at her. "Where should I sit? I'll write the story so you can make tomorrow's deadline." She knew the rules. First write the copy, then collapse.

But Walter Strutt said, "You come and sit here. Tom

Paulson will interview you. He's already got most of the details. You can fill in some color." The word color made her flinch. Red, then rusty brown. Vacant blue eyes.

Tom was older, maybe in his forties, with thinning red hair and bad teeth. He glanced at the clock and then only asked her to confirm the details he'd gotten from the police.

Vaguely, she thought she should insist on writing the article, but she didn't seem to have the energy to argue.

When Tom turned back to his typewriter, Walter Strutt said to her, "You go on home now. We'll keep your name out of it if we can."

She nodded, like a child taking instruction. He glanced around. "Hudson, go get Miss Dixon a taxicab." He dug in his pockets and pulled out some crumpled notes. "Here. You take her home and then come back."

"Yes, sir." Hudson was a skinny redheaded boy with freckles. He was probably not twenty yet and appeared to be some kind of gofer. He treated her as though she were his aged grandmother, holding her elbow and helping her into the taxi. "I'm very sorry, Miss Dixon," he said as they headed out in the darkness.

* * *

When she walked into the apartment, Vivian jumped up. "You're so late! Tell me all about it. Were the gowns beautiful? Did you meet—" She caught sight of Abby's face and said, "What is it? What's happened?"

Haltingly, she told the story. Vivian grew pale as Abby recounted finding Lillian's body and the ensuing interview. Finally, Vivian said, "There's blood on your skirt."

"I know. I have to change this minute. And I must have a bath. I want to at least be clean when they arrest me."

Viv put her hands to her heart. "The police don't really think you did it, do they?"

"They took my passport. And my notebook. They said I'd be hearing from them." She felt dizzy with shock and, if she was honest, with fear. "I think, perhaps, they do."

Vivian stood suddenly. "I'm going to run you that bath. And I'll give you the special new milled soap I was saving for a special occasion. It smells like lily of the valley. And in the morning, we'll get hold of the American consul. You are not a friendless girl here in Paris, as they'll soon find out."

"Thank you." She'd expected Viv to scream or faint, and here she was acting with more sense than Abby. She had to pull herself together, to think. "A telegram. I must send a telegram to Charles Abernathy. He'll know what to do."

Viv nodded. "Write it out. While you're bathing, I'll send the telegram." She took another look at Abby. "And get a bottle of brandy."

* * *

The next morning, Hudson arrived with a message from Walter Strutt. "Take the day off, Abigail. Take as long as you need. I'll be in touch. Here's an advance on your salary in case you're short of cash." He'd signed the note with only the letter W. Enclosed in the note was fifty francs.

Now what? If she didn't have work to distract her, what was she going to do all day? Wait to be arrested? She felt at once bored, with no prospect of going into the newsroom today, and that time was running out.

She went in search of a newspaper. The kiosk on the corner had two English-language newspapers. She bought both and carried them to the closest café.

"Bonjour, madam," the woman behind the counter said as Abby approached.

"Bonjour, madam," she parroted. "*Café crème, s'il vous plait.*" She decided to splurge and sit at a table, which was more expensive than knocking back a coffee at the counter. She even asked for a croissant.

She sat down at one of the round tables. There weren't many people here at this time of day. A couple of women chattered away in a corner. A man sat alone, a coffee at his side, reading a letter. From the look on his face, he'd received bad news.

She sipped her own coffee, ate a bite of flaky, buttery croissant and then resolutely looked at the front page of the paper. "Woman Murdered in Couture House" read the headline in her own paper. The write-up contained, as Walter Strutt had promised, just the facts. Still, it was difficult to read about a murder she'd discovered without adding a lot of extra drama to those facts. She was most interested in the final paragraph of the piece.

Inspector Henri Deschamps said, 'No arrests have been made, but I believe we will apprehend the killer soon.'

The last of the croissant stuck in her throat. She rose slowly from the table. There must be something she could do to proclaim her innocence.

She had never felt so much an orphan or been so homesick for Chicago as she trudged back up the stairs to the cold apartment. She had to wait for Uncle Charles's telegram. He wouldn't let her down, she was certain.

When the sweating delivery boy arrived with the telegram, she tipped him generously and then ripped open the buff envelope.

Abby had thought fate could have nothing worse to throw at her.

She was wrong.

The telegram wasn't the expected reply from Charles Abernathy.

She read the telegram rapidly and groaned aloud. "No."

To: Miss Abigail Dixon

Received spiritual visitation last night. Believe you are in danger. On my way to Paris. Much love, Aunt I.

Signed Ida Penelope Tumulty.

Aunt Ida was her mother's oldest sister, a formidable woman who was a renowned spiritualist in Chicago.

Since Abby did not believe that ghosts came back from the dead with messages for her aunt, she assumed the story had made the Chicago papers already. Aunt Ida was right about one thing. Abby was in real danger.

In France, murderers were punished by the guillotine.

* * *

Abby took a deep breath when she reached Les Deux Magots with its green awnings, jutting like the prow of a ship into the sea of activity that was Saint-Germain des Près—cars, buses, trams and people walking rapidly, huddled against the cold. One hardy artist, wrapped in a thick coat and wearing woolen gloves with the fingers cut out, sketched.

Abby tried to school her jumping stomach, her jangling nerves and her shaking hands to calmness. She imagined she was Nellie Bly as she pulled open the heavy door. She'd discovered that if she acted confident, people were more likely to help her. And she needed help in the worst way.

She needed Americans, other journalists, who could help her navigate this legal system she did not understand.

It was late afternoon, and the bistro was crowded. Most of the booths and tables were occupied by elegant Parisians, smoking and drinking tiny coffees or aperitifs. They were reflected in the long mirrors. A waiter in a black apron and white shirt approached, but she'd already seen a familiar face and gestured to the crowded table before heading toward it. Mr. Hemingway today wore a disreputable old green sweater, a pipe held between his teeth while he talked.

She recognized no one else at the table. There were no women sitting among the group of men. She wavered before approaching such an intimidating group. *Confidence*, she reminded herself.

He stopped talking when she grew close. "Excuse me, Mr. Hemingway, but I'd like to talk to you."

He squinted at her through pipe smoke, then smiled at her in recognition. "You looking for more bullet holes?"

"Hem, you're a married man." A portly man in a black suit turned to her. "You sure you aren't looking for me?"

She smiled briefly. "Actually, I'm looking for any journalist with ties to the United States."

Mr. Hemingway's smile disappeared. "Didn't you say you wrote for the women's page?"

A snort of laughter came from a long, lean man lighting a cigarette. "Hem knows all about fashion."

But he wasn't laughing. He stared at her with eyes that seemed far too old for his young face. "You in trouble?"

Thankful that someone understood something apart from foolish witticisms, she nodded. "May we speak somewhere? In private?"

He nodded once. Rose and ushered her to a tiny table in the far corner. He made some kind of signal, and instantly a waiter appeared with a jug of cold white wine.

"What's the trouble?" He didn't seem one to beat around the bush.

She glanced around and leaned closer, keeping her voice as low as she could, given the level of chatter. "I believe I am about to be arrested for murder." Then, briefly, she told him what had happened.

He sent her a level look with no hint of shock. "You kill her?"

"No. Of course not."

"What do you want from me?"

She drank the cool, light white wine to ease her dry throat. "I'm alone in a city, a country I don't know. I don't speak the language. I was hoping that you might be able to help." Her voice threatened to wobble so she swallowed more wine.

"If you're looking for sympathy, go home to your mother."

"My mother's dead. And they took my passport." She began to rise. "Sorry to trouble you."

When he smiled at her, she saw a charm that was at odds with his scruffy appearance. "Sit down. You wouldn't go home anyway."

Pleased that he understood even the tiniest bit, she shook her head and resumed her seat. "No. I wouldn't."

He poured more wine. "You like working for the women's page?"

"No. I want to write real news."

He sat back and gazed at her, those sharp eyes twinkling. "Well, kiddo, right now you're living a story. You've got a scoop. What are you going to do about it?"

"Do about it?" He was right. How could she have been so stupid not to see that if she wanted to write hard news, stumbling onto a murder and then being a suspect was a pretty darn good way to go about newsgathering.

"You want to be a real reporter? Show your editor you've got the guts and the drive."

"Honestly, I'm more interested in clearing my name. I don't

want my last article to be a first-person account of heading to the guillotine."

His lightning-swift smile lit his face again. "That's some good copy, 'Heading to the Guillotine.'"

"How can you make jokes about my possible demise?"

"Life is dark, kiddo."

"I'll go crazy if I sit around waiting to be arrested."

"Stop thinking like a victim. Act like a reporter. What's the story? If you didn't kill the dame, who did?"

"But—"

"Find the story. Then tell the story."

"But the police confiscated my notebook."

He leaned back, looked into the bowl of his pipe and then dug into his pocket for matches. "If you're going to give up that easily, you might as well pack what you'll need in prison." He lit the match and held it to the pipe, then puff-puff-puffed until it was drawing to his satisfaction.

She tried to hold in her irritation and sense of panic. Finally, he took the pipe from his mouth, pinched a bit of tobacco off his tongue and continued. "I've been writing stories for years. Fiction, I mean. Back in '22, my wife was bringing all my work to me in Switzerland. She packed everything into a small valise. Every page and scrap, including my copies. She got on the train with my life's work." He leaned forward. "My life's work. Every word. Tucked the suitcase under her seat. Then she went to buy a newspaper, and when she got back, the suitcase was gone."

"Gone?" Even in her own misery, she felt the shock of his loss.

"Stolen."

"Oh, my gosh. How awful."

"Some bum wanted the case, I guess. Maybe thought there were valuables in there." He shook his head. "Nearly killed me at the time. But it was the best thing that ever happened. You know why? I started over. Got sharper. This is your chance to do the same. You lost your notebook. All right. Start over. You write down everything you remember. You want to keep writing about tea parties and hats, or you want to write stories that matter?"

"Stories that matter."

"Then you get a good, clean notebook and you sharpen your pencil and you get back in there."

She felt her heart rate quicken. "I will, thank you."

"Look forward to reading your stuff."

She got up to leave, and he said, "Oh, and one more piece of advice. Don't talk to any of the other reporters, or you'll get scooped on your own story."

SIX

As Abby walked to the door, she caught a glimpse of a man watching her, his face reflected in the mirror. As their gazes connected, he lost interest, which didn't surprise her. In a city of sophisticated, well-dressed women, she hardly rated a second glance.

She pushed through the heavy door and back out into the cold, gray late afternoon. Still, she barely noticed the weather. She was rehearsing the argument she'd no doubt have with Walter Strutt when she tried to convince him to let her write the news story she had literally stumbled on.

Should she head straight to the newspaper office now and plead her case? *No*, she thought. Why, they hadn't even bothered to interview her further today, which made her certain that Uncle Charles and Walter Strutt were doing their best to shelter her from unpleasantness.

Better to take Mr. Hemingway's advice. He was a more experienced reporter. She would try to recall everything she could about the events she'd witnessed, details she'd noticed.

She'd barely arrived home when the second telegram arrived. This one was from Charles Abernathy.

Dreadful news. Hold steady, dear girl. Have alerted American consul. Hiring you best defense lawyer in Paris. Love, Uncle C.

She read it over several times and on each reading became more convinced that Uncle Charles believed she'd killed Lillian. His first instinct had been to hire a defense lawyer. If even he thought she'd murdered her stepmother, what hope did she have?

The clatter of Abby's typewriter filled the air as she related her ordeal to the readers of the *Chicago International Post*, feeling as though she were typing for her life. She'd been right there, this story should flow from her fingers, yet her initial efforts were terrible. She was yanking yet another sheet of paper out of her typewriter when Vivian walked in, bringing the scent of expensive perfume in with her.

Her roommate built up the fire and then she joined Viv on the sofa. "Did you hear back from your uncle?"

"Yes." She handed Vivian the telegram, and when she'd read it, Viv said, "That's wonderful news. I'm just sad that you'll be going home soon. I'll miss you."

"I'm not going home. I can't. Besides, a more seasoned reporter I met says I should write the story. I'm letting my own paper scoop me." She slumped back on the couch, feeling defeated. "But I don't even know how to begin. I should be writing a factual account of what happened, but really I want to tell the world I am not a murderess." She turned to Viv. "You believe I'm innocent, don't you?"

"Of course, I do." Which was more than Uncle Charles did.

"But Lillian was my stepmother, and I hated her. I could have killed her. I was there on the same day. It would have been easy to pick up those scissors and..." She couldn't finish the sentence. The vision of Lillian as she'd found her made the bile crawl up her throat again.

"Well, you don't hate me, so I'm not worried." Vivian

turned to Abby, and her blond curls bounced. "Anyway, if you did kill her, you could write one of those tell-alls. Like those dames on Murderess Row in Chicago." She sighed rapturously, clasping her hands together and holding them over her chest. "I loved those stories."

Abby rolled her eyes. She remembered all too well the string of women who'd been caught murdering their husbands or lovers in Chicago and then been lauded as celebrities. The female reporters who'd covered the trials were known as sob sisters because they'd befriended the jailed women awaiting trial, writing sensational stories about them.

It wasn't her idea of journalism, which was just as well since Uncle Charles had kept her writing about calmer topics. She wrote about the way Chicago was growing so fast it was sprawling into farmland and how the factories made the air toxic and barely breathable. Surely, these were issues that should engage readers.

But no. The glamorous murderesses had caught the public's attention in a way that civic planning never would.

In a way, Chicago had turned itself upside down since prohibition began. Alcohol sales had actually gone up, and when gangsters took over the booze trade, they became heroes, while married women who murdered their lovers, often while intoxicated, were heroines.

Vivian rubbed a spot of coal from her thumb and jumped up. "Wait right here."

She went to her bedroom and returned in a moment with a bulging scrapbook. She laid it on the trunk and opened the book. Onto the black pages, she'd pasted articles and photographs that interested her, mostly makeup tips and hairstyles. Here was a step-by-step guide to achieving the Marcel wave and then a photo of Vivian herself after a successful effort. There were photographs of movie stars complete with gossipy articles about their private lives. A newspaper clipping showed

Rudolph Valentino, sultry and mysterious as *The Sheik*, and Clara Bow, big-eyed and baby-faced. Vivian sighed over the young actress. "She gives people like me hope. She came from nothing and look at her now."

Viv turned pages carefully past a dried bouquet of flowers, a program from a Vaudeville show, a photo of Mary Pickford, until she stopped and pushed the scrapbook closer to Abby. "There. That's Belva Gaertner. She was so beautiful, and she dressed with such style."

Abby remembered the story well from the year before. "But she murdered her married lover, shot him in her brand-new Nash sedan." She'd been Belle Brown, a cabaret singer, when she married a wealthy and much older man. Soon bored with her new respectability, she'd begun drinking and running around with younger men until the night her married lover died in her car, killed with bullets from her gun. She'd claimed she was too drunk to know what had happened, as she posed for the cameras and chatted to journalists who'd followed her into Cook County Jail to record her every comment.

Vivian nodded. "Yes. But I believe she truly regretted her actions. She used to sing hymns in prison, you know. And she helped some of the other lady prisoners with their hair and showed them how to dress better."

Abby wasn't so starry-eyed. "She got away with murder, then showed the other gals how to do it."

She skimmed one of the articles Vivian had pasted into her scrapbook and read the following:

> "Why, it's silly to say I murdered Walter," she said during a lengthy discourse on love, gin, guns, sweeties, wives and husbands. "I liked him and he loved me—but no woman can love a man enough to kill him. They aren't worth it."

On the facing page was a step-by-step lesson on how Belva achieved her hairstyle, including diagrams.

Viv turned a few more pages until she came across a headline from the previous April from the *Chicago Tribune.*

Demand noose for 'prettiest' woman slayer.

Of course, Abby had seen the headlines and read some of the articles, but seeing them preserved and treasured by her roommate was like seeing them anew. The piece described how another murderess, Beulah Annan, had played a popular song on the phonograph, over and over, while the man she'd shot in the apartment she shared with her husband lay dying. She confessed to a drunken quarrel and that she'd shot the man because he'd threatened to leave her. Later, she changed her story to self-defense, even though he'd been shot in the back.

But what struck Abby, now that she felt some unwilling kinship for these women accused of murder, was the way they were described. Beulah was:

> The prettiest woman ever accused of murder in Chicago—young, slender, with bobbed auburn hair; wide set, appealing blue eyes; up-tilted nose; translucent skin, faintly, very faintly, rouged, an ingenious smile; refined features, intelligent expression—an "awfully nice girl" and more than usually pretty. She wore fawn colored dress and hose, with black shoes, dark brown coat, and brown georgette hat that turned back with a youthful flare.

She remembered feeling mildly horrified when Beulah, Belva, and several other women were found not guilty and set free, despite compelling evidence of their guilt. Viv tapped the scrapbook page with enthusiasm. "Those ladies became terribly famous. They got presents in jail, sympathy cards and flowers, even marriage proposals."

Abby didn't want flowers or proposals, but not being convicted would be nice.

Vivian said, "Those women needed reporters to tell their stories, but you could write your stories yourself. That would be even better."

"But I'm not a murderer." She felt she needed to be very clear.

"No." Vivian looked disappointed. "I suppose you couldn't pretend you killed Lillian Dixon? You'd be on the front page for sure. Even the papers back home, I bet." She looked Abby over critically. "And you could be as pretty as Beulah if you ever bothered with your appearance."

Abby felt a tingling in her typing fingers. "Viv," she said, jumping to her feet. "You're a genius."

Vivian looked pleased. "Gosh. No one's ever called me a genius before, unless it's about how I apply makeup. It's terribly exciting. Are you going to confess?"

She laughed, and it was the first time she'd felt like laughing since she'd discovered her stepmother's corpse. "No. Of course not. I'm innocent of this terrible crime. And I'm going to write about that!" She rose and began to pace back and forth in front of the fire as she plotted how to become her own sob sister. "Never mind the dry facts. Readers want pathos, emotion—golly, Vivian, you're right. They want a heroine." She pictured the headline. Stood and using the thumb and index fingers of both hands created an imaginary headline. "Girl Reporter, Embroiled in Murder!"

Her roommate nodded enthusiastically. "I'd read that in a minute."

She remembered what Ruth had told her when she'd been hired. If Japan sank on the same day a society hostess served oysters Rockefeller, the oysters would lead. If that was true, then surely an American girl reporter, telling her own heart-rending tale of being unfairly suspected of murder, would lead over a factual reporting of the incident by a male reporter who hadn't been present.

"And you will read about it. I won't write about my guilt but about my innocence. I'll tell the readers about my ordeal, hounded by the French police. Trying to clear my name."

Vivian nodded, approving the plan. "That's almost as good as if you did murder her." She touched her blond curls, thinking. "*Plucky* Girl Reporter," she offered. "In those true crime pieces, they always call the girls plucky."

"I'll be so plucky, I'll grow feathers," Abby vowed.

She felt a rush of energy, and her natural optimism began to return. "Thanks, Viv. That's a brilliant idea." She headed back to her room.

"But where are you going?"

"To work. I've a story to write."

Vivian's face fell. "But I thought we'd listen to the wireless and set each other's hair."

"I'll bring my typewriter out here if the noise won't bother you." And at least she wouldn't freeze to death.

She sat at the small kitchen table and began. In less than ten minutes, the bashing of typewriter keys ceased, and Vivian glanced up from the fashion magazine she was reading. "What's the matter? Did the plucky heroine run out of pluck?"

Abby tried to smile, but she felt as though she were writing for her life. When she fit her fingertips to the cold metal letters of her Underwood, she was reminded of steel bars in prison. Even the clacking of the keys echoing against the walls of their cheap flat sounded like jail doors clanging shut.

Inside, her emotions were as jumbled as her thoughts.

"No. There are no adjectives sufficiently pathetic to render this journalist sympathetic. The truth is, the sympathy will lie with the brave young widow slain after the tragedy of losing her husband."

"Then you're not a very good writer."

She sat back. She'd moved her typewriter into the front room so they could both enjoy the warmth of the fire and she could keep Viv company, but she had a second reason. Though she hated to admit it, she didn't relish being alone. Visions of death assailed her.

"You know what we learned in journalism school?"

"Who, what, when, where, why?"

She nodded. "That, of course. But also to be suspicious of coincidence. You know the kind of thing. If the congressman simply happens to be related to the president of the company that wins a hotly contested patent, perhaps it isn't a coincidence."

Vivian's pretty face creased in a frown. "I'm not sure what you're getting at."

"Simply this. Doesn't it seem odd to you that of all the couturiers in Paris, my father's widow should choose to be at the very place where I was covering the new collection?"

"But, Abby, how could she have known you'd be there?"

"I don't know. That's what's bothering me. Is this really a ghastly coincidence, or did she seek me out?"

Vivian put the magazine down. It was the latest *Vogue*, and the woman on the cover looked ready to jump into her roadster and speed off, her scarf floating behind her. Abby understood the impulse. "If she wanted to see you, why not come here? To the apartment?"

"Because she believed I wouldn't let her in?"

"Wouldn't you?"

"I don't know. I probably would have." She tried to think. "She always loved drama and being the center of attention. Perhaps she planned to confront me in the couture house."

"For what purpose?"

Abby reached forward and ripped the yellow paper out of her typewriter. She didn't need Charles Abernathy to tell her that she was writing purple prose. She screwed the page up and tossed it into the fire, where it flared for a moment, then curled and blackened. "I wish I knew."

"Come on, let's go out and get some dinner. My treat. A good steak frites is what you need. We'll go to the brasserie on the corner. Have some of that good red wine they serve there."

"I'm not hungry."

"You need to eat. You must keep up your strength. But I'm not going anywhere with you until you've combed your hair. And changed into a clean blouse," her friend admonished.

Abby reached for the comb on top of the dresser and glanced out the window as she did so. Two men stood on the street, smoking. They had the air of people who'd been chatting for a while and had run out of things to say. Both wore wide-brimmed fedoras and dark coats. She could not see their faces, but as she watched, one stamped his feet up and down as though he were cold. The other dropped a cigarette butt onto the pavement. There were several at his feet as though he'd been standing there a while.

A woman holding a child by the hand walked by, and the men shifted position to let her pass. As they did, the streetlight illuminated one man. He had a round face, black hair and small, dark eyes. There was something oddly familiar about him.

Think. She closed her eyes and mentally retraced her steps today. It took her a moment to place him, but she was certain she'd seen that man as she'd walked out of Les Deux Magots this afternoon.

He'd been drinking a coffee at a table near the door with another man whose back had been to her. Perhaps the same man he was with now. She remembered the moment their gazes had met in the mirror and he'd glanced away as though he'd found her not pretty enough to hold his attention. And here he was again, outside her home.

She began to think there was another reason he'd been watching her.

SEVEN

She ran out of her room and into Viv's. Where Abby's bedroom was sparsely furnished and lacking any personality, Vivian's room smelled of perfume, and there were clothes and hats on every surface. Two silk stockings hung over the wrought-iron headboard, and her wardrobe was so stuffed it wouldn't shut properly. A pink flounce of skirt peeked out as though begging to go dancing.

She grabbed Vivian's arm and said in a low voice, "Come and look out the window. Tell me if you recognize the two men who are outside our street door."

Vivian glanced up, clearly startled, but she put down her powder pot among the chaos of cosmetics on her dressing table and crept behind Abby to the window in her bedroom. She looked down. "Golly. Who do you suppose they could be?"

"Look carefully. Have you ever seen them before?"

Vivian shook her head. "I wouldn't know men like that."

As they stood staring down, the second man glanced up at their apartment. Abby took note of his long face and thin, drooping mouth as she pulled Vivian back from the window.

"Shall we stay in after all?" Vivian asked, sounding nervous. "There's bread and cheese in the kitchen."

"No. I want to see if they follow us. That's the only way to know if it's me they're watching."

"But—"

"No harm can come to us on a crowded street when all the world is heading out *pour le diner*."

"I hope you're right. But they've quite spoiled my appetite."

It took some convincing on Abby's part, but soon, the two women opened the street door. "Remember, pay no attention to those men. Pretend you don't even see them," Abby whispered.

Vivian nodded. They stepped out onto the cobbled street and walked the short distance to their local bistro. It was already half full. The windows were steamed, and a wonderful odor of garlic and wine wafted out as they walked nearer. Even with the noise of traffic and the babble of French voices, she heard the click of shoes following them.

She felt Vivian yearning to turn and stare, so she slipped her hand into the crook of her friend's arm and leaned in as though whispering girlish secrets. "Don't turn around. We'll get a good look at them if they follow us into the restaurant." Then she giggled as though she'd said something amusing.

Vivian's arm was stiff, but she played along. "I don't think I'm cut out for this spy stuff," she whispered back.

They crossed the street, and Abby pulled on Vivian's arm to slow her down and stop her racing into the perceived safety of the brasserie.

When they reached the restaurant, she immediately felt calmer. The familiar warmth, the waiters they knew by sight, the regular diners, the chalkboards scrawled with the daily menu, all these things were as comforting as a warm bath.

The waiters all wore crisp white shirts, ties and black aprons. One nodded to them and waved them to a table, too busy to stop. Abby settled herself with a clear view of the door.

Vivian collapsed into the seat across from her and gazed at her with wide eyes. "Well? Did they follow us in?"

She turned and pretended to peruse the chalkboard menu, keeping the doorway in her peripheral vision. "No. I don't think so."

Vivian let out a sigh of relief. "I couldn't have eaten a thing knowing those two ghouls were staring at us."

Abby didn't share that the long-faced man had paused in the doorway, scanned the diners as though contemplating entering, and then strolled past. She'd bet her Underwood typewriter that the two men were even now loitering somewhere where they'd have a good view of the door.

"Who would follow you anyway?"

"The police, I imagine." At least she hoped it was the police.

"Oh, Abby, I think you're terribly brave."

What choice did she have?

"Tell me about your date on Friday," she said to get Vivian's attention focused so she'd stop fidgeting and turning to the door every minute.

"He's taking me to the Ritz."

"He is?"

Viv dimpled. "Well, I asked Monsieur Chappelle where the rich people go to dine, and he said to start with an aperitif at the Ritz. Doesn't that sound divine?"

"It does." Monsieur Chappelle was Vivian's boss, a "nose" who created the perfumes Vivian helped to sell in the tiny shop on the Champs Elysées. He was a most elegant man, a Parisian by birth, and Viv consulted him on any matter of French etiquette or custom.

This was her third date with the man who'd met her when buying perfume for his mother. Or so he said.

Vivian glanced across the table and then fiddled with her silverware. "It's very sad. He's stuck in an unhappy marriage, and his wife doesn't understand him."

"I'll bet. She doesn't understand why a man she married is courting other women."

"He's asked and asked, but she won't hear of a divorce." She showed Abby a pretty pearl bracelet the man had given her. "It's very sad he's not free."

"Be careful, Viv. Nothing good can come of this. You could get yourself into trouble."

Her roommate was still regarding her bracelet as she said, "Not as much trouble as you're in."

The logic was twisted but unarguable. Abby wondered how long she'd remain a free woman. Now that she had detectives following her, she felt convinced the inspector was getting ready to pounce.

A good meal of steak frites with a half-liter of the house red improved their moods immeasurably. After dinner, they retraced their steps to their apartment. The two men slouched over from the opposite street corner, and once more she was followed by the echo of their footfalls.

Beneath their dinnertime chatter, she'd been thinking. Part of the reason her attempts at an article about the murder were so lackluster was because she lacked the most vital tools of the journalist's trade: facts.

She knew almost nothing about why her stepmother had come to Paris or why she had turned up at Paul Joubert's couture house.

She needed to know. Not only for her article but for some sense of how her father's wife had spent her last weeks and days on earth.

As she and Vivian climbed the stairs back to their apartment, Vivian turned to her, leaning against the wall for a moment to catch her breath. "I wonder why she was invited."

"I beg your pardon?"

"Monsieur Joubert wouldn't invite just anybody to get a glimpse of his new collection. If he did, I would have been there. But a famous couturier would only invite special customers and members of the press to see his collection before the official launch. Well? Why did your stepmother get an invitation? She must have been quite a customer."

Leaning against the wall and catching her own breath, Abby realized that Vivian was right. "Of course. How stupid I've been."

When they got back to the apartment, she went straight to her room, pulled out her Black's guide to Paris and searched the section on hotels. What she read immediately depressed her. "Paris contains above four thousand hotels, whose charges for board and lodging per day per head vary from fifteen to forty francs." Four thousand hotels? How on earth would she find out where Lillian had stayed if she had to search so many?

As they sat in front of the fire, she asked Viv, "What's the most expensive hotel in Paris?"

"I'm not sure. The Ritz? Le Crillon? Or maybe Hotel Meurice?"

She thought for a moment, trying to imagine what would have influenced Lillian's choice of hotel. "You follow the gossip. Where would British royalty stay?"

"If they're not staying in each other's houses, they put up at Hotel Meurice, I think. Why?"

"Because my stepmother followed the movements of British royalty like a religion. I'll start with Meurice."

Vivian looked concerned. "Start what?"

"I need to know why Lillian was in Paris. If I can get into her hotel room, maybe I'll find the answer."

Vivian grabbed her arm. "Abby, you can't! First, they've probably cleaned out her room already. There'll be nothing there."

She shook her head, freeing her arm from Vivian's clutches. "She'd have booked the hotel for a month at least if she was shopping for a couture wardrobe. I'm sure I've got some time."

"But—but the police. They'll have you arrested in a second if they find you breaking into a dead woman's hotel room. Especially since they already think you murdered her."

"Then they'd better not find out." She shucked off her coat and hat, then turned to her friend. "Don't you see, Viv? I've got no facts. Nothing to go on at all. The French police would love to pin Lillian's murder on me, but I know I didn't do it. That means the killer is still out there, and I'm going to find them. This is my big chance to prove I'm a real reporter." She sighed. "Also my only chance to prove I'm innocent of murder."

"I don't like it, Abby. I think you should sit by the fire and we'll break into the box of chocolates Edgar sent me." Edgar was her married beau.

Vivian had taken off her coat and hat and laid them beside her. She squeaked as Abby grabbed them up. "What are you doing?"

"We can't eat chocolates. I need your help. I want you to put on my coat and hat and the highest heels you own, then go downstairs and walk back to the bistro. Once you're there, you will ask if they've seen a packet of books you had with you and now you can't find. Of course, there is no such packet of books, but you'll have a look, anyway. Tell them you must have left them on the bus or the Metro. Then you'll come back here."

"Why?"

"Because those men out there will think you are me. While they follow you, I'll sneak out and head to the Hotel Meurice."

Vivian ran to Abby's bedroom window. "They're still out there?"

She nodded. "I need you to be my decoy."

"For what purpose? Abby, you might as well go to the police and confess to murder this minute!"

"No. I have to do this."

"You're crazy. We don't look a bit alike. This will never work. Those men are trained detectives. I'll end up arrested."

"It's dark out. Stay out of the streetlights and lengthen your stride. Walk like an American."

"I prefer to walk like a lady. I won't have any part of it." She crossed her arms over her chest and straightened to her full height, still a good few inches shorter than Abby.

"Please, Viv? Also, I'll need to borrow some of your finery if I'm going to get past the front door of a fancy hotel." She could sense Vivian about to refuse. She hadn't known her roommate for long, but she suspected she knew the way to her heart. "When I write my first-person accounts of my ordeal, I'll make sure they get your picture in the paper, too. We'll be heroines, Viv. Both of us."

With a hiss of frustration, Vivian stalked to her room and began pulling out clothes. "Everything will be ridiculously short on you."

However, by hanging a skirt precariously from her hips instead of fastening it at the waist, then putting one of her hats at an angle atop Abby's head, Vivian sighed and said, "This is the best I can do. Mind you put on some lipstick."

Abby hugged her friend. "Thank you."

"And if I get arrested, I will be seriously displeased with you."

"You know I'll bail you out," she wheedled.

Those big blue eyes did not look convinced. "Unless you're in the next cell."

However, a few minutes later, Vivian, wearing her highest heels, a dark scarf wrapped around her blonde curls and Abby's coat and hat, left the apartment. Abby stood to the side of the window in the darkened room, keeping the two men in sight. As instructed, Vivian crossed the street, keeping her back to them, and began to walk back toward the bistro.

She watched the rapid conversation between the two men. One hesitated and glanced up at the apartment window. She held her breath. If they left one cop to watch the apartment, then she'd never be able to sneak out. There was only the one front door to this building. But after a moment, the second man joined the first, and they followed Vivian.

With a quick breath out, she slicked on lipstick, grabbed her notebook, two fresh pencils and her tiny Kodak camera, pushed them all into her large leather bag, then slipped on her best gloves and left the apartment.

When she reached Boulevard Saint-Michel, the street was busier. Wrought-iron street lamps cast pools of light, and the cafés and bistros were bursting with life. She found an empty taxi and asked to be driven to the Hotel Meurice.

The taxi headed toward the river, and soon they were crossing the Pont Saint-Michel. Over the stone parapets of the bridge, she glimpsed the dark ribbon of the Seine. She could see the lights of a river steamer.

She let out a breath in the back of the black cab. Well, she was launched now. Whether on adventure or disaster, she wasn't certain. Once across the river, they turned toward the Louvre and Rue de Rivoli.

The taxi let her off at the elegant hotel beside the Jardin des Tuilleries. She was tenderly handed out by a uniformed hotel doorman. "*Merci*," she said.

She disclaimed any need of assistance and did her best to look perfectly at home. *Act like you belong*, she told herself. As she headed for the imposing entrance, a young man scooted ahead of her and held the door, beating out the liveried bellman. "Here you are. Allow me to do the honors," he said in a cheerful British accent. He sounded exactly like Edward, the Prince of Wales, looked a bit like him too, with his blond hair and delicate good looks.

"Thank you so much," she said, walking ahead of him.

"I say, you're an American."

"I am."

"I'm awfully keen on Americans. My grandmother was one. Charming woman. Everyone says so."

"Freddy!" An older woman's voice rang out from behind them. "Freddy, really. Who's to see to the bags?"

The handsome stranger shook his head at her. "Terrible deafness I got in the war. Can't hear a thing I don't want to."

She couldn't help but laugh. "But what about the bags?"

"Oh, heavens, Digby will see to those. Very efficient, my man, Digby. Mother insisted I accompany her shopping, but carry her parcels I will not. Well, goes to show."

She wasn't sure what it went to show but was too grateful to her companion for sweeping her into the hallowed lobby of the hotel to complain.

He kept up his sprightly chatter, complaining good-naturedly about shopping as he rather masterfully shepherded her toward the imposing registration desk. She was wondering how to slip away when the man behind the desk said, "Lord Ashton. Welcome back, sir. I hope you passed a pleasant day."

"Certainly not. Women and shopping." He made a comical grimace. "Key for me and for Miss...?" He glanced at her.

Well, this wasn't how she'd intended to get into Lillian's room. She had little choice now but to brazen it out as best she could. "Dixon," she said, airily. "Mrs. Lillian." She looked down modestly at her gloved hands, hoping the man behind the desk would be too busy dwelling in the glow of Lord Ashton to pay any mind to her. She was gambling that this was even Lillian's hotel, and for a terrible moment, she thought her heart might stop, but the desk clerk merely said, "Of course, Mrs. Dixon."

She'd planned to try and bribe a chambermaid to let her into the dead woman's room, after somehow discovering which room she was in. Instead, this lovely man dropped the key into her hand.

She and Lord Ashton stepped toward the elevator, both of them ignoring a large woman who was commanding several bellboys to take a mountain of packages up to her suite. "I say, are you really married?"

She hated to lie, but she reminded herself that an undercover reporter sometimes had to skirt the truth in the name of justice. "Widowed."

"Well, that's much better. I mean, terrible for you, of course, but, oh Lord, I am making a mess of things. Tell you what, let me take you for dinner on the seventh for a spot of dancing. I shall fall madly in love with you and propose marriage before morning," he said. "I'm Frederick Ashton, but everyone calls me Freddy."

Or Lord Ashton. She laughed, genuinely enjoying him even as her stomach fluttered with nerves. "Thank you, Freddy. May I ask for a postponement? I have something important I must do this evening."

"Of course, dear girl." He reached into his breast pocket and pulled out a silver card case with the initials FCA engraved on it. He flipped open the case and handed her a card. "Do please call me. I should very much like to see you again."

He ushered her into the elevator ahead of him, and the uniformed attendant shut the brass doors and whisked them up while his mother was still organizing bags and parcels. She stepped out at the fifth floor, thanks to a surreptitious glance at the key, and he continued skyward. "Hope to see you again soon," he said, doffing his hat as the brass door shut.

"I hope so too," she replied, wishing that life were different and she was the kind of woman who put up at a hotel like this and danced all night with charming titled gentlemen.

But, sadly, she was a reporter charged with murder. Her night would not include dancing.

EIGHT

Abby could feel the luxury as she walked down the corridor. The woodwork gleamed, the brass doorknobs shone, and tucked into an alcove was an ornate table holding an enormous arrangement of fresh flowers.

She was relieved to discover no police guard at the door of suite 505. With a deep breath and a surreptitious glance up and down the deserted corridor, Abby slipped the key into the lock and turned it.

She entered the suite and was immediately assailed with the scent of Lillian Dixon. It was a combination of Chanel No. 5 and cigarette smoke.

Her father's wife had claimed to be the first woman in North America to wear Chanel No. 5. Maybe it was even true. She'd certainly sprayed herself and her things lavishly with the stuff.

As Abby flipped on the light switch and a heavy crystal chandelier burst into life, she felt a wave of sadness. She hadn't liked Lillian, but no one should die like that.

"Settle yourself in the story," her favorite journalism teacher had admonished. By which she'd meant that the telling detail might take time to come forward. That the right question to ask an interview subject might not be the first question that came to mind.

Why had Lillian been in Paris? More importantly, why had she been killed? And by whom?

Abby stood very still, inhaling the perfume and cigarette smell, and realized there was a third scent, like a small voice intruding on a conversation.

She glanced around the suite. Opulent was the first word that sprang to mind. The rooms were furnished in Louis XVI style. Blue silk curtains hung from the windows, held back by gold ropes. Gilded molding patterned the walls, and a large oval, gold-framed mirror hung from one wall.

Armchairs and a settee were upholstered in the same blue fabric as the curtains. The paintings were tasteful and probably real. The tables were black chinoiserie, and the carpet was a pale patterned Aubusson.

A raccoon skin coat lay over one of the chairs, where it had obviously been carelessly thrown. Had Lillian worn it and discarded it or planned to wear it to *Maison Joubert* and changed her mind?

She stepped deeper into the suite, toward a door that must lead to a bedroom. As she approached it, she saw a pair of red satin dancing shoes and, on the chair, a pair of silk stockings.

She opened the door and saw the large bed. Sumptuous and regal. It was neatly made, which told her the maid had been in. Lillian had never been one to make her own bed.

Set yourself in the story. What was the story here, in this room? "Who killed you, Lillian?" she asked softly. She closed her eyes, and as she did so, she realized that the smell of scent was stronger in this room. Much stronger. Almost expecting to find Lillian standing in front of her, she jerked her eyelids open and once more saw the bedroom. The neatly made bed. Pink silk and lace peignoir folded into modesty on a nearby chair.

The silence was eerie, the smell reminding her too much of the woman who had caused her family so much pain.

She stood quietly and observed. Then she walked through the bedroom and into the bathroom. When she flicked on the electric light, she was almost overwhelmed by the luxury. The deep tub, the gold taps, the gilt-framed mirrors. Lillian's cosmetics were laid out on the marble countertop, from the mundane toothbrush and tooth powder to the exotic creams and lotions that promised eternal youth. Well, she'd achieved eternal youth in one way. Lillian Dixon would never know old age.

She returned to the bedroom, and as she stood there, the story began to play out in her head. She stepped forward and pulled back the pretty blue bedspread. Two pillows, plumped to perfection, revealed nothing but the efficiency of the chambermaid.

Swiftly, she flipped first one pillow and then the other. Underneath was nothing but fine cotton sheeting. She knelt and peered under the bed. Not so much as a ball of lint met her gaze. She pushed her hand between the mattresses. Nothing.

She opened the doors of the wardrobe and discovered it was packed with designer gowns, shoes, bags and coats. All appeared new. It seemed Lillian had spent the last of Edward Dixon's money on decking herself out. Two of the gowns bore the Paul Joubert label.

She systematically began checking bags and pockets, hoping for a clue, something. Lillian had never been tidy, and all the bags were crammed with visiting cards, notes and receipts.

In an everyday bag, the kind Lillian might take out when there was no one she wanted to impress, she found a silk cosmetics bag. It contained her lipstick, powder and a silver cigarette case embossed with a coat of arms. The case reminded her of Freddy's card case except for the crest. She opened the case and saw that it contained two cigarettes. She inhaled and, yes, here was that third scent she'd noted. It was from the cigarettes in the engraved case.

She closed the lid with a snap and then stood stock-still, her ears straining. She'd heard the click of a lock, she was certain of it. But this was a hotel, of course. People came and went day and night. And yet she was almost certain the sound had come from the outer door of this suite.

Perhaps it was the chambermaid come to turn the bed down. Except that a chambermaid would be moving about, bustling with no thought of stealth. A chambermaid would have knocked before entering.

She'd turned on lights and left them burning so anyone coming into the suite would know there was someone here. As her heart began to knock against her ribs, she thought of locking herself in the bathroom.

Abby was certain that the person on the other side of the door was standing still and listening, as she was. She felt the denseness of the silence between them. She slipped her bag into the larger one she'd found, closed the wardrobe doors silently, and withdrew her pearl-handled Browning 25 revolver. Pointed it at the door and waited.

She didn't wait long. Even though her straining ears heard no further sound from the outer room, she saw the brass handle of the bedroom door begin to turn.

Her heart pounded harder, but she steadied her aim and, as the door slowly opened, she pulled back the slide, which sounded loud in the silence, and thumbed off the safety.

A man walked in. A man she knew. Those world-weary eyes seemed less surprised to see her than she was to see him. He took in every detail of her appearance from her borrowed skirt to the pistol in her hand. "Bonsoir, Miss Dixon."

Her mouth was so dry, she could hardly get words out. She put the safety back on her pistol. "Inspector Deschamps. What are you doing here?"

A wintry shaft of humor crossed the frozen gray of his eyes. "I believe it is I who should be asking you that question, Miss Dixon."

She lowered the gun. Since she was perfectly aware she'd made herself look more guilty in the detective's eyes, she told him the truth. "I'm trying to find out who killed Lillian Dixon."

"And you do not believe that the police of Paris can do an adequate job?"

She shrugged her shoulders, noticing the tightness of her borrowed coat. "I have a personal interest in making sure the correct culprit is caught and that the wrong woman does not pay for a crime she did not commit."

He held out his hand. "May I?"

Reluctantly, she stepped forward and placed the pistol into his open palm. He studied the gun as though he were a dealer interested in buying it. "A very nice pistol for a lady, but why would you feel the need to carry such a weapon?"

Her smile was tight. "Before coming to Paris, I worked in Chicago, where there is approximately one murder a day. My father worried about me. He taught me to shoot when I was a girl. When I moved to the city, he bought me this pistol." She'd chosen the chrome-plated, pearl-handled model, even though her father had told her that a gun was neither a toy nor a fashion accessory and plain black was less visible.

"You are an unusual woman, Miss Dixon."

He did not sound as though he were paying her a compliment. He gestured to the item in her other hand. Foolishly, she was still holding the silver cigarette case. She should have dropped it into the handbag, now hanging from the crook of her arm, but she'd been too rattled. "Also a present from your father?" he asked drily.

Perhaps the man in front of her was working to put her neck beneath the guillotine, but she had to trust him to put justice over expediency. "I found it here, in this room."

"And you wanted perhaps a memento of your stepmother?"

She shook her head. Too many things reminded her of Lillian, and none of them were happy memories. "This isn't hers."

His eyebrows rose at that.

"This is a man's cigarette case. Lillian's was gold and enamel. No doubt you'll find it in the handbag she had with her when..." She took a quick breath. "When she died." She held out the silver case. "Look at the coat of arms on it. This case belongs to someone important."

As he took the case from her, he said, "I must have a word with my men. How did all of us overlook what you so easily found?"

"You forget, I knew Lillian. She was married to my father for five years." Trying to keep the bitterness out of her tone was like trying to stand still while a giant wave crashed into her. "She liked... souvenirs."

"Souvenirs?"

"Yes. When she first... entangled herself with my father, she took his favorite cufflinks and had them fashioned into earrings. She would wear them out at social events that my parents attended. Of course, my mother recognized them, and so did anyone who knew my father well. It was one of her many petty cruelties. Toward the end of my father's life, she taunted him with mementos from other lovers."

Her pathetic story didn't seem to affect him, but he perused the cigarette case more carefully. "And you believe this cigarette case is another such souvenir?"

"Yes. She may have planned to offer his wife a cigarette if the gentleman should turn out to be married."

As she had, he opened the case and regarded the two remaining cigarettes.

"I believe Lillian was in Paris to find herself another

husband. And, if I'm not mistaken, she intended to nab herself an English title."

He glanced at her with disbelief. "Miss Dixon, the British aristocracy do not usually marry American divorcées with dubious pasts."

"Lillian was a very determined woman. Maybe Lord Cigarette Case—or his lady—was determined to stop her?"

"You have made up quite a tale around a cigarette case," he said. "The owner could have dropped it on the street and she picked it up."

"That coat of arms could tell us who that case belongs to. There must be some organization that keeps track of these things."

"The Royal College of Heralds, I believe."

"So you think it's English?"

He didn't even glance at the case. "Yes. However, as I said before, it could have been dropped somewhere and Lillian picked it up."

She shook her head. "Didn't you smell the cigarette smoke when you entered her suite?"

"I smelled perfume."

She tsked with impatience. Pointed to the still-open cigarette case he held. "These cigarettes are particularly pungent. It's the same scent I noticed when I first walked in. I don't think they're French cigarettes."

"No. They're Egyptian."

"I'm positive that the man who owns this case was her lover."

"Perhaps he came to her suite with his wife and enjoyed an aperitif and a cigarette. He left, forgetting the case, and before she could return it, Madame Dixon was killed."

She felt that he was toying with her, testing her in some way. She shook her head. "Look at this." She scooped the peignoir off the chair. As the folds fell out, it was revealed as a sheer, gossamer garment designed to reveal rather than cover a woman's body. "Look in her closet. Lillian traveled with a series of silk nightgowns. This, she wore for a man. Probably a dark-haired man."

She held out the peignoir, where a strand of brown hair clung to the neckline. "As you will recall, Mrs. Dixon was fair."

He took the garment from her and carefully replaced it. "The single hair could also belong to the chambermaid who tidied the room or even one of my men." He turned toward the door, obviously about to throw her out.

"And what about the perfume?" she cried.

That made him pause, at least. "Perfume?"

"The Chanel No. 5. The smell is everywhere, but where is the bottle?"

His tone was as dry as her mouth as she tried to convince him she was not her stepmother's killer. "I feel sure you are about to tell me."

She pointed to the wall. "See? The slightly yellow stain on this wall?" He didn't move, so she grabbed his hand and pulled him toward the wall. "The scent of perfume is stronger here. She threw the bottle at her lover's head. Lillian always threw things when she was in a temper. The bottle broke, spilling the perfume."

He looked unconvinced.

"Why would she be in such a rage?" she asked.

"Why, indeed?"

"I don't know. But maybe whatever they were fighting about led to her murder."

"This is a most energetic story. One might even say the plot came from one of your American radio dramas."

She felt slightly downcast that he wasn't taking her theory more seriously. He opened the bedroom door and waited politely for her to walk through it. She felt like a schoolgirl in trouble as she made her way to the main door. Before he opened it for her, he looked down at her. "Miss Dixon, may I suggest that you go home and drink some warm milk and try to get some sleep?"

She put a hand on her hip and sent him her steeliest glare. "Are you patronizing me?"

His eyes were deadly serious. "I am trying to protect you. Not everyone in the police department is as broadminded as I am. You would do well to remember that."

"I'm trying to clear my name."

"Perhaps the police might be better equipped."

At his mention of the police, she remembered another beef. "Did you put a couple of gumshoes on my tail?"

"Gumshoes?"

"There are two men following me. Are they yours?"

He sighed. "Sadly, yes. And how easily you, ah, gave them the slip."

"I did." She cheered up at that. But then her brow clouded once more. "How did you find me?"

"I gave the hotel instructions to notify me immediately should anyone attempt to gain entrance to Madame Dixon's suite."

And she'd fallen into the trap like a plump partridge into a net.

NINE

Abby woke the next morning with her spirits as overcast as the sky.

She dressed and put the water on to boil for coffee, by which time Vivian had returned with several of today's papers under her arm, as well as a fresh baguette, still fragrant and warm from the bakery.

Viv had been cool when Abby had returned last night, saying merely that she had wanted to be certain her roommate was all right before going into her bedroom and shutting her door with firmness bordering on a slam.

"Good morning," Abby said.

"Not very," was the frosty reply.

Even though Abby's fingertips itched to take hold of the morning's papers, she took the time to brew coffee and warm the milk and cut up the baguette. She put the sliced bread in a basket, added a jar of jam, and brought it out with the coffees, setting it all on the steamer trunk the girls used as a table.

"Viv, I'm sorry," she said when her roommate joined her. "I shouldn't have asked you to pretend you were me and deceive the police."

Vivian turned to her, her blue eyes no longer cold but sparkling with anger. "Is that what you think? That I was worried for my own safety?" She shook her head so her blond waves shuddered. "I was sick thinking about what could happen to you. I don't know how to bail someone out of jail in France. And I probably wouldn't have enough money, anyway."

Vivian looked heavy-eyed and sneezed twice, no doubt from going back out into the cold last night.

"I'm so sorry, Vivian. And you were right, I never should have done it." In a rush, she told Viv everything that had happened the previous evening and watched her roommate's eyes grow as round as saucers.

"Abigail Dixon," she said when Abby was finished. "You pulled a gun on a police officer? You *should* be in jail."

"I know. Let's see what the papers say."

The murder was still front-page news. Her own paper had stuck to the facts, which were lurid enough.

Police Hunt for Slain American Widow's Killer.

The story that followed was factual and, she suspected, deliberately dry.

However, the front-page headline on one of the rival English-language papers, the *Paris Gazette,* screamed,

Knifed to Death at Couture House! Stepdaughter Present.

"No!" she cried aloud as she rapidly scanned the text. Her hand crept to her throat.

"What is it?" Viv asked. She'd taken the cast-off *Post* and turned the pages until she found the women's page.

"The *Gazette*! Someone must have leaked that I'm a suspect. And I've a good idea who that was." When Inspector Deschamps had let her go last night with only some terse words of warning, she had felt she was being treated leniently. But he'd found a way to punish her, by leaking her presence at the couture house to the press.

Why, Paris was as bad as Chicago for police corruption and the cozy back-and-forth that existed between those who supposedly upheld the law and those who reported on it. She read aloud:

> Widow Knifed to Death at Couture House! Stepdaughter Present.
>
> Lillian Dixon faced tragedy when her beloved husband died of shotgun wounds less than a year ago. The lovely young widow, with her blond curls, her shapely figure and her American optimism, left despair behind and removed to Paris for a new start.

Abby wanted to interpolate scathing comments but forced herself to continue reading the piece as it was written.

> Putting up at the Hotel Meurice, the wealthy young socialite had spent her short time in the City of Light refreshing her wardrobe. What a future she could have had, but her life was cut cruelly short in *Maison Joubert*, the very fashion house where she had ordered several gowns. The afternoon Mrs. Dixon was murdered, her estranged stepdaughter, Abigail Dixon, was also present in *Maison Joubert*. Sources report that Miss Dixon, a fledgling reporter for the *Chicago International Post*, was very angry to find her stepmother in the fashion house. By the end of the afternoon of February 6, only one of the Dixon women left *Maison Joubert* alive. The other was cruelly stabbed to death.
>
> Inspector Henri Deschamps says that the Paris police "hope to make an arrest soon."

By the time she'd finished reading, her voice had risen. "They've all but convicted me without a trial." She read the piece through again. "And how neatly they've sidestepped a libel case. They don't actually say I did it, but it's pretty heavily implied. There's even a picture." She shoved the paper at her roommate. A photographer had snapped her photo—it must have been yesterday—and she hadn't even noticed.

"That's a very poor photograph of you."

"Good likeness, though," Abby replied grimly. "I imagine everyone in Paris will point to me on the street and shout... What's the French word for murderer?"

Vivian's French was better than Abby's, but not by a large margin. "*Meutrière*, I think."

She pushed away her café au lait. "Why couldn't Lillian have been murdered in Chicago, where such things are commonplace? Where I know people?"

"What are you going to do?" Vivian asked, biting into a piece of bread lavishly spread with strawberry jam.

"The only thing I can do. The *Gazette* wants to sling words at me? Words provided by Inspector Deschamps? Well, I'll do some word-slinging of my own."

"Promise me you'll be careful. Remember, Lillian's killer is still out there."

When she walked out the street door, two men who'd been standing talking on the street corner turned and walked in the opposite direction. She shook her head. Where did the police find these men? They were like actors in an amateur drama playing policemen.

She walked quickly, not willing to wait a minute. When she arrived at the newspaper office, she went straight to the editor's desk. Walter Strutt was on the phone, but at the sight of her, he said, "I'll call you back," and replaced the receiver with a thunk.

"Abby. I told you to stay home. Rest up." He seemed at a loss for what else to say. "Get over the shock."

She slapped the *Gazette* onto his desk. "Not a chance. I've got a job to do. And a great idea of how to do it."

She seated herself at the desk across from him without an invitation. He glanced at the *Gazette,* but she knew he'd already seen the piece. He had all the papers delivered to the newsroom. He looked peevish and very sorry he'd been forced to hire her. "No offense, kid, but I don't have a story for you."

"No," she said, feeling the tingling in her fingertips so strongly she clasped her hands together. "I have a story for you. I am going to write a first-person account of being accused of murder in Paris. I, a young, friendless girl who just arrived in the City of Light, am facing the darkest ordeal a girl can go through."

All her earlier attempts to write the story had ended up on the fire, but now that the *Gazette* had identified her and put her at the scene of the crime, she was burning to tell her tale.

He heard her out. First, in boredom, and then she knew the moment she had him. She reminded him of the popularity of stories about Murderess Row in Chicago. "Those stories are still fresh in readers' minds. I'm suggesting something similar, only, in this case, the accused murderess is also the reporter."

"You aren't accused yet."

She tapped the *Gazette* front page with her fingertip, and he said, "Not officially."

"I have to fight back. My only weapon is my typewriter."

He dragged on his cigarette and then watched the stream of smoke he exhaled as though the answer was written there. "You do it?" Then he shook his head. "No. Don't answer that."

"Of course, I didn't."

He stubbed out his cigarette and called out, "Ruth, come on over here."

Ruth walked the short distance and said, "I thought you'd be on your way back home by now."

"She can't leave the country," Strutt said. "She's a witness in a murder case. Possible suspect. Flics took her passport." He shot Abby a sharp look. "Make sure you go carefully. Until you're arrested, you stick with how it feels to be in this position. I don't want you accused of libel as well as murder." It was difficult to tell from his tone which of those crimes he'd think was worse.

He glanced up. "Grab a chair, Ruth."

She did. The editor grabbed a pad of paper, began to scribble. "Have to call Abernathy and get his okay on this."

That was one more hurdle she'd have to jump, and it would be a high one. "If he gives you any trouble, let me talk to him," she said with a firmness she didn't feel. Inside, her guts felt like jelly.

"Fill Ruth in," he told Abby.

She did, though she left out her evening visit to the Hotel Meurice, knowing she'd gone beyond the boundaries of an ethical journalist when she'd obtained entry to her stepmother's room by impersonating the dead woman. However, there was plenty of drama in coming forward to tell her story. When she was done talking, Ruth said, "You sure you know what you're getting into?"

Abby answered honestly. "No. But I have to do this."

Ruth's forehead creased in a frown. "You'll get hate mail. Crazy people will ask you to marry them. The anonymity of being a reporter will be gone. You will *be* the story as well as covering it."

Walter Strutt waved Ruth's objections aside like so much cigarette smoke. "This kind of story happens once in a lifetime. Or more often, never." He tapped his pencil on the page. "We publish Abby's firsthand accounts, what? Once a week? Twice a week? How long can we drag this out?" He glanced between the two of them. "Think of the headline. 'Girl Reporter Stumbles on Stepmother's Body.' He tapped the pencil again.

"What's that word they always use when the courageous young woman faces a terrible ordeal?"

Ruth and Abby answered at the same moment. "Plucky."

He snapped his fingers. "That's it. Plucky Girl Reporter Stumbles on Stepmother's Body. Then, subhead, 'First-person account.'"

He scratched that out. "No. I got it. 'In her own words.'" He glanced at the clock. Scratched his balding head. "You've got an hour. No more than a thousand words. I want shock, horror." He shook a finger at her. "But no details the police haven't released. You found her dead. Murder suspected. You're interviewed by police. Terrible ordeal. First week in Paris. They took your passport."

"Got it. Now I live in the shadow of the guillotine." She was already on her feet.

"Good line. Use it. Ruth, find her a good typewriter. Turf somebody out of their desk if you have to. Every time she finishes a page, you edit it. Then hand it to me." He picked up a cigarette, then tossed it down. "I gotta move the front page around."

* * *

Ruth put her at her own desk. "Need coffee? Water?"

"Nothing." She picked up a sheet of yellow typewriter paper, rolled it into the machine. She had no time to choose her words carefully, no time to think. She went with the basics she'd learned in journalism school. Who, what, when, where, why?

"I arrived at the studio of Paul Joubert, couturier, to cover women's fashion. What I saw was murder."

Her prose might be purple, but if Walter Strutt wanted a plucky girl reporter to put on the front page, she'd give him one. As she forced herself to relive the terrible experience, she had the competing sensations of remembered horror and the pressure to write about it in clear, direct sentences.

She finished the first page, blindly waved it over her shoulder with one hand while reaching for the next sheet of paper with the other. Ruth took the page from her and sat just behind her. She began typing. In the pause between words, she heard Ruth mutter, "what I *witnessed* was murder."

Yes, she thought, that was a better word than "saw." And, convinced she was in good editing hands, she put her attention back on the next part of her story.

She was interrupted when Hudson, the copy boy, was sent to fetch her. Walter Strutt was on the phone with Charles Abernathy, and she could hear the argument as she grew closer to the managing editor's desk. He looked relieved to see her. "Abby is here now. You tell her yourself."

Then he pushed the black receiver her way, shaking his head.

Abby was not going to be turned away from her path, not now and with so much at stake. Like her freedom.

"Uncle Charles," she said cordially into the phone.

"Don't you Uncle Charles me, young lady. What's this I hear about you writing stories? I told you, we're hiring the best lawyer in Paris, dash it, in all of France. You're not a seasoned reporter. You could end up in hot water, girl. Hot water." She heard him clear his throat. "I never should have sent you to Paris. I want you home the second you get your passport returned."

She could hear the worry echoing through the transatlantic call and felt a sudden rush of homesickness. She tried not to take offense at how little he trusted her. Instead, she set about soothing his worry. "Uncle Charles, the other papers have published details leaked about me being there." She grew hot at the back of her neck thinking of the cold-eyed inspector giving information to a rival paper. Maybe he'd sold the story, which made him greedy as well as vindictive. "It's too late for me not to be in hot water. I'm already being boiled for dinner. The *Gazette's* dinner. At least you should let me cook up stories for our paper." She felt she'd stretched that metaphor so thinly it was in danger of snapping, along with Uncle Charles's temper.

"I don't like it," he said, and she realized that telling him the *Gazette* was already writing about her involvement had upset him. However, she wasn't sure whether he was more worried about her, or was reacting to the horror of being scooped by a rival paper.

"Please let me do this, Uncle Charles. Walter Strutt is going to edit all my pieces himself, so he won't let me say anything foolish."

"Strutt would hang you by your ankles from the washing line if it would sell a paper, and don't you ever forget that."

She tried another tack, with one eye on the clock, where the minutes to deadline were ticking away. "Honestly, Uncle Charles, I need the distraction. I'm going crazy sitting in my apartment waiting for the knock on the door."

"Good Lord, yes." He seemed quite struck by that image. "If those Frenchies want to arrest you, let it be from the newsroom of a major American newspaper. Have a photographer stationed there to catch the moment. We'll do everything we can to protect you and to clear your name."

Knowing she had turned him to her way of thinking, she sighed. "Maybe my stories will help."

He made a rude noise. "Don't get ahead of yourself, Abigail."

"I won't. Thank you, Uncle Charles."

"Oh, very well. But the minute your passport is returned, young lady, you'll be on the next boat back to America. Understood?"

"I understand."

"You're not to worry. You're not without powerful friends."

"Hopefully my articles will boost circulation enough to pay for the lawyer."

"Now, don't you worry about that." She could hear his sigh rattle across all the miles between them. "Abby, if I'd had any idea you'd get yourself in trouble, you know I wouldn't have sent you. Your father must be rolling in his grave."

Along with her stepmother.

* * *

Walter Strutt sent her back twice to rewrite the final paragraph before he was satisfied. Hudson was standing waiting when he finally signed off on the finished story. The kid took off at a sprint for the typesetters.

"Good job," Walter Strutt said. "Now, go on home and rest up. You look tired."

She didn't want to rest, but she was happy to be excused from the newsroom. The other reporters kept eyeing her, and she didn't want to talk to any of them. They either thought she was guilty or they hoped she'd spill details. She was safer out of there. Besides, she had something to do, and she didn't want Walter Strutt or anyone to know about it.

She walked home to change her clothes and, to her surprise, found Vivian there. She'd changed from her chic black dress into warm woolen trousers, a wool sweater and a shawl, which she'd wrapped around herself. She huddled on the sofa with a magazine in her lap and a handkerchief in her hand.

When she saw Abby, Vivian sneezed violently.

"Are you all right?"

Her roommate said, "No. I have a cold. When I got to the perfume store, Monsieur Chapelle sent me home again. He's terrified he'll catch my cold and that will ruin his 'nose.' She used her fingers to draw an imaginary shape around her own petite nose. It looked like a large sausage. "He doesn't want me back until I'm completely well."

"I'm so sorry. It's all my fault for sending you back out into the cold." She immediately added more coal to the puny fire. "Can I get you anything? Perhaps some coffee?"

"No. Talk to me. What happened at the newspaper?"

She recounted her day so far. Vivian nodded in approval as she described her conversation with Uncle Charles and how he and Walter Strutt had agreed she could write her first-person accounts. She grinned at her friend. "You'll have more stories to paste into your scrapbook."

"Well, that's exciting."

"Not as exciting as what I'm doing next. I'm going back to the couture house."

Vivian choked on a reply, which made her sneeze and she blew her nose. "You're doing what?"

"I have to do something. Lillian was murdered there. Maybe I'll find a clue that was missed."

"Didn't the police tell you not to interfere?"

She tossed her head. "Then the police should have given me back my notebook. I have to finish my article. It was my first assignment. I'm a professional."

Viv wrapped her shawl tighter around herself. "No one's going to believe that."

"Well, that's my cover story. I'm going back because that is where Lillian died. Why? Why there? Why at that moment? The cigarette case definitely belonged to a man. A rich one, with a title. No doubt she was spending my father's money on outfitting herself to lure yet another rich man. I need details. Facts. Somewhere to start."

"Do you really think they'll let you back in?"

Her hopes were, in fact, dim, but she refused to give in without a fight. "I can ask, can't I? You have heard that suspects are innocent until proven guilty?"

"I have, but I'm not sure about the French."

TEN

The damp cold was bone-chilling and wafted up from the river. The Seine itself seemed to be moving slower, as though too cold to work up any enthusiasm. The other pedestrians were huddled into woolen coats and mufflers, fur if they could afford it.

Once more, her steps took her to Rue Faubourg.

Abby was even less excited about ringing the bell at *Maison Joubert* than she had been the first time.

Then, she'd been afraid of boredom. Now she was digging into the sordid details of a murder in which she was the prime suspect, interfering against the very strong advice of the inspector in charge.

She supposed she was being foolish, but now that she'd begun to delve into the mystery of Lillian's death, she couldn't think about anything else.

Abby stood outside *Maison Joubert*. The damp chill crept through her woolen coat and seemed to penetrate her very bones, but still, she didn't ring the bell. The image of her grisly discovery insisted on intruding. She had to force herself to ring for admission.

At least the two detectives following her would be stuck out in the cold. She'd considered trying to lose her tail, but she couldn't ask the ailing Vivian to be her decoy, and besides, perhaps it would be as well if Inspector Deschamps knew she was not going to sit idly by while he fed details that made her look guilty to a rival newspaper.

To her chagrin, the door was opened by the same disapproving woman who appeared to be wearing the same disapproving black dress and accusatory pearls. Once more, those fine French nostrils flared. "Mademoiselle Dixon." The words dripped with contempt.

Abby held her handbag tightly in her hands. "I would like to see Monsieur Joubert."

"But it is impossible. He cannot have the likes of you polluting the very air of his atelier."

She would not indulge in a common brawl on the street. Instead, she pulled herself to her full height and looked down on the woman. "Please tell *Monsieur* I am here."

The woman didn't open the door wider. She put her palm flat, ready to slam it in Abby's face. Abby pushed her foot into the doorway. Fortunately, she was spared any injury to foot or footwear when she heard Paul Joubert's voice. The horrible crow immediately turned to the sound of her master's voice. Abby used her moment of inattention to push her way into the foyer.

"Excuse me for coming by without an appointment," she interrupted, with her best attempt at a winning smile, "but we never finished our interview. I still have an assignment to complete."

Paul Joubert looked astonished to see her. No. If she were being accurate, which a reporter ought to be, the word was not astonished but horrified. But in a moment, he had recovered his poise. "But of course, I am very happy to see you again."

The woman in black clutched at her chest, and Abby made

out the shape of a crucifix beneath the black fabric. She directed a tirade of French, far too fast for Abby to follow, at the designer, but he merely shook his head at her and replied in one sentence. The woman glared at Abby, made the sign of the cross, then slammed the front door and stalked into the haberdashery.

"You must forgive us, Miss Dixon. Nothing so terrible as murder has ever happened to us. Madame Lafitte lost a husband, a brother, and both her sons in the Great War. The experience has left her bitter and suspicious."

Abby wondered whether a bitter and suspicious woman was the most appropriate person to greet customers and guests who might visit Paul Joubert's atelier.

He seemed uncertain what to say or how to conduct himself and merely stood looking at her.

His eyes seemed sunken in his head and shadowed with blue, as though he were not sleeping. His colorful waistcoat had been replaced by a sober gray one. Even his mustache seemed to droop with sadness.

"Is there somewhere we could talk in private?" she asked.

For a moment, his exhausted-looking eyes narrowed and his face grew hard. Then the mask-like rigidity passed and he said, "But of course."

She followed him all the way to the top floor, where he kept his office. It was a spacious room that took full advantage of the skylights letting in the seeping gray. Two wire mannequins stood on one side, each sporting a stunning, almost completed evening gown. One gown had obviously been inspired by a peacock's tail. It shone with rich blues and greens, and dashes of black and silver glowed like jewels. The other gown was as hot as the peacock dress was cool. And relied on red satin with a feathered hem she could picture swirling around a dance floor.

His desk was large and simple and had nothing on it but a telephone and a duplicate of the costume book she had seen in the supply room with the fabrics. Across from his desk was a small seating area, and she could imagine top staff settling themselves around the table and discussing the next collection or the needs of a particular client. He gestured her into a chair, and instead of settling himself behind his desk, he took the chair beside her.

"And how may I assist you, Miss Dixon?"

"Please, call me Abby. Everyone does."

He nodded.

"I want to finish my assignment. The police confiscated my notebook, so I have none of my notes or my sketches."

"You wish to begin again? To what purpose? My collection is a disaster. A murder has been committed on one of my clients in my very salon!" He threw up his hands, and she saw that they were shaking.

She looked him straight in the eye. No doubt her gaze also reflected the strain and worry of the past few days. "I have an assignment. To be honest with you, this was my first assignment for my newspaper. I must finish it or risk losing my job."

He gazed at her inscrutably for a moment, his narrowed eyes squinting at her as though he could see right into her thoughts. Then, as he had before, he relaxed and said in his usual charming way, "I seem to have a great deal of time on my hands. I will help you in any way I can."

Rapidly, she reviewed the people she'd met on her first foray into the couture house. "May I request that the English girl, Suzanne, tour me through your facility once more?"

He seemed startled by the request. "Allow me to see if she is available."

He left, and she wondered why he hadn't simply summoned the young woman. And then she realized that the poor girl had stumbled upon Abby kneeling by the dead woman. Perhaps she believed she'd been chatting away to a murderer and would refuse.

Then what would Abby do? Her French wasn't good enough to interview the employees here on her own. She needed Suzanne's help.

She drew out a fresh notebook and flipped it open to her carefully penned questions. Mr. Joubert was gone a very long time. Restless, Abby rose.

She walked to where the two dresses stood in the corner, looking like beautiful girls all dressed for a dance that hadn't yet begun. They were so exquisite, she couldn't resist the urge to touch. The silk was heaven against her fingertips and shimmered in the light. She longed to slip into the peacock dress and twirl. A hitherto unsuspected love for fine clothes was beginning to rise.

When Paul Joubert re-entered his office, he was alone. "Please excuse my absence, Miss... Abby." When he said her name, he put the emphasis on the last syllable, which made her name sound so much prettier. "Suzanne is delivering a gown." He shrugged. "To a client who is understandably reluctant to come here. Suzanne will return shortly. In the meantime, let me devote myself to you."

She smiled at his quaint use of English. "I don't want to keep you from your business."

His expression was as empty as his salon. "When one's business is the site of a spectacular murder, one becomes suddenly less busy."

"But your new collection is about to launch."

He shook his head. "I have postponed its release. My custom orders have flown away. No fashionable lady wants to set foot on the premises where such a violent crime was committed on one such as herself."

He gestured to the two dresses she had been admiring. "Those gowns, *par exemple*, are virtually worthless to me now. And the woman who ordered them is taller than the normal and slender." He threw up his hands. "She cancels the order. With only one fitting left to go."

"But that's awful."

He shrugged in a purely Gallic fashion. "*C'est la vie.*"

He did not seem inclined to rush into their interview, and it occurred to her that having a murder suspect cover his collection was hardly ideal.

She made a gut-instinct decision to trust him. "*Monsieur*, I have not been entirely truthful with you. I'm here only partly to complete the research for my article. I'm also trying to clear my name." She leaned forward impulsively. "I didn't kill Lillian Dixon. But I'm determined to find out who did."

He did not seem overwhelmed with joy at her admission. "And may one ask why you do not trust our very efficient police, our judicial system?"

She thought she detected a hint of sarcasm in his words. "So long as the police are putting their efforts into convicting me, the trail of the true killer grows colder."

"You make a very passionate defense. I make no doubt that when you have your say in front of the magistrate that you will sway him in your favor."

"I hope to find the killer before I end up in front of a judge. I would like to talk to the rest of your staff. Perhaps someone saw something they didn't think important. People talk to me. It's one of the reasons I'm a good reporter. They might be more relaxed around me than they would be around a police officer."

He played with his pencil without answering.

"Please, will you help me? I need the names of everyone who was working here that day and anyone who could have accessed the second floor. Lillian's driver, the other ladies in the salon, customers in the shop below."

His lips were forming a refusal when there was a soft knock on his door and the bitter woman in black entered carrying a small stack of mail. "*Monsieur*, here are your letters." She shot a poisonous glance at Abby as she set the mail on his desk.

The woman's body all but twitched with loathing as she made a wide berth around Abby's chair and exited the office. Abby noticed this but vaguely. All her attention was on Paul Joubert. He glanced down at the stack of letters and grew pale. His eyes were wide with what looked like shock and fear. He shrank back in his chair as though his stack of mail was so many poisonous snakes.

ELEVEN

"*Monsieur?*" Abby asked. "Is everything all right?"

He pulled himself together with a visible effort. He reached out with a shaking hand, grasped the entire stack of letters and shoved it into the top drawer of his desk. He attempted a smile, but it was a sad effort. "Bills. Always bills."

"I can imagine this is a very difficult time for you." But she didn't think the correspondence that had so affected him was a bill. When she'd glanced at the uppermost letter on the stack, she'd seen a plain white envelope with the direction written in careful cursive handwriting. There was no return address on the envelope. Abby was fairly certain that in France as well as in her own country, most bills arrived in typewritten envelopes.

He seemed to debate with himself for a moment, and she remained quiet. At last, he nodded once, pulled himself up straight and said, "I prepared such a list as the one you request for the police. As it happens, I had an extra copy made." He unlocked the lower drawer in his desk and removed the carbon copy of the typewritten list. He glanced at it for a moment before pushing the pages across the shiny mahogany surface of his desk toward her.

"Thank you."

She began to peruse the list and was daunted by the number of names upon it. He leaned across the desk, and his finely manicured index finger gestured to the first block of names. "These are all the employees who were in the atelier that day."

She nodded and made a note with her pencil.

He pointed to the second, smaller grouping of names. "These are the ladies who were in the salon. Beside each of the names is that of the servant or driver who accompanied her."

She made another note.

Silence reigned for several seconds. Gently, he said, "And, of course, you were there. I do not believe you had a driver."

She shook her head. It was jarring to see her own name on the list of possible suspects, even though she knew that in the police's mind she was number one.

This next block of names were the people on the lower floor.

It was a brief list, but one item caught her attention. "Who is this English milord?"

He shrugged. "A customer."

"Please. May I speak to whoever served this Englishman?"

"But of course. I shall have the young man fetched."

"Thank you." Maybe it was a long shot, but that cigarette case had belonged to a rich man. If she knew Lillian, she'd come to Europe to bag a title as well as a fortune. As a penniless woman with no social standing or pedigree, Lillian had enticed Reginald Dixon away from his wife and family and into marriage. But she'd come to Paris as the widow of a prominent businessman and with enough money that she could maintain the façade of wealth until she'd claimed her next victim. Lillian would have aimed high.

Once more, Paul Joubert rose and left her. She doubted that he would go all the way down to the street level to fetch this young man. He'd find one of his underlings to do it for him. She didn't have very long, so she grabbed her camera from her bag.

Her heart banged, not only with the stress of possible discovery, but because she was acting like a thief. With the same speed she showed on the tennis court, she jumped to the other side of the desk and opened the drawer where Joubert had put his mail.

Quickly, she picked up the envelope that sat on top. She laid it on the desktop, snapped a photograph of the front of the envelope, then flipped it over and snapped a second photograph. She'd just shut the drawer when the door to the office began to open. She had no time to return to her seat or put away her Kodak. She turned the camera that was still in her hand toward the peacock dress.

"I hope you don't mind," she gushed as she snapped a photograph. "I love that dress so much."

"Not at all." He looked her up and down in a professional way. "In fact, it would suit you well." He resumed his seat beside her, and she settled herself once more. "The young man, Eugene, is on his way."

Soon, a deferential knock sounded on the door. "*Entrée*," said Joubert.

The young man was thin and wore a worried expression. She imagined he did not often find himself called to the great master's private office.

"Eugene, Miss Dixon has some questions for you. About the Englishman you served the day of the unfortunate incident."

The young man's thin, nervous shoulders shuddered slightly. "Of course. I am happy to help."

"You speak English," Abby said, relieved. "How wonderful."

The young man turned to Paul Joubert as though looking for permission to speak. The older man nodded encouragement.

"Many of our customers are English. It is a great help if we can speak their language."

"This Englishman that you served on the day of the murder, what can you tell me about him?"

It was clear the young man had thought of little else; she had the feeling that not much happened in his life that catapulted him into the limelight. "He was dressed with great elegance, in the English style. He came in saying he wanted to buy some handkerchiefs. As I was showing him some samples, he said that he thought he recognized one of the cars waiting outside. That it belonged to a particular friend of his. He asked who the ladies were upstairs." Here he shot the couturier a nervous glance. "Naturally, I could tell him nothing."

Paul Joubert nodded, and Eugene continued. "We treasure the privacy of our clients." It was obvious from the way his eyes darted to the floor, to the wall, anywhere but to her face, that he was lying.

"What was his name? This Englishman?"

"I do not know, madame. He bought three handkerchiefs and paid in cash."

"But the list referred to him as an English lord. Why is that?"

He shrugged helplessly. "It was in his manner, his very excellent dress. He was certainly the gentleman."

"And did this gentleman wait to see whether he knew this lady?"

He shook his head. "That I cannot say with any certainty. He paid, I gave him his parcel, and then several more customers came into the shop. I did not see him leave."

"Thank you."

She scribbled some notes in her notebook. "Do you think Madame Lafitte might have seen whether this Englishman penetrated the atelier?"

"You think it could be important?"

She nodded. "I do."

But when she was consulted, the woman vociferously denied letting any person up to the higher levels. Her stream of quick French, with much shaking of the head, rolling of the eyes and gesticulating with the hands, told Abby that the woman was denying any knowledge of this Englishman as effectively as though she had understood every word.

When Madame Lafitte had stalked out, Monsieur Joubert said, "Well, it seems we are out of luck with our English milord."

"Madame Lafitte could easily have turned her back for a moment, greeting another customer at the door. It would only take a moment for this Englishman to dart past her and run up the stairs." Then somehow find Lillian, kill her and stroll back downstairs and out the door without anyone seeing him? As a theory, even she felt it was far-fetched.

"No one else mentioned seeing him." Apparently Paul Joubert also felt that her theory lacked credibility.

"Have they been asked specifically? I've always found that people sometimes need their memories jogged for the incidents they've witnessed to resurface."

He shrugged helplessly. "Me, I make pretty dresses."

"I wonder."

"You wonder?"

She'd been thinking and suddenly leaned forward and clasped Paul Joubert's wrist. She had an idea so bold, so mad, that Nellie Bly herself might have thought of it. "Monsieur Joubert, what if I were to wear one of your very pretty dresses to the Hotel Meurice? If I were to dine and dance with a titled Englishman? Do you not think I might draw attention to your wonderful creations?"

He narrowed his gaze on her in that penetrating, slightly sinister manner that had unnerved her earlier. "To what purpose?"

"Two purposes. One, the Hotel Meurice is where the titled English stay. Perhaps I'll be able to discover something about the man who came to the shop. The second purpose is to help your business. I feel somewhat responsible that my stepmother and I have hurt your livelihood."

"Pardon my lack of subtlety, Abby, but you wearing my gowns can only remind the swirling dancers of the tragedy that took place here."

"Exactly!" She felt quite enthusiastic about her plan. She'd liked Paul Joubert the moment she met him. He'd been more than forbearing with her when she'd acted so oddly at their first interview.

He could have banned her from his premises instead of speaking with her again. "You know about fashion, but I know newspapers. If the readers here are anything like those in Chicago, they'll love reading about the murder. If you saw the *Gazette* today, then you know I'm already front-page news."

He inclined his head.

"I'm writing about my ordeal for my own newspaper, which is paying for a defense lawyer and proclaiming my innocence. I'll make sure our photographer takes pictures of me in your gown. What if one of them made the front page? You can't buy that kind of publicity." She motioned to the lovely gowns in his office, imagining herself wearing them. "You said yourself, those gowns are nearly worthless to you. The woman who canceled her order was taller and slimmer than most."

She sat as straight as she could in her chair. "I am five foot ten inches in my stocking feet, and I've played sports all my life."

She saw that he was looking her over critically and pushed on with her crazy plan. "When society sees that you have gowned me, they won't be able to resist. I can't promise you'll get your business back, but I will do my best to make sure that I am photographed from every angle in your gown. You might even give a statement yourself proclaiming your belief in my innocence."

His full lips twitched. "Are you so certain I believe you're innocent?"

"Not at all. Consider this a publicity stunt. Like the Citroën motor car company lighting up the Eiffel Tower to advertise their automobiles." She'd been rather shocked when she'd arrived to see that three sides of the Eiffel Tower were illuminated every evening in yellow bulbs advertising the French car maker.

Monsieur seemed genuinely amused by her idea, and for the first time, she saw him relax. "You liken yourself to the Eiffel Tower, Miss Dixon?"

Her lips twitched in spite of herself. "Well, at home they used to call me a beanpole. I suppose the Eiffel Tower is an improvement."

"I think it is a mad idea, and for that reason, it appeals to me." He raised a finger. "My business is ruined unless I can, how do you say it? Turn the tide?"

"Exactly."

"However, I cannot allow you in one of my gowns unless you put yourself in my hands completely. You will visit a hair salon of my choosing. You will have your face made up by a cosmetics artist. Hose, undergarments, shoes, all must fit the image."

A tiny niggle of panic danced across the back of her neck, under the weight of her hair. She touched the heavy mass that she'd worn either in a long braid or, from the time she was sixteen, pinned into a roll. Her mother had brushed it when she was young and called it her glory. It was long enough that she could sit on it. "What exactly do you have planned for my hair?"

He made a tsking sound. "A long curtain is very good for a window. But for a stylish young lady? *Non, non, non.* Your hair will be cut into a style suitable for a fashionable young woman in Paris. You shall be bobbed."

Her hair, her beloved hair. She was about to argue with him or bargain, but she could see that it would be useless. He was a man of strong artistic opinions. And she felt that if she were willing to sacrifice her hair, he might go along with her plan. It cost her a pang of sadness, but she nodded. "I will put myself and my hair into your hands."

"A very wise choice."

"So we have a deal?"

He shook his head. "So very American. Yes, madame. We have a deal." He rose and walked toward the lovely peacock-colored dress and considered it. He turned back to her. "May I suggest a pre-dinner drink at the Ritz bar?"

"Why, Monsieur Joubert, I think you have mastered the publicity stunt."

TWELVE

"May I use your telephone?" Abby asked Monsieur Joubert.

"But of course."

She rang through to the Hotel Meurice and was relieved to find herself rapidly connected with Frederick Ashton. She could hear muted revelry in the background and suspected she had found him in the bar. "Freddy?"

"It is he. And who is the divine creature on the other end of this apparatus?"

"It's Mrs. Dixon. We met in the hotel the other night."

He recalled her with flattering speed. "And a jolly good thing you've called me. I've tried your room several times, you know, and you're never there. I do hope you're taking me up on my offer for dinner and a spot of dancing."

She was delighted that he'd recalled his offer and she hadn't needed to remind him. "I am not staying at the Meurice any longer. But I'd love to join you for dinner."

"Capital. What say you to tomorrow night?"

"I can't think of anything I'd like more."

"Wonderful. Let me take down your address, and my driver and I will come and fetch you."

She didn't want anyone who had "Lord" in their name fetching her from her tiny walk-up flat. Thankful to Paul Joubert for his suggestion, she said, "Why don't we meet for a drink in the Ritz bar?"

"Marvelous idea. Simply marvelous. Say, seven o'clock? Then we'll pop on over here for a spot of supper and a twirl around the floor."

"That sounds splendid." When she ended the call, Paul Joubert, who had listened unabashedly to her conversation, said, "Tomorrow? We've not a moment to lose. Let's get you into a fitting room right away."

Abby believed passionately in the cause of the suffragettes, and she had rejoiced when women in her country were finally accorded the vote. She had been named for Abigail Scott Duniway, an advocate for women's rights and a friend of Abby's mother. Her heroine was Nellie Bly, who had raced around the world in seventy-two days with only one dress. She'd feigned madness in order to expose the terrible conditions in a notorious insane asylum. Women like those were Abby's inspiration. They did not for a moment consider fashion and beauty to be the primary considerations of a woman.

So Abby was somewhat ashamed when she found herself enthralled by the glitter of beads, the swish of black fringe and the cool luxury of silk. It was the English girl Suzanne who arrived to help her out of her sensible tweed suit and into the glorious gown. Suzanne looked at her warily, and her eyes widened when she heard that Abby would be fitted for a Joubert gown, but she agreed to help.

She led Abby to a fitting room that was the farthest away from where Lillian had died. A rope was stretched across the hallway to prevent anyone from going down there. She wondered if they'd be able to get the stains out of that carpet. No doubt it would have to be replaced.

Paul Joubert left her with Suzanne, who brought with her a

simple but beautiful black silk step-in chemise. While Abby swiftly undressed behind a painted screen and slipped into the chemise, she heard voices arguing outside. Paul Joubert and an angry Frenchwoman who was not Madame Lafitte. She peeked out, and Suzanne mouthed, "Madame Bernard. The *première*."

Abby stepped out from behind the screen, feeling practically naked. Suzanne assessed her with a professional eye and nodded. "You're the perfect shape for Paul's creations. You should see the way some of our clients have to squeeze themselves into full-body corsets in order to wear one of our gowns."

The arguing ceased, and soon the door opened. Madame Bernard carried the peacock dress into the fitting room as though it were made of spun sugar and would break if she so much as breathed on it. Suzanne oh-so carefully lifted the gown from its wire form and helped Abby into it. Then she stepped back and glanced at the *première* nervously.

Madame Bernard stared at Abby, and her gaze was so pointed, she could stitch a hem just by looking at it.

It was clear she believed this American journalist and possible murderer no more belonged in a Joubert gown than the Arc de Triomphe belonged in Iowa.

Her shoulders drooped as though the weight of every Frenchwoman who could not afford a Joubert gown was upon them. Together, she and Suzanne pinned and conferred. Abby scarcely dared to breathe. Finally, Suzanne said, "There's really very little to do. The dress could have been made for you."

"It's the loveliest thing I've ever worn."

When Madame Bernard made a sound like a boxer who'd been punched in the kidneys, Abby knew she understood English.

At that moment, Paul Joubert knocked politely and, when bade to enter, looked Abby up and down critically. He made a circular motion with his index finger, indicating she should turn. She did, and the brush of silk, the whisper of luxury, seduced her senses.

"It's perfect," she cried, unable to contain her emotion.

"But of course," he replied. He made Suzanne move a couple of pins and then professed himself satisfied. He wagged a finger at Abby. "Tomorrow, you will present yourself at three o'clock for the preparation."

"But I don't have to be at the Ritz until seven," she protested.

His brow clouded, and for a terrible minute, she thought he would snatch the gown back and banish her from his kingdom of silk and bugle beads. Then, he said, "Do you believe I waste my genius on someone who has not the time to prepare herself properly?"

Behind his shoulder, Suzanne shook her head as though Abby might have trouble choosing the correct answer. She knew one thing. She was not giving up her chance to wear this beautiful dress. Hanging her head, she said, "No."

He didn't forgive her immediately. His lips remained compressed. "And you will arrive at my atelier at three o'clock? Most promptly?"

"Yes."

"Very well." Paul Joubert bade her farewell and left. Then the two women carefully helped her out of the dress.

Madame Bernard left without a word, carrying the gown as though it were a victim of terrible persecution. As Suzanne was about to say goodbye, Abby put a hand on her arm. "Can I ask you a couple of questions?"

"I suppose." She opened the door and stepped out into the hall. "Come out when you're dressed." Abby supposed she couldn't blame the woman for not wanting to remain alone with her in the fitting room. The last time she'd seen Abby in one of these rooms, she'd been sharing it with a dead woman.

Abby left the chemise in the fitting room and emerged in

her own clothes, feeling very much like Cinderella after her gown had turned once more into rags. "It's about Madame Lafitte."

Suzanne immediately relaxed her wary stance and made a rude noise. "That old toad. Don't let her worry you. She hates everyone. We're supposed to feel sorry for her because she lost her husband and both her sons in the Great War, but she's bitter and twisted. No one knows why Paul keeps her, except he knew her before the war." She glanced down the empty corridor in the direction of the stairs. "Her and Madame Bernard. I'd be a much better *première*, but he's loyal to these miserable women he worked with in the old days." She shrugged, pushing her ambition down.

"There was an Englishman here the day of the murder. He was downstairs buying handkerchiefs, and he asked about the ladies upstairs. Madame Lafitte swears she never saw him run up the stairs, nor would she have allowed it. Could she be lying?"

Suzanne glanced rapidly down the corridor to make sure they were alone, then lowered her voice. "Of course she could. The woman is obsessed with money. Grease her palm with a few francs and she'll do anything."

"You're certain of this?"

She nodded, then leaned close, nearly whispering. "She marks down what time we all arrive. It's not her job, but she does it so she can report to Paul if anyone's tardy. It's understood that if you're late and you pay her five francs, she'll mark you down in her book as having arrived on time."

"Thank you." Suddenly her theory that the English gentleman had been able to get upstairs was gaining credibility.

"Why are you interested?"

Once more she found herself proclaiming her innocence of murder and her determination to find out who did kill Lillian Dixon.

"Goodness. How brave of you. And you think this Englishman could be the one who..."

"I don't know. But I'd love to discover whether anyone saw him up here that day."

"Let me see what I can find out."

She nodded, feeling that one more person was willing to give her the benefit of the doubt at least.

* * *

When Abby got back to the apartment, trailed by her two plainclothes officers, she ran all the way up the stairs and burst into the apartment so she could tell Vivian the news. "You won't believe what happened at *Maison Joubert*."

Vivian dabbed her red nose with a pale blue hankie. "After the last time you said those words, I don't think I want to know."

"You'll want to know this." And she related the plan she and Joubert had cooked up.

Vivian dropped the newspaper she was reading and jumped to her feet. "Abby, it's like, well, it's like Cinderella."

"Except Cinderella caught herself a Prince Charming, and I hope to catch a killer."

Vivian shuddered. "Oh, don't say that. You could be putting yourself in danger."

Refusing to face that unpleasant truth, she said, "And there's more." She struck a pose like one of the girls on the front of Vivian's *Vogue* magazines. "I am going to have my hair cut and set professionally."

Viv clapped her hands. "Oh, I can't believe it. I finally got through to you about that old-fashioned hair." She sneezed. "Will wonders never cease?"

She didn't have the heart to tell her roommate that Paul Joubert had forced the haircut on her.

"Tell me every single thing about that gown. Oh, I'm so

envious I could—" She sneezed explosively, and they both laughed. Then, feeling more girlish than ever before, Abby described the dress, from the feel of the silk to the rich colors to the exquisite beading.

When she was done, Vivian giggled. "Why, Abby, you sound as though you're falling in love."

She nodded, slowly. "I believe I am. With French fashion. You look better," she said in an effort to cheer her roommate up.

"I don't feel so bad. What I am is awfully bored." She put on her prettiest pout, and it was so pretty Abby suspected she practiced in the mirror. "I mustn't go out into the cold, but I need something to do."

"I have something we can do, but you won't like it."

She sat back down and cast the newspaper aside. "Anything's better than lying here with nothing to do."

Abby took off her coat and hat, went into her bedroom and returned with a leather handbag, which she placed on their wooden table. Then she made a confession. "When I was searching Lillian's room, Inspector Deschamps interrupted me."

"Don't remind me," Viv said, giving an artistic shudder.

"Well, I had Lillian's handbag at the time, and in order to keep a hand free for my gun, I shoved my handbag into hers and then looped the bag over my arm." As Vivian continued to regard her with her wide, blue, innocent gaze, she said, "I still have Lillian's bag. I brought it home with me by accident."

Vivian looked shocked. "Why haven't you given it to the police?"

"I only realized it when I got ready to go out this morning. I want you to help me sort and catalogue everything in that handbag."

Vivian looked as though Abby had just asked her to perform a lewd act on Boulevard Saint-Germain. "We can't go through a dead woman's things. It would be wrong."

Abby was having the same thoughts. "Honestly, Vivian, if

I'd been thinking straight, I'd have put the handbag back before the inspector came into the room. It all happened so fast. I thought it was Lillian's murderer standing on the other side of that door, so I was more concerned about getting my gun out than worrying about which bag I was holding."

The handbag slouched as though divining that its owner was no more and its days of being paraded around the fashionable streets of Paris were over.

"But now that I've got it, the police will assume I've gone through the bag anyway. If I'm going to be blamed for wrongdoing, I should do something wrong. Besides, I knew Lillian. I may see things that the police wouldn't. And when we've finished, I promise to take the bag straight to the police station and explain." She swallowed against a suddenly dry throat. "I'm sure they'll understand."

"I am saving up for a new black dress so that I will have something decent to wear to your funeral," Vivian said to her quite sternly. Then she sat down at the table and sighed. "Tell me what you want me to do."

Abby fetched a fresh notebook and sat down opposite Vivian. "I believe the best way to begin is to study each piece of paper, visiting card, each receipt, photograph, anything that's in this bag. Perhaps we can piece together some idea of Lillian's final days."

"All right, but I'm doing this under protest and because I'm so wretchedly bored."

"I understand completely, and I honor your objections."

Then, with a deep breath, she reached into the dead woman's handbag and removed a handful of papers. She handed these over to Vivian, instructing her to put things in chronological order if possible, bills and receipts in one pile, any personal correspondence in another, and a third pile for miscellaneous.

Abby began with Lillian's leather change purse. She

repressed a shiver when the unmistakable scent of Chanel No. 5 assailed her. Opening the purse, she discovered French francs, American dollars and British pounds all mixed up together. The American dollars and French francs were easy to explain, but why the British pounds? Was Lillian planning a trip there?

She considered organizing the money into separate currencies and counting up the amounts, but she thought the police would prefer to see this bag as close to its original state as possible so she resisted the urge. She did, however, remove the visiting cards, crumpled bills and bits of paper, keeping a mental idea of where they'd been in the handbag and, as she had instructed Vivian, began to pile them into three wobbly stacks.

She found a newspaper clipping and, on smoothing out the paper, discovered it was from the *Post*. It was the record of who was arriving and on which boat. Lillian had torn out the account of her own arrival, which seemed entirely in keeping with her self-obsession.

Abby rolled her eyes and placed the account in the miscellaneous pile until it occurred to her that Mrs. Lillian Dixon, widow of Mr. Edward Dixon of Chicago, would not have wasted her voyage. She scanned through the rest of the names and noted faint underlinings in pencil. Were these shipmates Lillian had become friendly with? Or those she had hoped to become close with in Paris? There was a Mrs. Ernest Peabody on her ship, and that name was underlined in darker pencil.

She found another newspaper clipping, this one describing the parties and salons of wealthy expats in the city. She let out a cry of triumph that startled Vivian, who'd been carefully lining up the edges of her pile of receipts. "Heavens, what is it?"

"I told you Lillian was determined to insinuate herself with upper-class English people. Look. Here's the proof." She stood and leaned over the table, turning her newspaper clipping around so that Vivian could read it. "Do you see here?" She tapped her finger on the relevant society event, which Lillian had underlined. Vivian glanced at her and back at the page and read aloud, "The Duchess of Cirencester will be entertaining close friends, including Mrs. Ernest Peabody of Boston and Lady Eleanor, Marchioness of Witney, at an evening party at her townhouse on the Rue de Rivoli."

She looked up, clearly confused. "I don't understand. What's a duchess going to do with Lillian? She wasn't on the boat, was she?"

Abby shook her head. "No. She wasn't. But her dear friend Mrs. Ernest Peabody, of the Boston Peabodys, was on the boat. And I'll wager Lillian used all her charm and flattery on the Peabodys to get herself an introduction to the duke and duchess." She was really quite pleased with this bit of deductive reasoning. "And that is where she met the owner of that cigarette case."

Vivian put her head back and stared off into the middle distance as though judging the force of Abby's evidence. Finally, she said, sounding dejected, "No wonder I never meet eligible men. I don't use the right strategy." She looked up at Abby, her big blue eyes a curious mix of innocence and cunning. "I wasted my time on my voyage over. I see that now. I was looking for single men when I should have been making the acquaintance of society women. The kind who hold luncheons and soirees." She sighed. "If only I had done that, I could be married by now."

Abby had no time for such sentimentality. "Look where Lillian's social climbing got her." In case Vivian couldn't follow her train of thought, she took her right to the final station. "Dead."

THIRTEEN

Scissors. Gleaming silver, sharp and deadly. Abby'd dreamed of them, and now they were coming toward her. Aimed not at her throat but her long, lustrous hair. Hair her mother used to brush faithfully, one hundred strokes a night.

When Abby heard the first cut, she experienced a moment of panic. She curled her fingers around the arms of the hard chair in which she sat in order to prevent herself from jumping up and running. But as the scissors continued and she heard the grinding noise of each strand of hair being severed, she wondered whether shedding all those pounds of heavy hair was akin to shedding the weight of her past.

Her childhood and girlhood had been happy, but the past few years had been difficult, painful, and each physical and emotional blow of her family's disintegration seemed to have reached its nadir with her current predicament.

In coming to Paris, she'd attempted to run away from her past, but the past followed. The one person in all the world she'd wanted to avoid ever seeing again had forced herself most unpleasantly into Abby's life. The perfect irony was that even in her own tragic demise, Lillian had managed to cause Abby further suffering.

As the mound of dark brown curls on the floor grew, she felt a corresponding lightness. She could hold her head a little higher without the burden of all that hair pulling her down.

The little man busy with the shears chattered in French, and she nodded and smiled and tried to answer sensibly. Then he came at her with styling products and hot irons and she closed her eyes. When he finished, she wanted to ask for a mirror but didn't know the right word.

Then the makeup stylist began. She was a middle-aged woman with thin, beringed fingers, thick eyebrows and a beauty mark she'd painted above the corner of her upper lip. The woman looked at her with narrowed eyes, then said, "Smoky."

Smoky. She understood the word but didn't understand how it related to cosmetics. The woman's hands were quick and light as she creamed, powdered, painted. Abby grew bored and wondered if she'd be in time for her date. She was finally offered a large hand mirror.

To say that she didn't recognize herself was, of course, absurd. But even though she'd seen her own face reflected back at her most days of her life, still she thought, if she were an acquaintance, she'd have had to take a second look to be certain the woman staring back at her was Abigail Dixon.

When she moved, her smooth, gleaming hair brushed her jawline. She now wore a bang across her forehead, something she'd never had before, and that took some of the height off her forehead and seemed to focus attention on her eyes, which did indeed look smoky. Charcoal and silver added mystery to her brown eyes. Her lashes were long and silky. The fullness of her lips had been emphasized with a plum lipstick. She looked almost embarrassingly sensuous. Also stylish and fashionable.

The trio of experts stood staring at her, seeming anxious for her opinion, but she was dumbstruck.

Finally, the hairstylist said, almost as though the words burst from him, *"Madam, qu'elle est belle!"*

It was a revelation. She turned her head this way and that, regarding herself in the mirror. She nodded once, liking the bounce in her hair. "Do you know, I believe I am."

The makeup woman clapped with delight and then pressed on her the cosmetics she would need to re-create this look.

When she returned to the couturier, Paul Joubert took one look at her and kissed his hands to his lips, more like an Italian gentleman than a French one, and made a loud smacking noise. Then he broke into a broad grin. "Come, the dress, she is ready."

While other girls had read fairytales, Abby's grandmother had pressed on her pamphlets about the suffragette movement. Her mother, her poor mother, had encouraged her daughter to read poetry and the classics. However, the story of Cinderella was not unknown to her, and as she stepped into the gown sparkling with beads and hinting at all the colors of a peacock's tail, she understood the power of transformation.

She stepped into the black and silver shoes provided for her, and finally, *Monsieur* slipped a black silk cape lined with vivid blue silk over her shoulders.

He stood back. "Abigail, you may be my finest achievement."

Before she could resist the impulse, she leaned forward, touched her cheek to his and planted a kiss. Then she laughed, for she'd left a perfect Cupid's bow imprint on his cheek.

She picked up her handbag, and he let out a cry of rage. *"Non, and non and non."* He picked up the evening bag that matched the dress. The *tiny* bag that matched the dress.

"But, *Monsieur*, there are things in that bag I need. My notebook. Pen."

He folded his arms beneath his chest and tapped his foot in

annoyance. "Suzanne, please tell Miss Dixon what belongs in a lady's evening bag."

Suzanne raised her shoulders, letting Abby know she couldn't help her, and replied, like a schoolgirl reciting a lesson: "One's calling card, a handkerchief. A few francs. A small comb. A lipstick, a powder compact."

"That is correct. And that is all that is permitted."

"But—"

His pleasant expression hardened. "Miss Dixon, we made a deal. If you want to wear my beautiful gown, you follow my rules." Here was the finicky perfectionist Suzanne had warned her about that first day. "When you wear a Joubert gown, you are my ambassador. *Non.* You are my muse."

He let the word muse sink in. No doubt the notion of being a Greek goddess of inspiration made his clients swoon. She didn't feel like swooning. She wanted to argue. She needed her notebook and pen. She felt naked without them. "I'm a reporter. I must have my notebook."

He was unmoved. "You will agree to my terms or I must ask that you return the gown."

She could say yes and then flout his rules, but she knew she wouldn't. They'd made a deal. "All right," she said. "But what about the door key to my flat?"

He looked as though he'd eaten a bad oyster. "Is it a large one?"

"No. Quite small."

"Very well."

"Then I agree to your terms."

"*Très bien.*" He was the charming couturier once more. He pulled the gold watch from today's red and gold waistcoat and said, "And the timing is perfect. We've an hour left for you to practice."

"Practice what? I've been wearing clothes all my life."

He raised his Gallic nose in the air. "Not my clothes."

She was escorted to the main showroom, where he'd summoned one of his models. "Giselle will demonstrate for you how to walk." And then in stalked the *première*. "And Madame Bernard, she will teach you." The *première* eyed Abby with almost as much critical attention as Joubert himself. She walked forward, put her hand under Abby's jaw and her other at the back of her head, under the smooth sweep of hair, and tugged, lengthening her neck. Then she put her hands on her shoulders and held them back. ",*iComme ça*," she said.

Paul Joubert left them to it. They practiced standing, which reminded Abby of her short time learning ballet as a child. The position of the foot was very important to the line of the dress. No one cared how uncomfortable she might be. Every line of her body was to be posed in a way that would best showcase the gown.

They made her practice walking, behind the model, imitating her every move, while Madame Bernard issued terse instructions that Suzanne translated. "Relax your mouth and jaw. You mustn't let your teeth touch. You can part your lips slightly if it helps."

Madame watched her for a moment and came forward to push Abby's shoulders down. Madame let out a stream of quick French, and Suzanne said, "Confidence. It's all about confidence. You must look as though you and the dress are one. The head is high, the spine straight, hips slightly forward.

"Now, we walk. Feet straight and one foot directly in front of the other. Think of a tightrope walker. But don't look down," she cried as Abby tried to watch her own feet, which had never felt so clumsy.

It felt strange being so free within the dress. Her body felt loose-limbed and caressed by the fabric rather than constrained by it. Madame Bernard pushed her hips forward, and Giselle demonstrated again and again how to place her feet, one in front of the other, so her hips swayed. "The arms are relaxed, and we hold the handbag so." It was looped over her wrist and held away from the body so it didn't interfere with the view of the gown.

"I never knew walking was such hard work," she said.

"Be glad you're wearing that gown and just had your hair done, or Madame Bernard would put a book on top of your head, just like deportment lessons at finishing school."

"I never went to finishing school."

Suzanne chuckled softly. "Yes. I think that's obvious."

They were running out of time, and Abby felt that she'd stood, walked, sat—stood, walked, sat over and over so many times, she was ready to scream. Madame Bernard was never satisfied, but with a glance at the clock, she sighed and said something that Suzanne translated as, "And the final lesson, *the arrival*."

She said it as though it were a religious event, and Abby almost expected her to cross herself. "The arrival?"

"This is not some frock you ordered from a clothing catalogue. It is a piece of fine art. And you are merely the frame."

Abby formed a mental picture of herself walking around within a large wooden frame and found she wasn't far wrong. "When you enter a room, you pause. Center yourself inside the frame of the door or between pillars at the opera house. And you take a moment. You lengthen the spine, you place the feet so, and you count to five in your head."

She motioned for Giselle to demonstrate, and Abby saw the way that deliberate pause allowed the dress to fall into place. It made a statement.

"Look into the middle distance so the head remains elevated. And then count, slowly. Then you can move as you've been shown."

She practiced the entrance, feeling, each time she paused so dramatically, as though she should launch into song or recite a poem. Paul Joubert came in as she was practicing yet again, and he said, "Madame Bernard, you are a miracle."

Abby thought that was unfair. She was the one who'd been doing all the standing, walking and posing. He turned to her, looking pleased. "And you are ready for your grand adventure?"

"Yes. I've just enough time to get a taxi to the Ritz."

"No taxi, madame. My own car will take you to the Ritz. My driver is yours for the evening."

She was stunned by his generosity. "Oh, but Monsieur Joubert, I can't take your driver. You might need him yourself."

"I will not. Besides, he will ensure you do not walk about in the streets and dirty the shoes or gown."

She smiled, feeling the unfamiliar stickiness of lipstick. "Very well. But I thank you anyway." She thought about her discarded garments and her bag. "And my things?"

He shuddered visibly. "In my opinion, they should be burned. But my driver will carry them, and you, home at the end of the evening."

She thanked him once again, feeling all the silk and swirl of her borrowed feathers, her tiny handbag containing only the allowed items.

"I'll walk out with you," Suzanne said. As they walked down the stairs to the street level, the English girl said, "I asked around. One of the seamstresses, Nicole, is certain she heard two women arguing in a fitting room when she went downstairs with extra pins."

"She's certain it was two women? One couldn't have been a man?" She'd been so pleased with her theory that the English lord had run upstairs and managed to get Lillian alone.

"I'll ask her again."

"They were arguing in English?"

Suzanne paused, her hand on the banister, and closed her eyes for a moment. Abby waited.

Suzanne shook her head. "No. She could make out only a

few words, she said. They were speaking in French." Well, darn. Another theory died on the vine.

Abby touched the girl's arm. "Thanks. I want to talk to Nicole myself, perhaps tomorrow when I return."

"Of course."

As she swept from the couture house, Madame Lafitte said, in a heavy French accent, "Fine feathers, mademoiselle."

Abby wasn't fooled for a moment that this was a compliment. At least her feathers made her look like a peacock. Not a bitter black crow.

FOURTEEN

Abby arrived at the entrance to the Ritz bar on Place Vendome in all the glory of her borrowed designer gown. When she moved, the silk skirt brushed her calves, and crystal beads caught the light.

It had been bad enough practicing her entrée at the couture house, but in a public place, it was excruciating. She already felt half dressed with most of her hair missing and in this slip of a dress. Still, she'd promised, and she tried to be a woman of her word. She paused in the entrance to the bar, her feet in third ballet position, head high, jaw relaxed, gazing off into the middle distance. Or in this case, the rows of bottles that stretched to the ceiling behind the long bar. She was so accustomed to prohibition that her eyes widened to see such an exuberant display of alcohol.

She remembered the *première's* directions as best she could and let her shoulders and arms relax, her tiny bag swinging gently from her wrist. Slowly, she counted in her head to five.

A pianist in tails played Gershwin on a grand piano, and at round tables, the beautiful of Paris were here to see and be seen.

She felt glances flick her way, casual at first, and then

people began to whisper and stare, whether because of her fabulous gown or her sudden notoriety as a murder suspect, she wasn't certain.

Freddy caught sight of her from the bar and waved a cheerful hand her way. He strode forward, and an expression of delight suffused his handsome countenance. He took both her hands and said, "I shall be the envy of every man in Paris tonight."

A hovering waiter led them to a table for two against one of the long windows. Freddy glanced at her. "Champagne?"

Even though she was in the middle of a murder investigation, it was impossible not to enjoy the notion of drinking champagne at one of the most famous bars in Paris. "Why not?"

The waiter fetched a bottle and opened it, not with the sound of a gunshot and an eruption, but with a quiet sigh. He poured foaming wine into two glasses. Freddy tapped the rim of his glass on hers. "To the most beautiful woman in Paris." He leaned forward with easy grace. "Now, tell me everything about the mysterious Mrs. Dixon."

The waiter, who had been so respectful and effusive moments ago, snarled in French. She and Freddy both glanced up to find two lean and hungry-looking men being ejected from the table closest to theirs. One of the men looked ready to argue, but the second one grabbed his arm and dragged him toward the standup bar. It was as clear to Freddy as it was to her that the men had stationed themselves so they could keep an eye on her and probably eavesdrop on her conversation.

"Whatever is the matter with those two ghouls? Are they bothering you? Shall I have them thrown out?"

He was about to rise when she laid her gloved hand on top of his. "No. I believe those two men are with the police force." She took a deep and fortifying drink of her champagne. "I think I had better explain."

"Only if you care to. No wish to pry into your affairs."

Since she didn't know where to begin, she said, "I thought perhaps you might have recognized my photograph from the newspapers."

"Not unless you're one of those wonderful female jockeys, a golfer, or perhaps a tennis professional. I only look at the sporting news. Can't abide politics nor the terrible things people do to each other."

"I am not a professional athlete."

"Pity. You've got the build for it."

Oh, he was hopeless. Obviously one of those handsome but not very bright rich Englishmen she enjoyed reading about. In fiction. "Freddy, I am suspected in the murder that happened at the *Maison Joubert*."

His pale blue eyes nearly started from their sockets. "Oh, by all that's wonderful, are you really?"

"Yes." She leaned in and lowered her voice. "I most earnestly assure you that I did not kill that woman, but it was she who was Mrs. Dixon. I'm afraid I told you a fib the other night."

"Do I gather that you are not a widow?"

She smiled a little at that. "I am not. I'm a single woman. Abigail Dixon. My friends call me Abby."

"I hope I may count myself among their number. Extraordinary coincidence, what? You having the same surname as the dead woman?"

"I'm afraid that wasn't a coincidence. She was my late father's second wife. The awful twist of fate was that we both found ourselves in *Maison Joubert* on the very same day." Wanting to make a clean breast of things, she added, "It was I who discovered her body."

"Jolly bad luck." He sipped reflectively. "Gory business, death. I saw too much of it in the Great War. Well, we all did. Senseless brutality—and all for what?"

A prickle of guilt that she had taken advantage of his good

nature made her say, "If you would prefer not to be seen with me, I would understand perfectly."

His eyes had assumed a troubled expression that suggested he'd spent the last moments revisiting some of what he had seen and experienced in the war. He shook off the momentary melancholy. "What nonsense is this? A night out with a good meal and a spot of dancing is exactly what you need. Get your mind off this dreary business."

He might not be too bright, but he was exactly what she needed. "Why, I do believe I will."

"Good girl. Drink up now and let's scamper out of here while the lead-footed coppers do their best to follow. They'll never be allowed up on seven, you know. Not dressed for the rooftop. I shall have a word with the maître d' anyway. I will not have you bothered."

Perhaps there was more to Freddy than charm and good looks. When he glanced back at the two cops tailing her, his mouth hardened, and she suspected a streak of ruthlessness might lie beneath his easy manners.

He motioned for the waiter, and after a discreet paying of the bill, they rose and he slipped her black silk cloak over her shoulders. He tucked her hand into the crook of his arm as they walked nonchalantly out of the Ritz. She did not so much as cast a glance behind at the latest pair sent to trail her.

* * *

Walking into the seventh-floor dining room of the Hotel Meurice was like entering a film set. Conversations hummed, crystal chandeliers sparkled, laughter tinkled. Women held cigarettes in long, dainty holders, and hers was not the only designer gown in the ornate room. Indeed, the feeling of being on a motion picture set intensified when she recognized Clara Bow, the It Girl herself, enjoying herself at a table of admirers.

She had to stop herself from staring at the film star. She treasured every detail to tell Vivian when she got home.

The maître d' treated them with flattering enthusiasm. "A pleasure to have you with us tonight, Lord Ashton."

He bowed his head in a courtly fashion toward Abby, including her in his general benevolence. "I believe we will have the pleasure of welcoming both Lady Eleanor and your brother tonight." He led them to a table on the edge of the dance floor.

"Quite a family party." Freddy dropped his voice and spoke softly to the man, slipping him a coin.

"I shall take care of it personally, sir. Those men won't get past the door."

"Good man, Boney, and start us off with a bottle of champagne, will you? You know the one I like."

The man bowed once more. "With the greatest of pleasure."

She was going to have to take it easy on the champagne or she'd end up being carried out. They'd barely sipped their first glass of champagne when the band struck up a Cole Porter tune. "I'm very partial to this song," Freddy said. "Can I persuade you to dance?"

"Of course." She was beginning to sense that he couldn't sit still for long. Still, she was happy to oblige, since she had seen a photographer working at the edge of the dance floor. Her own paper was supposed to send someone, too. She might not be a movie star or legitimate celebrity, but a photo of a woman accused of murder would sell a lot of papers, especially one as well-dressed as she. She was conscious that everything from her bobbed hair to the soles of her well-shod feet screamed fashion.

It was a pleasure to dance with Freddy; he had the natural rhythm and grace of a sportsman. He wasn't a great deal taller than she, so they were eye to eye in her heels and well matched. "Will you dance me to the other side of the floor, Freddy?"

"There's a nasty photographer over there. He bribes his way in, you know."

"I have my reasons for wanting to be photographed."

"Right you are, then. Hold on and prepare to twirl." He made everything fun, and by the time he'd gracefully maneuvered her to the edge of the dance floor, she was laughing. The photographer, who had watched their approach with glee, snapped a picture. In the instant it took him to change the bulb, the music stopped and her escort obligingly posed with her. She gave a dazzling smile as the camera went off once more. The little man behind the camera called, "Miss Dixon, tell us what happened. Did you kill her?"

"I did not. And for more on my harrowing story, you will need to read my own articles in the *Chicago International Post*. Thank you."

"Wait, where'd you get the frock?"

She made sure to speak slowly and loudly enough to be heard. "*Maison Joubert*, of course."

The band struck up again. Freddy grinned at her. "Do you Charleston, Miss Dixon?"

"Why, yes. Do you?"

"Of course." And they were off. It was an athletic number with a great deal of kicking and hopping, and she was laughing and flushed when he finally led her back to their table.

"Miss Dixon, you are a pleasure to dance with."

"Please, call me Abby," she said. "And so are you."

Freddy was an entertaining companion. He recounted amusing anecdotes, often about other Englishmen present, which she encouraged, believing that one of them might have been Lillian's lover and possibly her killer. While Freddy paid her outrageous compliments and made her feel like the most beautiful woman in Paris, her attention was always partly on the other diners and dancers. Not only was she looking for clues to her stepmother's murder but for copy for tomorrow's front page.

She believed that the more people who read about her

plight, the more careful the police would be in proceeding against her. Her paper had taken up her cause as an innocent American persecuted in a foreign land and was offering a reward for information leading to the conviction of the real killer, a brilliant stroke of genius cooked up between Charles Abernathy and Walter Strutt.

She had awoken from a nightmare to find herself famous. Or infamous, depending on one's viewpoint.

She became aware that a young woman was standing beside their table. When she glanced up, the girl blushed. "I'm sorry to bother you," she said in an American accent, "but I think you're so terribly brave."

"Thank you," Abby said.

"Could I—would you mind—that is, I'd love to have your autograph." And she pushed forward the folded front page of the *Chicago Post*'s International Edition.

Plucky Girl Reporter Discovers Murdered Stepmother

She'd argued with Walter Strutt about being called a Girl Reporter. He'd told her she was lucky to get a front-page story and some kids had all the luck. "Make sure your story is *harrowing*," he'd said, then rearranged her copy to make sure of it. The first paragraphs leapt out at her.

> The first thing I saw was the blood. Lillian Dixon, my father's second wife, lay in a pool of her life's blood. Murdered! I hoped she might still be breathing, but when I attempted to revive her, it was clear that my stepmother had breathed her last.
>
> My dreadful ordeal was only beginning. When the police arrived, it was me they questioned, me they suspected.

"Good Lord," said Freddy, reading over her shoulder.

She sighed and borrowed the young girl's pen since her own tiny bag did not have room for one. "The things a girl will do for a byline."

She signed her name and handed the paper back to her young fan, who said, "I know you're innocent. Good luck."

The young woman had barely left when an older lady bore down on them, trailed by a fashionable young man. She was a faded version of Freddy, wearing an old-fashioned blue dress with an ermine stole. Abby was fairly certain she'd been the one left with the bags when Freddy had first met Abby.

He rose as she approached. "Mother, darling. Allow me to introduce Miss Abigail Dixon. Abby, this is my mother, Eleanor Ashton." At his mother's sharp look, he said, "Lady Eleanor."

"How do you do, Lady Eleanor?"

His mother looked taken aback and disapproving. Clearly, unlike her son, she read the front page of the newspaper. She held out a soft white hand. "Do you make a long stay in Paris, Miss Dixon?"

"I live here."

"How pleasant for you."

The man standing behind her could only be Freddy's older brother. The resemblance there was even stronger. He didn't have as charming an expression, and his hair was dark, but the bone structure, the shape of the mouth, and even those pale blue eyes were similar enough that she could hazard a guess they were closely related. "And my brother, of course. Larry."

"Only informally, of course, my dear. Lawrence is properly referred to as Lord Lambridge. He's the Earl of Lambridge, you see." And if the woman was trying to make Abby feel like an insignificant nobody, she was doing a good job.

"Only a courtesy title," Freddy said. He turned to Abby. "Borrowed from our revered papa."

"Well, when your father dies, Lawrence will be the

Marquess of Witney, as well as the Earl of Lambridge," his mother explained, again no doubt for Abby's edification.

"How de do?" Lawrence said, clearly bored with an argument that sounded to Abby's ears as though it played out often. "Call me Larry."

Since the two were standing with obvious intent, Freddy had no choice but to say, "Won't you join us?" And in moments, their party of two became a party of four.

Larry said, "Mother and I were thinking of the entrecote with béarnaise sauce, and Boney says there's some early asparagus. Perhaps with that French way they do potatoes."

"Yes, fine. Abigail?"

"That sounds wonderful."

While the brothers argued about which wine to choose, Abby was subjected to the most delicate inquisition. She felt as though she were being dissected with a feather as Freddy's mother asked questions in her soft, well-bred voice about her background, her parents, and probably calculated to the last centime how much her Joubert gown had cost.

Or maybe she was looking at Abby because she had her legs crossed and wasn't sitting with her ankles and knees pressed together as a proper young lady should. "And what brought you to Paris, Miss Dixon?"

"A job. I'm a newspaper reporter."

The older woman's eyes widened. "So you work? For money?"

She bit back the urge to say, "I didn't inherit it from generations of inbred landowners who exploited the poor." That would never do. So she simply smiled and nodded.

"Who introduced you to Frederick?"

Freddy had been arguing for a Chateau Margaux, but at the sound of his name, he glanced over. "Fate introduced us, darling Mother. Fate."

Darling Mother looked as though Fate would from now on be her sworn enemy.

Freddy's brother drew out a plain silver case and flicked it open, offering her a familiar-looking cigarette. "Not now, Lawrence," his mother said. "You know those awful Egyptian cigarettes make me cough."

With muttered impatience, he snapped the case shut, and Freddy said, "What happened to the silver case Papa gave you? The one engraved with your borrowed crest?"

Larry's face creased with petulance, and he glared at his brother in a way that promised vengeance later. But his shrug was casual. "Left it at home. Too many pickpockets in Paris." A certain ruddiness to his complexion, though, suggested he was lying.

Abby did not believe he had left his cigarette case in London. She had a very good idea she knew exactly where it was. In the possession of the French police.

Dinner was a difficult affair with all of them at cross-purposes. Freddy clearly wanted the conversation to flow. He wanted to charm and be charmed. Darling Mother wanted to show up, at every opportunity, how much Abby did not fit into their world. She did this with no subtlety whatsoever. "Did I tell you boys that the Duchess of Cirencester has invited us for tea next Thursday? It's in aid of her latest charity. A dreadful bore, of course, but one has obligations." Then she turned to Abby. "Of course, anyone who's anyone in Paris will be there. Will we see you, my dear?"

Freddy stepped in to save her. He said, "Abby is a working girl, Mother. She doesn't have time for tea parties." As if she'd been invited. "And I won't be able to attend, I'm afraid. I've got to dash back to London for a spot of business."

Larry seemed agitated. He kept glancing around as though looking for more interesting people to talk to. Thanks to Freddy's tactlessness, she was near certain that Larry had been in

Lillian's room and it was his cigarette case she'd discovered there. She wished she'd thought to study his face when Freddy introduced her, to see if he flinched hearing her surname.

She was certain he and Lillian had been intimate, but that didn't mean Larry had killed her. Had he been the man who'd purchased handkerchiefs at *Maison Joubert*?

How would she find out?

A second young woman came up to Abby and asked her to sign her autograph book. She said, "I'm going to write a letter to your newspaper telling them how swell I think you are. And I know you're innocent."

"Thank you."

When the young woman went away with her autograph book clutched to her chest, Lady Eleanor said, "Such a sordid thing to have a murder in one's family. I'm so sorry, dear. Lillian Dixon was your *stepmother*, I believe?" The tone she used for stepmother suggested that having one of those in the family was even more sordid than having a murder.

Larry's attention was brought back instantly. He turned to Abby. "I didn't realize. Did you say you were related to Lil—the dead woman?"

Here was her opportunity. She'd never be an actress, but she put a hand over her eyes and said in a choking voice, "So difficult. My stepmother. Murdered." She put out a hand toward Larry. "I'm sorry. Would you have a handkerchief?" She pressed Freddy's foot with her own, hoping he understood the message. She did not want him to give her his hankie.

"Really, Lawrence," said his mother. "It's not like you to be tactless."

Peeking through her parted fingers while she pretended to be desolated, she saw Larry dig in his coat and then he passed her a handkerchief. "Oh, thank you," she said, dabbing delicately at her dry eyes, careful not to smudge her makeup. "So kind."

Then she put the cloth into her lap and stared down at it as though in great distress, running her hands over it, folding it. She wished she knew more about the world of fabrics and much more about the stock for sale in Joubert's store.

The fabric was fine cotton but otherwise seemed uninterested in revealing its secrets. Feeling a little like her stepmother, she slipped the hankie into her tiny bag, hoping the young man who worked in haberdashery at *Maison Joubert* could tell her if it was one of those purchased by the English gentleman on the day Lillian was murdered.

Perhaps she was breaking Paul Joubert's rules about what she could carry in her tiny evening bag, but she felt he might make an exception if she dropped a piece of evidence into that bag that could help convict a killer.

FIFTEEN

Larry was clearly less interested in his handkerchief being returned than in excusing himself from their company. Abby wondered if it was a guilty conscience and he didn't want to be around her any longer, knowing she was being blamed for a crime he committed.

Whatever the reason, he gazed around the room until he spotted someone clearly more palatable. "Mother, do you mind if I excuse myself? I see Miss Lexington and her chaperone in the corner. I should like to ask her to dance."

"By all means, my dear. Do give her my love and ask her to tea with us tomorrow."

He left, and she turned to Abby with gentility as false as her smile. "Perhaps you know Miss Alexandra Lexington? She's from New York. Her people are in shipping. Or is it lumber? She's a great heiress, in any case."

"Ships or trees, she's a stranger to me."

Now that his brother had abandoned them, Freddy obviously didn't feel that he could do the same to his mother by asking Abby to dance. They made strained conversation for a few minutes, while she was given an opportunity to note that his brother danced as well as Freddy himself. His partner wasn't as light on her feet and looked rather humorless.

Freddy tapped his feet to the music and made a helpless face to Abby. She understood perfectly how he felt. She would also rather be twirling around the floor than sitting with his mother, who so clearly disapproved of Abby. Lady Eleanor seemed determined to protect her son from such a dangerous influence and so she decided to excuse herself and leave.

But Lady Eleanor was ahead of her. Suddenly, Freddy's mother clutched at her chest and slumped back in her chair, putting a hand to her forehead. "Oh, dear. Freddy, I'm not feeling at all well. I'm afraid I shall need you to escort me back to my room." She took a shuddering breath and glanced with sharp eyes at Abby. "I'm so sorry, my dear. It's my angina acting up."

Abby thought the angina wasn't the one doing the acting, and Clara Bow could have taken lessons from the suddenly ailing Lady Eleanor.

Freddy didn't look very sympathetic. "I should think it's indigestion, Mother. You did insist on eating two helpings of the asparagus in butter sauce."

"No. It's my angina." She sighed. "Of course, I never complain, but I'm afraid I must ask you to take me up to my room to get my pills."

"But couldn't Larry—"

"And sit with me for half an hour to make certain I don't need a doctor."

"I say, really, Mother—"

"It's all right," Abby said, not wishing to be part of a scene. "I have a car here. You must look after your mother." She was so grateful that Paul Joubert had lent her his car and driver tonight and insisted the driver remain with her all evening. She'd felt he was overprotective of his gown, but now she was merely thankful.

"No, really. I must see you home."

Behind her, a new voice intruded. "It would be my pleasure to escort Miss Dixon home."

She turned, startled to find Inspector Deschamps standing just behind their table, where he'd obviously overheard the last scene. She shouldn't have been shocked to see him, since his men had been following her everywhere, but still, she felt as though she'd been cornered.

It was also disconcerting to see the inspector in evening clothes. He looked surprisingly at home in this well-heeled crowd.

Even as Freddy tried to argue that it was his responsibility to escort Miss Dixon home, his mother was speaking over him, thanking the inspector for his kindness.

Freddy did not look as grateful to the inspector. While his mother explained her ailment to the inspector, Freddy said in a low voice to Abby, "I'm so sorry. At least give me your address. I've no way to get hold of you otherwise."

She couldn't think of a way to avoid giving it to him without appearing as though she had something to hide. Poverty wasn't a sin, she reminded herself as she scribbled her address on the back of one of Freddy's visiting cards, then watched as he carefully placed it into his breast pocket.

Lady Eleanor required the assistance of both the inspector and Freddy to get to her feet, then leaned heavily on her son's arm as they moved toward the door. Inspector Deschamps seated himself where Freddy had been. She raised her eyebrows at him. "Did you come here for the food, Inspector, or the dancing?"

Instead of answering her, he said, "That is a stunning ensemble you're wearing tonight, Miss Dixon."

She was certain he'd recognized the gown. No doubt he'd seen the dress in Paul Joubert's private office, as she had. She said, airily, "It's a Paul Joubert."

"No doubt you are well paid by your newspaper."

He must know perfectly well that a reporter's salary would never cover a Joubert gown, not if she saved every penny for thirty years. She smiled sweetly. "Monsieur Joubert lent me the gown."

"I wonder why he would provide a gown for a woman suspected of a murder within his atelier?"

"Because he believes in my innocence."

His smile was swift and cynical. "I think you are not quite the ingénue you appear to be, Miss Dixon."

"I'm a journalist, Inspector Deschamps, and I'm very interested in asking you a few questions about the murder of Lillian Dixon."

He seemed quite startled at her bold request. "I shall tell you what I've told every other journalist who has asked me questions. The investigation is ongoing. I cannot comment further."

"And yet somehow, the *Gazette* was given my name and enough details that it looked as though the police were about to arrest me. If you'll slip information to the *Gazette*, why not the *Post*?"

His icy gray eyes narrowed on her face. "I assure you I did not slip any information to anyone."

"Then how did the *Gazette* get details of the murder?"

His face was cold and hard. "You would know better the tricks a reporter will get up to than I would."

She searched his face, but it was unyielding. Had she been wrong about him? Did the *Gazette* coax the sordid details from someone else? And if so, then who? The only other possible source was someone in the couture house.

Not Paul Joubert. Please let it not be Paul Joubert.

* * *

The following morning, Abby received a bouquet of white roses. The note that accompanied it said:

Smashing evening last night. So sorry I couldn't take you home personally. Show you forgive me by taking a jaunt to the Ballet Russes with me Saturday. Warmest regards, Freddy.

She was torn between the pleasure of seeing him again and the horror of knowing her wardrobe would not stretch to another society event.

A second bouquet of flowers arrived for her. It was extravagant and brimming with color. The note said, "My heart is at your feet!" It was signed, Paul Joubert.

She puzzled over the note for only a minute before running out the door.

She headed straight for the newsagent, where she purchased all the English newspapers. It was somewhat shocking to see her own photograph staring back at her from the front page, or this new version of herself. The *Gazette* headline was:

Murder Suspect Leads Police a Dance.

The caption beneath the photo said:

Miss Abigail Dixon dines and dances in a Paul Joubert couture creation. The American journalist is a person of interest in the recent murder of society widow Mrs. Lillian Dixon, who was the reporter's stepmother.

Her own paper had also put her photograph on the front page with a much more sympathetic caption.

Putting on a brave face, in spite of personal tragedy, *Post* reporter Abigail Dixon shows off not only her courage, but a couture gown by the legendary Paul Joubert.

When she arrived at *Maison Joubert*, the black crow frowned but this time let her in without argument. She was left to stand in the foyer while an underling was dispatched to find the designer. Within moments, he was running lightly down the stairs, beaming and looking much happier than when she'd seen him the day before.

"Mademoiselle Dixon, you find me your devoted slave." He kissed her soundly on both cheeks, and she drew back with a laugh.

"The dress?" she asked.

"But *non, non, non*. You in the dress. Have you seen the papers? You are front-page news, along with my humble creation. And today I have three orders from new clients and one woman who canceled her order previously has changed her mind." He twinkled at her. "A woman's prerogative, of course."

"But that's wonderful." She chose her words carefully. "I'm sure being seen in the company of an English aristocrat also helped."

"But *non*, it is your beautiful self," he replied gallantly.

"*Monsieur*, Lord Frederick has invited me to the Ballet Russes on Saturday." She glanced down at herself, drab in a brown tweed skirt and straw-colored sweater. Only her bobbed hair suggested she was a daring, young, fashionable woman.

He understood her dilemma at once and she saw him pause and narrow his gaze at her for a moment. Then he nodded as though they had conducted an entire argument or perhaps a long conversation and he agreed with her. "It would be my honor if you would allow me to clothe you for this outing. You will be my muse."

She let out a sigh of relief. "It is I who would be honored," she said.

As he led her upstairs, he said, "Couture clientele occupy a small world. The women who can afford a gown by me, or Miss Chanel or Lanvin, are as desperate to be different as they are to fit in with the current fashion. Is this comprehensible?"

"Yes, I think so." She thought back to her night at the Meurice and the Ritz bar. "There's a certain look that a woman must have, but within that, she wants to appear unique and eye-catching."

"*Exactement*. You, this fresh, young, American beauty, tragically and falsely accused of murder, a journalist who will recount the history of your wrongs, *bien sûr*, I believe you will become the toast of Paris. And, naturally, every young woman of style will copy your hair, your shoes and *absolument*, your gowns."

"And I shall make sure, at every opportunity, to mention that my gowns are designed by Monsieur Joubert."

He raised one finger and gazed at her with his penetrating eyes. "Exclusively designed by Monsieur Joubert."

Of course, if his prediction was true, he would not be the only designer offering her their wares. But not only did she love Paul Joubert's designs, she felt great loyalty to the man who had allowed her back into his atelier after the murder and who had already provided her with one gown.

"But of course, *Monsieur*. I shall be your muse. Only yours."

He smiled his charming smile and bowed slightly. "We understand each other. Now, come, I will show you some designs."

"Designs? But, *Monsieur*, the Ballet Russes is Saturday." She tried to remember what day it was; so much had happened in a short time. "Why, that's tomorrow."

He dipped his head. "One will work miracles."

She thought of the red dress that had been canceled by the same woman who'd ordered the peacock gown. "Perhaps the red dress?"

"*Non.* You will be photographed by every camera there. You will not appear as a pretty girl in a fancy frock. You will be a goddess."

He led her to the room where he kept bolts of cloth and a design book. As they walked, they passed the *première*, carrying a completed garment before her with the same reverence as though it were a religious statue. When her gaze followed the woman, Paul Joubert said, "That is a gown for another lady who attends the Ballet Russes. In a moment, I must go down to her."

But Abby was not interested in the current client, but in a previous one. "*Monsieur*, where is the gown that my stepmother was trying on in the fitting room the day she was murdered?"

His footsteps slowed and then stopped entirely as he turned to her, a frown gathering. "Madame Dixon was not here that day for a fitting. She came, as you did, to view the fall collection."

"So she had no reason to go to a fitting room?"

"None at all."

Then why had Lillian been in that fitting room?

What had lured her there? Or who?

SIXTEEN

"Suzanne?" The voice was imperious.

"Yes, Paul."

"Come and help me. We must design and create a gown in twenty-four hours." They swept into the fabric room, Suzanne's shoes tapping behind them as she raced to catch up. His gaze roamed this treasure chest of fabric. "The silver patterned silk for the bodice, I think."

He grabbed a sketchbook, ordered Abby to "Stand there and do not move." He was abrupt, his movements swift and keen as he flipped to a fresh page and began to make fast sweeps with his pencil. His concentration was fierce. "Square neck." He stared at her. Nodded, went back to his pad. "Good arms, *bon*, we shall be sleeveless." All she could hear was the scratching of pencil on paper. Once, he shook his head, muttered something and flipped to a fresh page. Then he began again.

"Perhaps the chiffon. Black on top, quite flat front and back, and then the skirt, she flounces. Alternating rows of black and—"

"Pink?" Suzanne offered.

"*Non.*"

She scanned the bolts of chiffon. "Blue? Red? Green?"

"*Non,* and *non.*" He flipped to another page. "It must be perfect."

"Paul, your gowns are always perfect," Suzanne said with patience, as though this routine was not unusual.

He glanced around the room more slowly and then at Abby. Finally, he nodded once. "The coral silk crepe. Bring it down, please."

Suzanne fetched the bolt, slipping on white cotton gloves before touching the beautiful fabric.

"Hold it next to Abigail," he said. As she did so, pulling a length of the silk and holding it in front of Abby like a sheet, he nodded. "Yes. The color is perfect." He sketched once more, rapidly. And then he began to add more detail, and Suzanne sighed in what looked like relief. *Monsieur* had found his way.

"You go to the Ballet Russes, and I am inspired by Diaghilev himself and his love of the orientalist style." He chuckled. "If you see him, Abigail, tell him that he is my inspiration for this gown. He will be delighted."

She doubted she'd meet the founder of the Ballet Russes, the great Serge Diaghilev, but she thought the coral silk was beautiful, and anything Paul designed for her would be lovely, she was certain.

"Warn Madame Bernard, there will be much beading to be done. It makes no matter if we work all night. This dress will be a revelation."

Suzanne walked behind him to look at his sketchbook, and Abby was bold enough to do the same. What she saw was a long, elegant slip of dress with sweeps of fabric down the sides and patterns that she presumed would be beading at the neck and on the skirt. Even in pencil it was gorgeous.

He gestured with the end of his pencil. "Two long, sleeveless panels with matching undergarment visible, yes?"

They both nodded.

"And then here, you will follow this design. Tiny pearls and white and bronze glass beads in this design around the neck and on this section of the bodice, and for this area on the skirt, small, circular shisha mirrors and crystal beads."

"It's a lot of work," Suzanne pointed out.

"Yes. And it must be done by tomorrow afternoon. *Bon.* We must begin *immediatement.*" He became busy with his sketchbook once more. "And for the head, a little beaded turban, *comme ça.*"

Not wishing to incur the wrath of the *première*, who would have to arrange this miracle of a dress to be cut, sewn and beaded within twenty-four hours, along with a matching turban, Abby left the atelier. However, when she reached the ground floor, instead of leaving by the street door, she walked into the haberdashery. Fortunately, Eugene, the young man who'd told her about the English gentleman buying handkerchiefs, was on duty.

He immediately recognized her and came forward. "Miss Dixon. How may I help you?"

There was no one else in the shop, so she felt comfortable bringing out the handkerchief she'd taken from Larry and showing it to Eugene. "Is this one of the handkerchiefs that the English gentleman purchased from you on Tuesday?"

She hardly dared to breathe as Eugene took the white square from her and studied it. But after turning it over and studying the edges, he said, "It is impossible to say. It could be one of ours, but we are not the only shop selling men's handkerchiefs of this quality."

That was disappointing, but he hadn't told her it wasn't one of theirs. Wanting to be absolutely certain, she said, "But it definitely could have come from here."

"Oh, yes." He opened one of the wide, flat drawers on the wall behind him and pulled out a handkerchief and set it on the counter beside the one she'd brought in, which looked identical apart from the creases. "You see, it is the same. It could be from this shop, but I cannot be certain."

She thanked him and headed home once more.

If Larry had been involved with Lillian, and she was certain he was, then she was going to keep digging. She knew she had to give Lillian's handbag to the police and that she should do so today, but she wanted one more look at the contents.

When she arrived home, Vivian was at the table cutting Abby's photograph and accompanying article from the front page of the *Post* to paste into her scrapbook.

"Oh, Abby. You're so famous. It's very exciting. Why, I don't even mind having to stay home with a cold. It would be terribly dull to stand in the shop and sell perfume when I can help a plucky girl reporter clear her name."

"I'm so glad you said that. I want to take another look at Lillian's handbag. I had an idea."

Viv shut her scrapbook with great care and turned around in her chair. She was bundled up in wool trousers, a thick sweater and the same shawl she'd worn the day before. "I thought your idea was to take the bag to the police."

"And I will, but I want one more look."

She'd told Vivian all about meeting Lord Lambridge and how he'd definitely looked shocked when he discovered she was related to the dead woman. "He slipped and said 'Lill'—then stopped himself and called her Mrs. Dixon."

Vivian leaned closer. "That's very significant."

"I think so, too." Then she told Viv about how she'd managed to get hold of his handkerchief. "And today I asked Eugene, and he said it could have come from Paul Joubert's haberdashery."

Vivian looked saddened by this news. "Gosh. To think of a nice English lord being a killer. It's very hard being a single girl who only wants to find a man who can give her a good home."

She pondered more deeply on her future husband. "And nice jewelry and fashionable clothes."

Abby went to her room and, after removing her coat and hat, pulled Lillian's handbag from the armoire in her bedroom and returned with it. "I want to check something." She removed the contents of the bag, which she'd attempted to return to the state in which she'd found it. She dug out a newspaper article and spread it out onto the table. After reading it over, while Vivian watched her, she said, "Yes. I thought so." Then she pointed to the listing of the Duchess of Cirencester and her evening party. "What do you bet that Lady Eleanor and at least her elder son were there? And that's where Lillian met them?"

Vivian seemed quite taken with this idea. "If only you could find out who was at that party."

"I know. Ruth at the paper only finds out who's entertaining, where, and which of the most important guests will be in attendance. I doubt she ever finds out afterward who was actually present. But I'm sure Lillian was at that party, Viv." She tapped her chest. "Right here, I'm sure of it. And if there was a marriageable titled Englishman there, she'd have had him in her sights the moment he walked into the room. Not that she'd care if he was married, but she'd obviously prefer the younger, single man."

"But what about his mother?" Viv wanted to know. "If the mother turned up her nose at you, she must've swooned with horror at the idea of her beloved son in the clutches of a woman like Lillian."

"Don't forget, I'm a penniless working girl. Lillian would have passed herself off as a rich, young widow, not one who's spending all that remains of her late husband's money on catching the next one. Besides, knowing Lillian, she probably acted the role of a heartbroken widow with no thought of ever marrying again. Then, when she'd flattered Lady Eleanor and disarmed her, she made a date for later, when Larry's mother wouldn't be around, so she could show Lord Larry the side of herself that she only showed to men."

Viv, who'd been in Paris longer and was more practiced at meeting men than Abby, shook her blond curls. "That's too obvious. If it was me, I'd have accidentally bumped into him somewhere, some evening when I just happened to be looking my best." Vivian stood, held out both arms, mimicking a hunting rifle, closed one eye as though sighting down the barrel and said, with relish, "She tracked him the way a hunter stalks big game."

"I'm sure you're right. That's exactly what she did with my father." But she'd been thinking, too. "Now, we know that Lillian arrived in Paris three weeks ago. She immediately went about meeting and seducing Lawrence."

Viv said, "But why did neither your friend Freddy nor his mother seem to know who Lillian was if they met her at the duchess's house?"

"You make an excellent point, Viv. Lillian's plan must have gone awry. Maybe she didn't go to the party after all. Perhaps Mrs. Peabody didn't get her an invitation. However, if Lillian didn't come here specifically to lure Larry into marriage, then she had in mind someone very like him. He's rich, handsome, British and titled. He's perfect. As you said yourself, she'd have hunted him like the big-game trophy he is."

"If he's so perfect, then one has to wonder why he isn't already married. There aren't enough rich, single men to go around as it is. Believe me, I know. A man like that has his choice of women."

"Well, his brother isn't married either. Perhaps they enjoy playing the field too much to settle on one woman."

"But Freddy is the younger. He's not under the same kind of pressure. Larry, as the eldest son, is expected to marry and begin producing heirs as soon as possible. You can bet his mother has pushed every marriageable aristocratic female under his nose. I read about such things all the time."

"Well, if his taste runs to women like Lillian, no wonder he hasn't married some British blue blood." She thought of the dull heiress he'd been pushing around the dance floor the evening before. "You don't suppose his mother killed Lillian, do you? To stop her son from marrying the wrong woman?"

"Seems a bit drastic."

"You're right. She wouldn't have to resort to anything so vulgar. Lady Eleanor would stab a person with veiled insults, garrote them with the long and aristocratically connected family lineage and bludgeon them with *Debrett's Peerage*."

The two women were silent as they continued scrutinizing the clutter they'd found in Lillian's handbag. After rapidly scanning the bills for gloves, lingerie, hats and shoes, Abby began to grow frustrated. She dug into the handbag once more, looking for secret pockets, something fallen into the lining. It took her a minute, but she felt something hard. Slipped into a side pocket was a slim, leather-bound notebook.

"Oh, this is good. Her appointment diary."

Eagerly, she flipped through the pages. Lillian had a few notes written in the pages, but more often seemed to have shoved bits of paper with scribbled notes into the notebook. Mostly she seemed to have jotted down hair appointments, and there were scribbles that were indecipherable. She showed the book to Viv. "What do you make of that? Is it a word?"

Viv squinted at the small notation that appeared, at first glance, to be a cramped scrawl, but then she said, "It's a kind of shorthand, I think."

"Oh, no wonder I couldn't read it."

"Why would she use shorthand?"

"Perhaps because Larry was not the only man enjoying her company. If she accidentally left this diary out, no one would have reason to be jealous."

She was making her way through the notes when she discovered one that made her pause. "Meet with priest."

"Look at this," she said to Viv. "What would Lillian be doing seeing a priest?"

"Well, I don't think she was planning to become a nun."

Abby carefully noted down the time of Lillian's appointment, which had been just over a week before she'd been killed. She added it to the list of names and places Lillian had frequented and which she also wanted to check out. The list was daunting. Fashion houses, parties, hair appointments, doctor appointments. She could understand why the police simply wanted to pin the crime on Abby. It was much easier than doing this massive sifting through detail.

"She was seeing the doctor rather a lot. Almost as often as the hairdresser."

"Do you think she was ill?"

She'd seen the doctor the day before she was killed at five in the afternoon. "No. I'm beginning to think it was another kind of code. 'Doctor' was one of her lovers, perhaps. As was the priest. The hairdresser another." She noted down the times and dates but was interrupted by a knock at the door. Not many visitors braved the four flights of stairs. She and Viv both looked at Lillian's handbag and all its contents heaped on their kitchen table. Viv gasped and put her hands to her heart. In a desperate whisper, she said, "It's the police. It must be. And now I'm an accessory to murder."

Abby felt jumpy too but tried to reassure her friend. "No doubt it's another telegram. You tidy this stuff away and hide the bag, just in case. I'll deal with whoever's at the door."

"All right. But if it is the police, make sure you inform them that I urged you to turn the bag in."

SEVENTEEN

When Abby opened the door, it wasn't a certain cool-eyed inspector standing there, as she'd feared, but her Aunt Ida, hanging on to the doorjamb, trying to get her breath back. She took one look at Abby and cried, "Oh, thank heaven you're not dead."

Aunt Ida Tumulty was a tall, thin woman who wore loose, flowing, vaguely Oriental-looking clothes. Her gray hair she also wore loose and flowing. She was nearly as tall as Abby and wore a great deal of makeup. Her most compelling feature was her piercing green eyes. Aunt Ida was the president of the Chicago Spiritualist Society and a minor celebrity. Since she was the widow of a wealthy man, she mostly did what she liked. She specialized in connecting the living with their dead loved ones with mixed success. Some clients left her front parlor séance room with thanks and tears of gratitude, while others left with blank faces and dashed hopes.

Abby didn't think of her aunt as a fraud so much as an unreliable communicator with the dead. Although, of course, Aunt Ida blamed the communication problems on the other side. "It's not like dealing with Western Union. The departed don't find it easy to get their messages across." She would spread her hands wide and say, "I am but an open conduit."

She pulled Abby in for a hug, strongly smelling of sandalwood and bergamot. "Oh, my dear, I've been so worried about you. I received a message that you were in great danger. I had to come and see for myself."

Abby strongly suspected that her aunt had read of her troubles in the newspaper and said so.

Aunt Ida studied her. "You look tired, dear. The strain is showing. I did not read about your terrible trouble until I was already aboard the ship that brought me here. I wired you from the ship." She put a hand to her forehead in dramatic fashion. "I was terribly shocked when I heard about Lillian's death, of course. I knew the spirits had sent me here for a reason."

"Did the spirits by any chance tell you who killed Lillian? That would be the biggest help they could give me."

Aunt Ida shook her head sadly. "The spirits don't deal well in direct communication. But never mind. I'm here now, and we shall soon get to the bottom of this mystery."

Abby invited her aunt into their tiny flat and introduced her to Vivian, who looked as guilty as though she'd been caught in mischief. The curtain that hid their few cooking utensils bulged, and a handbag strap peeped out. Viv would never find success as a criminal.

Aunt Ida settled herself on the tiny settee. Although she didn't comment on the poor accommodation, after glancing around, she said, "I am putting up at the Hotel Meurice."

"You are? Do you realize that's the hotel where Lillian was staying before she was killed?"

"I wasn't certain, but I had a premonition that's where she would have stayed."

"Why would you want to stay in the same hotel as Lillian?"

Seeing Abby's obvious confusion, Ida smiled gently. "Don't you see? We'll have a séance, right in the hotel, which we know was Lillian's last address. There's a chance that she hasn't passed over yet and may be able to help us in our investigation."

"If you ask me, there's nothing Lillian would like more than to see me charged with her murder."

"Even if you're innocent?"

"Especially if I'm innocent. Let us not forget that she was not a nice woman."

"No. And, of course, terribly jealous of you. She didn't like that you were younger than she and that your father loved you. She was an odd woman. However much admiration she had, she couldn't bear for another woman to have even a bit of her man's affection. Not even if that woman was his own daughter."

Before bitter memories could claim her, Abby said, "I do have some acquaintance in that hotel myself." She told Aunt Ida about Freddy and his family. She was tempted to warn her aunt that Freddy's older brother was very high on her personal list of suspects but then decided it wasn't fair without any proof. Even if Larry had killed Lillian, he had no reason to do away with Aunt Ida. So long as he didn't take her prying and her séances seriously.

"But that's wonderful, dear." Her bright eyes gleamed as green as emeralds. "Is he an interesting young man?" Aunt Ida wanted nothing more than to see Abby settle down with an appropriate husband. In her way, she was as bad as Lady Eleanor.

"I'm much too busy trying to clear myself of murder to worry about courting."

"Nonsense. A young woman should always be thinking about courting."

"That's what I say," Vivian interjected.

Abby introduced the two women, and Aunt Ida thanked Vivian for being a good friend to her niece. She looked Abby up and down and said, "Apart from looking a little tired, you appear remarkably well. You've adopted that boyish new hairstyle, I see, but it rather suits you. As do these lovely French clothes you were wearing in today's newspaper photograph. They must be paying you well in Paris."

She snorted. "Hardly." Briefly, she explained about the deal she'd made with her newspaper to publish harrowing stories about her ordeal, and with Paul Joubert to clothe her. Aunt Ida, surprisingly, approved of her plan. But then, as she too often forgot, Aunt Ida wasn't very much like her sister.

She offered her guest coffee and was turned down.

"No, thank you, dear. I must get back to the hotel. I'm organizing a séance for this evening. I want you to come."

Abby felt her eyes open in surprise. "So soon?"

"But of course. It's the best way I can think to help you. We must move quickly if we are to contact Lillian's spirit before she's left this realm."

Abby thought that the quicker Lillian's spirit was gone, the better for all of them. She'd been a destructive influence when she was alive. The last thing Abby needed was the malevolent spirit of Lillian haunting her. However, since she didn't give much credence to Aunt Ida's spiritualism and she knew the woman genuinely wanted to help her, she agreed.

"Come at eight o'clock, dear. I'm in room 605."

A shiver ran down her arms. "Do you realize that room is right above the one where Lillian was staying?"

A delightful trill of laughter greeted her. "Of course, I do. I fell into conversation with one of the guests in the lobby and found out quite a bit. Everyone loves a good gossip about a juicy murder. The woman knew the room number, and it was an easy enough matter to book the room above it. I don't think too many people relish staying in that room."

"I certainly wouldn't," Vivian said, looking nervous.

"But, you see, I make friends with the spirits. That's why they talk to me. You're welcome to come along this evening."

She rose. "Would you care to accompany me, Abby? We

can have a good catch-up, and you can help me prepare for the séance."

"I'd love to, Aunt Ida, but Uncle Charles has hired a defense attorney for me here in Paris. I'm seeing him this afternoon."

Aunt Ida drew on her gloves. "Good. I told Charles Abernathy that he will have me to deal with if anything happens to you."

* * *

Monsieur Tremblay's offices were near 26 Quai des Orfevres, the imposing edifice on the banks of the Seine that was also home to the *Police Judiciaire de Paris*. Before meeting Monsieur Tremblay, Abby made a stop at police headquarters. Vivian had insisted she return Lillian's handbag, and she knew her roommate was right.

Abby tried to shake off the feeling of nervousness as she stepped into the beautiful building. She had asked for this meeting, she reminded herself. She hadn't been summoned here by the police. Still, she'd be glad when she was back out in the fresh air.

A young officer escorted her up a broad flight of steps and down the hall to an office. He knocked politely on the door and was invited to come in. The young man opened the door and stood back for her. She walked in to find Henri Deschamps behind a desk, paper spread in front of him. At her entrance, he rose politely and came around to offer her his hand. She shook it briefly and then sat in the chair he indicated.

"To what do I owe this pleasure?" he asked, slightly sardonically.

"Well, I haven't come to turn myself in, if that's what you were hoping."

"A pity."

She supposed sarcasm wasn't a wonderful tactic given that she was here to give him evidence she never should have taken out of Hotel Meurice. She wasn't quite ready to face his wrath, so she studied his office instead. Apart from the desk, there were shelves behind him, filled with books and neatly stacked papers. There were built-in cupboards on one wall, a window on the opposite side, and a coat rack with one coat on it and one hat.

He hadn't offered to take hers, so he clearly didn't want her to stay. On the top shelf behind him was a clock and beside it, a photograph of a beautiful woman. From her clothing, it appeared to have been taken before the war. "Is that your wife?" she asked, pointing.

He turned and regarded the photograph. "Yes."

"She's very beautiful. You're a lucky man."

"I've always thought so." He turned back to her and raised his eyebrows. She couldn't delay any longer, so she stood up. She was carrying two handbags. She put Lillian's bag on his desk. "I'm very sorry, but I accidentally took this from Lillian's room the night you found me at the Hotel Meurice."

He looked at the bag and then at her, and his pleasant expression faded. "Accidentally? Do you know that it is a crime to tamper with a murder scene, Miss Dixon?"

"Well, technically, that wasn't the murder scene." At his forbidding look, she blew out a breath. "I am truly sorry. You startled me when I heard you in the other room. I thought it might be Lillian's killer returning, and without thinking, I pushed my bag into her larger one. I didn't realize I'd done it until I got home."

"Have you removed anything from the bag?" Oh, he could do cold and intimidating well.

"No." At his raised eyebrows, she added, "I won't pretend I didn't peek. But everything is where I found it." She nibbled her lower lip. "There's an appointment diary that's easy to overlook."

"Thank you," he said, making *thank you* sound like a threat.

She smiled brightly. "Well, I've got a defense attorney to see, and you've got more evidence to sift through, so I'll leave you to it."

"I hope your attorney is a good one."

EIGHTEEN

Monsieur Tremblay was a very tall man with luxurious black hair. He heard her tale in silence, making very few notes. When she told him about her visit to Hotel Meurice and then returning the bag to the inspector, he looked less than pleased.

"Miss Dixon, there is no real evidence against you. It was an unfortunate coincidence that your stepmother should be murdered while you were in the same building. That is all one can say with any certainty."

"Oh, thank goodness." She felt very relieved until he pointed his index finger at her.

"However, if you continue with unwise actions, such as going to your stepmother's hotel room and removing her belongings, you put quite another complexion on the matter. Do you understand this?"

"Yes, sir."

"You make yourself look guilty, in fact."

"I was only trying to find out what happened to her."

"In Paris, we are very proud of our police. Please allow them to do their job unimpeded." She felt as though she'd been sent to the principal's office at school and was being lectured for bad behavior. She couldn't wait to get out of this richly paneled office lined with law books and smelling faintly of cigar smoke.

"I'm sorry," she said.

He continued to regard her. "I will refuse to work on your behalf if I hear of any further interference in this police investigation."

She hung her head, doing her best to look contrite. "I understand."

"Very well. We will not need to meet again unless you are formally arrested."

And that was very good news.

He'd said "unless" she was formally arrested and not "until."

* * *

When Abby arrived at Aunt Ida's room that night with Vivian, she was surprised to find several people already there. She'd assumed it would be only her and Aunt Ida, but she should have known not to underestimate her formidable aunt. An older, prosperous-looking couple sat side-by-side on the sofa in the parlor of Aunt Ida's suite, which she could see at a glance was larger than the one below it and featured a dining room, which Aunt Ida had prepared for her séance.

She introduced the couple as Mrs. Amelia Harris and her husband, Brendan Harris. "They met Lillian several times in this hotel and are very interested in my work, so I invited them to come tonight."

Abby shook hands and mustered the social inanities that one does on meeting new people.

"We're so sorry you've been falsely accused of murder," Mrs. Harris said to her, hanging on to her hand. "But I'm sure with your famous aunt's help, you'll clear your name."

"I hope so."

"I understand that Paul Joubert himself is helping you. I'm tempted to order a gown from him myself." She adopted a virtuous look. "Simply to encourage him in his laudable work."

"That's very kind of you."

In a moment there was a timid knock on the door, and two uniformed chambermaids came in, looking wretched and unsure of themselves. They popped identical curtsies and then stood uncertainly as though wishing they had dusters or brooms to keep themselves busy.

Aunt Ida bustled forward and thanked them for coming in loud and appalling French. Their names were Celine and Sophie. They had been the maids who'd cleaned Lillian's room one floor below.

"And now, we may begin. Please, come into the séance room." Aunt Ida had brought with her what appeared to be an entire trunkful of candles, which she'd placed around the dining room. There was a circular table in the room suitable for a small dinner party, and around this they seated themselves.

Aunt Ida turned out the electric lights, and they settled around the table, the flickering candlelight dancing on the polished surface.

Aunt Ida sat, majestic, at the head of the table, and Mr. Harris settled opposite, like a good host. Only instead of being served delicious French cuisine, the hope was that they would be served up ghosts. Abby loved Aunt Ida but was always mortified when she was forced to join the séances. She felt her aunt would've been a very successful actress and, instead, had followed her talents into taking on the roles of the dearly departed.

Aunt Ida breathed in and out a few times, and then she said, her voice clear and strong, "I ask each of you to clasp the hands of the person on either side. Close your eyes. Clear your minds of all thoughts, all memory, all wishes for the future or regrets of the past. We open ourselves in our circle to the spirits of those who have left our mortal world. I call on you now, spirits of the departed." In the silence that followed, Abby heard the breathing of the other participants and a horn from the street below. "Spirits, are you with us? Lillian Dixon, I call on you. Lillian? Are you with us?"

Mr. Harris sat on her left. He had hesitated before reaching for her hand, and against her palm, his felt leathery, dry and rather cool. On her other side was one of the chambermaids, and as Aunt Ida began to speak, the girl's hand grew hot and clammy and began to tremble. Poor girl. She was probably a staunch Catholic and horrified at the idea of calling on the spirits of the dead. Aunt Ida should be ashamed of herself, dragging these poor girls into a séance. No doubt they hadn't been able to refuse.

Even though they'd been told to keep their eyes closed, Abby half-opened hers. She didn't believe Aunt Ida could really channel spirits, but just in case, she hated the idea of them being around her while she was blind.

The nerve-stretching silence continued but for some rustling and the sound of Vivian clearing her throat. Abby felt she was trying not to cough. After another long, dramatic minute, Ida called once more. "Are the spirits with us?"

To Abby's astonishment and some horror, she saw the candlelight flare. There were plenty of fake spiritualists who used tricks, but Aunt Ida had never done that. No doubt a good fake could make candles flare by doctoring them somehow, but why would her aunt do that with so few of them in attendance?

Aunt Ida said, in a higher tone than usual, "The spirits are with us."

Celine's hand twitched in hers.

Aunt Ida said, her eyes still closed, "We seek your help. Spirits, what can you tell us of the murder of Lillian Dixon?"

There was a silence. Through her partly open eyes, she saw

her aunt's face crease. "Oh, dear. It's all in French," she said, half to herself.

"Spirits, we ask if there is anyone there who speaks English?"

She waited a beat. Then sighed. "Apparently not."

"Could you speak more slowly?" Aunt Ida asked, sounding half exasperated, half hopeful.

"*Lentement*," Vivian offered her the word.

"*Lentement*," Aunt Ida repeated.

Then she grew more animated. "Ah, a little more *lentewhatsit*, if you please. Wait, I'm getting something. I'm getting a name. Louise. Yes, Louise, that's right. *Oui*. Louise is here. And there's something else. What's that? Poodle-faker was spike-bozzled. I beg your pardon? Oh, now you're laughing. Why is that funny? Oh, Gott strafe England." She twitched and sighed. "Don Jay.

"Don Jay." She repeated the words. Then she opened her eyes and straightened in her chair. "They've gone now. But that's something. Perhaps it's the name of the real murderer? Or perhaps a witness?"

Abby and Viv glanced at each other, and then Abby asked, "Was the spirit maybe saying *danger*? That's danger with a French accent."

"But who is Louise?" Vivian asked as Abby turned the lights back on.

"That's Abby's middle name. She's Abigail Louise Dixon."

"And now we know I'm in danger," Abby said.

"But what were those other words?" Vivian asked, her blue eyes wide. "What does spike-bozzled mean?"

"Those were terms from the war, I think," Mr. Harris offered. "Gott strafe England, or God strike England, was a bit of German propaganda."

"I've no idea what spirits I roused," Ida admitted. "But I must work on my French."

The evening broke up, and Abby and Vivian rode the bus back to the Latin Quarter.

"The spirit knew your middle name, Abby," Vivian said, when they'd returned safely home. "That's given me a chill down the back of my neck."

Abby liked Vivian, but sometimes she could be very naïve. "Aunt Ida knows my middle name. She thinks she hears voices, but it's all in her head." She shook her own head. "I deal in facts, not dubious visits from the departed."

"But you will be careful? I'm worried about you. She said you were in danger."

"How can I worry about a séance when I have the Ballet Russes to look forward to tomorrow night?" She intended to take Vivian's mind somewhere more pleasant, and her plan was an instant success.

Viv put her hand to her heart. "The Ballet Russes. And in a Joubert gown."

* * *

The next evening, Abby swept into the Ballet Russes on Freddy's arm for a performance of *Le Train Bleu*. She felt as though every conversation stopped and every eye turned to stare at her. A kind of electric current, what the French would call a *frisson*, shivered through the crowd.

"My dear girl, you take my breath away," Freddy said, gazing at her with frank admiration.

He barely had time for more when the photographers began to close in. She became half blinded by the flashes but gamely kept her smile and turned obligingly each time a voice called out, "Over here, Miss Dixon."

"Is that another Paul Joubert gown?" a woman reporter asked, stepping forward.

"It is. Monsieur Joubert is the only designer for me," she

said, as though she could order a gown from any designer she liked.

"Tell me, how are you holding up under the strain of a murder investigation?" the woman asked.

Abby shrugged, so the beads and tiny mirrors on her dress shimmered. "I'm doing my best. For the details, you'll have to read my personal account of my harrowing ordeal in the *Chicago International Post.*"

Freddy stood gamely by her side and then, as though he'd been blinded long enough, said, "I'll fetch you a glass of champagne. Won't be a mo."

Now she was alone and posed quite happily for a few more photos.

"How will you plead to the murder charge?" another reporter pressed her.

A voice from her left calmly said, "Mademoiselle Dixon has not been charged with any crime." In a moment, the spotlight of attention shifted from her to the elegant man in evening dress.

"Inspector Deschamps, what can you tell us? Are you going to arrest Abigail Dixon?" He was suddenly in the center of the mob of reporters. He repeated the same words he'd said again and again. "Our investigation is ongoing. We hope to make an arrest soon."

Then, as suddenly as they'd appeared, the crush of reporters and photographers was gone.

Inspector Deschamps stepped toward her. It annoyed her to have to look up at him as he gazed down at her with a sardonic glint in his eye.

Oh, she could do sardonic as well as he. "You're a fan of the Russian Ballet, Inspector?"

"I am."

"What a coincidence that you should keep turning up wherever I am. But then I don't believe in coincidence. Did your spies tell you where I was going to be tonight?" She glanced behind him. "I don't see them."

"There was no need. Your attendance here was reported in the papers."

Her skin burned briefly at the thought of Freddy reporting to the press that she'd accepted his invitation, but even as the thought crossed her mind, she knew Freddy would never do such a thing. The news had to have come from Paul Joubert.

The inspector seemed amused by her sudden discomfiture. "You are becoming quite a celebrity in Paris, you know."

"Are you here to make sure I don't commit a crime during the ballet performance?"

"On the contrary. I am here on a more pleasant errand." He stood back to admire her latest Joubert creation. "Why, you could be on stage yourself in such an elaborate costume."

She gave what she hoped was a withering smile. "*Le Train Bleu* is about the idle rich going on vacation, Inspector," she said, glad she'd had a chance to peruse the program. "I don't currently have time to vacation. Or a passport."

He seemed more amused than offended. "Of course. My mistake."

Freddy returned at that moment with champagne, and the inspector bowed, wished them a pleasant evening, and was gone.

She drank the champagne with relief. Freddy looked after the inspector in concern. "Awfully sorry to have abandoned you before a battle. I'd have stood buff if I'd known he was hanging about ready to pounce on you."

"It's all right."

"It's not all right. Who wants a copper turning up everywhere one goes? Gave me a nasty turn, seeing him again, I can tell you."

"He claims to be a ballet enthusiast."

"Oh, he does, does he?" Freddy said, not looking convinced.

But, as they headed to their seats, she saw the inspector ushering an older woman to her seat. The woman had a similar upright bearing, and her features, though softer, were enough like the inspector's that Abby suspected he'd escorted his mother to the ballet. No doubt he was also here to spy on her, but in spite of herself, she was charmed.

Le Train Bleu was modern, energetic and unlike anything she'd seen in Chicago. The Russian dancers were athletes, an impression reinforced by the costumes designed by Coco Chanel. They danced not in tutus and tights but in golf trousers and even a bathing costume. She applauded enthusiastically. At the intermission, a slim, dark-haired woman wearing a short black dress with several strings of pearls came up to her. Thanks to Vivian's fashion magazines, Abby recognized her as Coco Chanel.

Dark, sparkling eyes regarded her, and the woman said, "Miss Dixon, I presume?"

"Miss Chanel. It's an honor to meet you. Your costumes were wonderful."

She ignored the gushing praise and gestured with her small, restless hand up and down, from the tip of Abby's head to the hem of her gown. "My old friend Paul Joubert has outdone himself. I could make up my face in those little mirrors on your skirt, but the effect is admirable. Very Grecian goddess."

"Thank you. I'll pass on the compliment."

The woman chuckled, and it was low and husky. "A little word of advice. Wearing the same designer too often is like keeping a lover too long. One needs a change to stay *au courant*." She handed Abby a card. "This is my personal number. Call me. I should like to design you a dress. Much simpler, but you will love it."

Even though Abby wanted to support a woman who was making a success of her business in a man's world, she'd made a promise. "As flattered as I am, I am Monsieur Joubert's muse. I cannot stray."

The designer half-closed her eyes and shrugged her shoulders. "Keep my card. Perhaps you will wear my signature perfume? It is the scent of style, I promise you. And there is no perfume du Joubert."

Since the scent of Chanel No. 5 would always remind her of Lillian, she refused once more.

"*Eh bien,* I find you amusing and very beautiful. You must come to one of my parties." She cast a glance at Freddy, who had struck up a conversation with another Englishman. "And bring your very handsome friend."

"That I can do," she said, delighted.

Coco Chanel had changed everything by throwing aside convention in couture, in business and in her personal life. If Lillian were truly going to bring herself into vogue, she'd need to add Chanel to her wardrobe.

"Miss Chanel—"

"Call me Coco. Everyone does."

"Coco. Did Lillian Dixon come to you for gowns? Did you ever meet?"

"Lillian Dixon is the woman who they think you killed, yes?"

Not how she would have put it, but... "Yes."

The woman put her shoulders up and her hands out in a dismissive gesture. "I would not have seen her personally. No. There are only very few clients I handle personally."

"Of course." Lillian hadn't been important, rich, or influential enough to have Coco Chanel's personal service. But she'd have aspired to become one of those very special clients.

"You, however, should you change your mind, I will design for you myself."

Was the woman under a misapprehension? "I'm a reporter. I don't earn much money. I'm not influential or important."

The woman chuckled. It was a low, smoky sound, "At this moment, my dear, you are the most famous woman in Paris." She paused. "After me."

"I only wish to prove my innocence."

"I admire your spirit. You remind me of myself when I was younger. You have taken this terrible thing that has happened to you and turned it to your advantage. Very good. But—a tiny word of advice—be very careful. Trust no one. Those closest to you may turn out to be your deadliest enemies." Then glancing past Abby, she caught sight of someone and waved. "I must go. *Bon soir.*"

Abby watched her go. Would she have said more? Had she had someone in mind? Someone who was close to Abby and might turn out to be her enemy?

NINETEEN

The letters began to pour into the newspaper office. They offered support, money for her defense and, as Ruth had foreseen, one even offered her marriage.

One letter arrived in a plain envelope. She tore it open and scanned the contents. Her croissant dropped to her plate. She read the letter again.

Mademoiselle. Your life is in danger. You must go back to America.

It was signed,

a friend.

She'd seen an envelope very like this one in Paul Joubert's office. She'd had the photographs developed by the newspaper and they sat in her files at home. She thought whoever had written to her was simply fear-mongering. Still, she didn't throw the letter away but put it into her desk drawer.

It seemed the more she learned, the more confused she became.

She turned back to her typewriter. Since she had yet to be arrested, her articles were more about how she kept herself busy and her spirits up. She'd tried to talk Walter Strutt into letting her do a series of articles on female prisoners in France, but he'd shot her down immediately.

"The girls in Iowa and Illinois don't care about French girls in prison. They care about you. So keep doing what you're doing."

"I haven't been arrested."

"Don't sound so disappointed."

He was right, but she was beginning to feel like a fraud. And yet, she was still followed by detectives, and there had been no arrests or breakthroughs in Lillian's case.

Her reports were growing shorter, and more space was being taken up with photographs of her at social events. So long as it sold papers, everyone seemed to be happy. Especially Paul Joubert, who'd asked her to come in for a fitting today. Freddy had invited her to a party hosted by an American millionaire, and Paul Joubert had been tickled. "Everyone, but everyone will be there. And they will be people who have money to spend."

He'd told her he had something special in mind, but it was more than she'd bargained for.

"Show me your back," he said, as soon as she was in her usual fitting room.

Abby was startled. "I beg your pardon?"

"Your back," Paul said in some irritation. "Is it an asset?"

"It carries my neck and head. I guess that's an asset."

He shook his head, turned to his assistant. "Suzanne, put her in something to preserve her modesty and let me see her back." He sketched while she and Suzanne retreated behind the modesty screen.

She raised her brows in a silent question, which Suzanne answered. "He'll only design you a backless dress if you have the right body. He's very particular."

"A backless dress? But what would I wear for underwear?" she whispered.

Suzanne shook her head, trying hard not to grin.

"You mean, nothing?" Abby was shocked. She wasn't a puritan by any means, but it wasn't her back she was worried about. If her back was bare, what was her front going to look like with no support?

She emerged in a hastily donned dressing gown Suzanne had reversed, pulling the lapels apart. Abby felt the coolness on her naked back as Paul Joubert inspected her. He took his time and then announced, "Yes. Perfect. Lean musculature and delicate bones."

"But the, um, front?" She had to ask.

"The female form is not to be trussed up and confined, my dear Abby. You want the freedom to vote and the freedom to act as you please in public. You should have the freedom to move in your clothing."

Suzanne said, "Luckily, you don't have too much cleavage. Don't worry." She dropped her voice. "There won't be any bounce."

When she arrived home, Vivian was signing a work order, and a uniformed man took the paper, nodded to Abby and left.

Vivian's eyes twinkled, and she grabbed her hand. "Come and look!" She tugged and dragged Abby into their main room and waved her hand in the manner of a conjurer. "Will you look at that? Our own telephone."

"Golly!" She stared at the elegant piece. "But how can we afford it?"

"We can't. Charles Abernathy paid for it. And he left a message that he'll telephone you tonight."

"Maybe he's phoning to yell at me." Possibly he'd heard that she'd been snooping where she shouldn't.

"It's an expensive way to shout at someone." They both stared at the phone.

"Look, you can't miss that call. I need to run out and get a few things before the shops close. When I get back, you have to tell me everything."

As Vivian prepared to leave, Abby glanced out of the window. "I see the two detectives are still there."

"Yes."

She went to her purse and pulled out some francs. "Get them a bonbon each, my compliments."

At that moment, the phone began to ring, making them both jump.

She resolutely approached the shrieking telephone. She picked it up. "Hello? Abigail Dixon speaking."

"Terrific work, Abby. Terrific." It seemed Uncle Charles wasn't phoning to yell at her after all, but to compliment her. "Newspaper sales increased drastically last year with that spate of glamorous murderesses in Chicago. But this? Sweet young American reporter unfairly accused of murder? And it turns out the dame was her evil stepmother? People can't get enough of it. I've had to hire extra staff on the circulation desk."

"I'm glad you're happy."

"Not just me. The readers are going crazy. They're phoning in, walking into the newspaper office. Some of the suffragettes are planning a campaign."

She was oddly touched. "That's nice."

"Nice? It's better than nice. Circulation's up, and half the women in this city want one of those fancy French gowns you've been wearing."

"Oh, Monsieur Joubert will be pleased."

"He darn well better be pleased. Now, I want to make sure you're still the prime suspect?"

"As far as I can tell, I'm the only suspect."

"Good. Good." She heard the wheeze as he inhaled his cigar.

"Good? It's not your neck on the line, or I should say, the guillotine."

"Don't worry. We're on your side. Tremblay's the best there is to deal with that cockamamie legal system."

"Thank you."

"Now, you keep up the first-person accounts. The more harrowing and pathetic the better. What does it feel like to be under the cloud of suspicion? The woman who broke up your family, alone and frightened in a foreign country, that kind of thing. Keeping up your spirits by attending the ballet and so on wearing those pretty dresses. As fast as you can write them, I can print them. Also, your hair."

"What about my hair?" She touched her fingers to her short locks.

"Get whoever cut it to write out how it's done. Get it translated and send it to me. Every woman in America wants her hair like yours."

"American women are copying my hairstyle?"

"Abby, I don't want to puff you up, honey, but you're a sensation."

There was a lightness inside that lifted the heavy weight of being suspected of a terrible crime, but not for long.

She had trouble sleeping, and when she did sleep, she'd picture herself looking up at the sharp blade of the guillotine about to drop. The steel was cool and wicked, and in her dreams there was always a basket beneath waiting for her severed head.

She'd hear the barked command and wake up with a start, her heart pounding and her throat parched. Still half asleep, she'd put her hands to her neck, as though making certain it was still attached. Still, being told she'd created a sensation, even for such a grim reason, was still something. "Golly," she said.

"That fashion piece for the women's page, we're changing it."

"Oh, but you have to run it. Poor Monsieur Joubert has been through so much. It would be devastating if we didn't run the feature."

"Oh, Joubert will be very pleased if he's half the businessman I hope he is. We're redoing the feature. We want you to model the gowns."

"What?"

"Come on, what did you learn in that fancy journalism school, Abby? Nothing sells papers like a young gal in a bind. The young wife whose husband murders her lover, the woman sentenced to hang for poisoning her ugly pig of a drunk husband, you know the stuff people go for."

"But surely I can use my fame for some noble purpose. Like bringing attention to the plight of women here in France. They don't have the vote! Or the plight of the many young women and children whose husbands and fathers never returned from the Great War. France lost more young men than any other country in the world."

"Honey, when the murder rap dies down, we'll see about letting you take on some other stories. In the meantime? You are the story. Got it? You're experiencing something that no other gal has ever experienced. She gets to live through you. It's like a penny dreadful, only real. Now, have other papers been after you to write for them?"

"Well, a nice man approached me on Rue de l'Opera the other day. He writes for the *Gazette* and said they'd be interested in talking to me, but of course I told him I already have a job."

"Good. R.J. has approved a bonus. Since you've boosted sales and become a murder row celebrity—"

"Oh, please don't use that term." The words made her shiver deep in her being. Still, it was nice that R.J. Hunnicut, the man who owned her paper, was personally making sure she was rewarded.

"Don't go getting soft on me, Abby. Murder, a young innocent American accused, the death penalty hanging over you, and in Paris, it's pure gold."

He was right. She couldn't falter. Not now. "You said something about a bonus?"

"How does one thousand American dollars sound?"

She couldn't speak for a moment. In the sudden silence, she heard a sound that might have been angels singing. "One thousand dollars?"

"That's right. And he's doubling your salary. You sign a contract that says you publish your stories exclusively with us. R.J. has an idea to get you to write a book about your experience when this is all over." R.J. was a notorious tightwad.

"Is he that afraid of losing me?" She didn't want to talk the newspaper's owner out of an incredibly generous bonus, but she was stunned.

Uncle Charles chuckled. "Not R.J. His wife. She's as hooked on your story as every other woman. She told him he had to give you the money. Of course, that's confidential. The whole thing is on the quiet. If reporters get wind of the bonus and increase, they'll all go out murdering relatives they don't like."

"Of course. Please tell R.J. and Mrs. R.J. how grateful I am."

"Now, you just keep your head on your shoulders."

"What if I can't?" She tried not to be a crybaby, but she was followed everywhere by police, and if there were other suspects, she had yet to hear about them. "What if they chop off my sweet American head first and ask questions later?"

"Not going to happen," he said in a tone so hearty, she knew he was bluffing. "Abby, we've got the best lawyer. You've got the support of the American people. I've heard that the first lady, Mrs. Coolidge herself, has taken a real interest in your case."

"That's nice."

"So, what do you say? Do we have a deal? A thousand bucks and double your salary is a lot of green."

She put a hand to her neck. "I'd better spend the money fast."

In fact, she knew exactly how she was going to spend it. Paul Joubert had opened his atelier to her and gowned her exquisitely, but she needed the rest of her wardrobe to match. Lingerie and even nightclothes. And wearing couture outfits up four flights of stairs was a crime against fashion.

"Abby?"

"Yes. We have a deal."

TWENTY

When Vivian returned, Abby told her the good news. Her roommate squealed, and she beamed with happiness. Then her face fell as suddenly. She was like a balloon that was overfilled and then popped. "I guess you'll be moving. Well, I don't blame you, but gosh, it was nice having you as a roommate."

Abby glanced around the shabby apartment. She might not have long to live, and if that was so, she was certainly going to spend her last days in style. "I was thinking along the lines of a few new nightgowns and some silk stockings. But with a thousand dollars, why, we could move somewhere much nicer. Maybe with an elevator."

"Oh, don't tease. I promise to be happy for you since the money came from such an awful tragedy, but don't taunt me with elevators."

"And endless hot water."

"No."

"A doorman to collect the bouquets of flowers and greet our callers."

"Now you're just being cruel."

She laughed. "Vivian, I wouldn't move without you."

"But I don't have a thousand dollars! I think I have about fifty dollars in the world."

"You'll pay the same as you pay here for half the rent, and I'll pay the rest."

"No. That wouldn't be fair."

"Of course it's fair. You've stuck by me and believed in my innocence, and besides, you're my only friend in Paris. Please say you'll continue to be my roommate?"

Vivian jumped up and hugged her friend. "Of course I will. And as soon as my ship comes in, I'll pay more toward the rent."

Since Vivian spent every cent of her earnings on clothes and magazines, Abby doubted that was going to happen anytime soon, but she'd meant what she'd said. She found Paris to be like a castle on the outside, elegant and ornamented, but once inside, there were twisting passages and dungeons so she had to be very careful where she turned. Vivian was her friend and her ally in a glittering but dangerous world.

"The only thing is..." Her words slowed, and she stopped to gnaw on her lower lip.

"The only thing is what?"

"If I'm convicted," she said in a rush, "I'd leave you the rest of the money, but I'm not sure how long it would last."

"No," Vivian said. "No. I will not believe that, and you're not to believe it either. They haven't arrested you. We both know they don't have enough evidence, and they'll never get enough because you didn't do it."

"I get so scared. I feel like Inspector Deschamps has a personal mission to separate me from my head."

Vivian shivered and sat down. "I don't like that man. I don't think he likes that you're making a fool of him and his men. That's why he's trying so hard to gather evidence against you."

"Sometimes I wish I'd never left Chicago."

Vivian sighed. "Most of the time I wish I never had to go back."

"Well, instead of sitting around feeling sorry for myself, what do you say we go and get some dinner? Somewhere flashy and fabulous. And I'm paying."

"Oh, Abby, I don't want you spending money on me. Let's go to the bistro on the corner."

"No. I'm blue, and I don't like being blue." She nudged her friend. "And now that I'm starting to get to know Paris, I even know where to go without asking you."

"Oh, where?"

"Maxim's, of course." She struck a pose. "Plucky girl reporter keeps up spirits in Maxim's."

"And thanks to Paul Joubert, I won't have to blush to be seen with you in those awful clothes."

* * *

Abby had a good desk with a good chair in a prime spot in the newsroom. How things had changed. A keen reporter eager to do good work got whatever chair was currently vacant, but a woman suspected of murder? That earned her a promotion in the newsroom, also a fat bonus.

Aunt Ida had been as delighted as Abby and Vivian to learn that they could afford to move and, with her usual energy, soon discovered a furnished apartment that would suit them admirably. It was on Rue Saint-Hyacinthe, only a couple of blocks from the *Post's* editorial offices. Their apartment was on the fifth floor, but there was an elevator, which seemed like the ultimate luxury. The flat also boasted polished parquet floors, tall windows, high ceilings and furniture that was a mixture of French antiques and modern pieces.

There were two large bedrooms, a smaller one for guests, a functional kitchen and a luxurious bathroom.

They moved their belongings in two taxi trips.

Abby was using the time when she wasn't writing articles

about her harrowing ordeal to try and discover who, apart from her, might have wanted Lillian Dixon dead.

She put in a call to Charles Abernathy from her home phone. "Uncle Charles, I need you to do something for me."

"Anything at all, my dear."

"Can you get someone to look into Lillian's background?"

"Now, Abby," he started in his avuncular way.

She cut him off. "Uncle Charles, the police have no leads. I know I didn't kill Lillian. There's something she's done or seen that made her a target. Do you remember when she met Father?" It was difficult to bring up that awful time. "Where did she come from? I know she met him at the golf club, but who introduced them? Did she ever talk about her people? Please, put a researcher on it."

He cleared his throat. "I've always believed he was sorry, afterward. That woman bewitched him."

"Yes. I believe he was sorry, too. It was as though she'd bewitched him, but I wanted him to be a better man and to remain true to Mother. I was so enraged by Lillian's behavior and what the divorce did to Mother that I never even tried to know her. Now I'm at a loss. Where did she come from? Who was she? Can you help me?"

"I'll do what I can, Abigail."

"Thanks."

* * *

A frequent visitor to their new home was Freddy.

"Are you in love with him?" Vivian asked when he'd returned her from dinner one evening.

"No. But he's very amusing company, and we have fun together."

"Well, it looks to me like you could be Lady Freddy if you

lifted your little finger. Ask him if he has any titled, rich friends for me."

Abby laughed and promised she would, but one of the things she liked most about Freddy was that he seemed perfectly happy for their relationship to stay casual. He might flatter her and show the world his heart was at her feet, but she sometimes felt it was an act.

However, his light courtship suited her perfectly. She was much too busy trying to solve a murder to worry about romance. And she didn't believe he was in danger of a broken heart, so she was happy to encourage him.

One afternoon, as they were driving to the country to visit friends of his, she pondered the little she knew so far about Lillian's murder. The odd phrases from Aunt Ida's séance played in her mind. Not that Abby believed her aunt was communicating with the other side, but she was leaving no stone unturned.

She said, "Freddy, if someone said 'a poodle-faker was spike-bozzled,' would that mean anything to you?"

He looked at her curiously. "It would take me back to the trenches is what it would do. A poodle-faker was a soldier who wanted to go on leave to chase the girls. Not that we all didn't, of course, but if he was too keen about it, he got called a poodle-faker, and sometimes they wouldn't let them go if he didn't have a better reason."

He looked over his shoulder and maneuvered the car between a bicycle and a taxicab. "And spike-bozzled, well, if something is completely destroyed, could be a gun or an airship, we'd say it was spike-bozzled."

"So if you put those two things together, you'd have a ladies' man who was destroyed?"

He shook his head. "It's not a sentence I would ever say. Who did?"

"It was at one of my Aunt Ida's séances. She was trying to

reach Lillian, but instead she came out with the strange phrases. The last one was 'Gott strafe England.'"

His normally humorous face went hard. "That was a bit of propaganda. Bloody Jerry used it in posters and even on postage stamps. I think they thought God might like to punish England, but it was the bombs and grenades and machine guns that did that."

He blasted the horn as a dog ran in front of his car. Then he looked at her. "Do you believe all that, then? That the dead come back with messages?"

"No. My aunt certainly does, though. If she's a fake, she's not a deliberate one. She genuinely believes she is channeling communication from the dead."

"Blimey. Who would want that gift?"

She laughed. "Well, it's made my Aunt Ida a great deal of money."

* * *

She was running over her latest piece, crossing out the word "terrifying," as she'd already used it twice, and replacing it with "awful." Which was so awful, she crossed that out, too. The truth was, her ordeal was no longer terrifying. If anything, there seemed to be a lull. She knew the police continued to investigate, but if there were any new leads, she wasn't hearing about them. Neither was Tom Paulson, the crime beat reporter who was covering the police angle.

"Knock it off, Abby," he asked her when she pestered him yet again for an update. "When I find something out, I'll tell you."

In frustration, she began to go through her mail. This was a daunting task, as every day, English-speaking women all over Europe wrote to her. Now the mailbag from the States came with plenty more letters and cards for her. They were from women who supported her, who believed in her. Women who'd had run-ins with the law and, annoyingly, women who wanted beauty tips and hairstyle advice.

Suddenly, she was in demand, not only for beauty and fashion tips but as a guest in various salons and tea parties. She ripped through the envelopes, casting a quick glance at each invitation before tossing it into the trash can. One, however, made her pause.

It was the coat of arms on the heavy vellum card stock that caught her eye.

The Duchess of Cirencester invites you to a charity tea in aid of fallen women of Paris

Abby would've tossed that in the trash with the rest, but even as her hand hovered over the top of the round garbage receptacle, she paused. This was the same party Freddy's mother had made sure to mention in her hearing as a place she would never be invited to, thus proving her social unfitness as a companion for her son. The fact that this, of all events in Paris, was the one that she had mentioned suggested to Abby that it was, in fact, an important social event on the calendar of wealthy expats.

It was the kind of event Lillian would have targeted in the hunt for her next husband, so Abby thought she would do well to attend.

Underneath the formal print of the invitation was a handwritten note that said,

My dear Miss Dixon, forgive the late notice, but I have read about your plight and wish to do anything in my power to help you. I hope you will

accept this invitation to my little salon and offer me the opportunity to become better acquainted with you.
  Your friend,
   Sarah Barncastle, Duchess of Cirencester.

Abby tapped her fingers on the desk. Perhaps she was cynical, but she doubted very much that the Duchess of Cirencester would ever have concerned herself in Abby's plight were she not becoming something of a celebrity. No doubt the duchess was one of those people who liked to be in the forefront of every trend. However, Abby had her own reasons for going to the duchess's salon.

TWENTY-ONE

Abby worried that Paul Joubert would slam shut the lid on this endless treasure chest of clothes, but she found her fears to be groundless. When she explained to him that she'd been invited to the charity tea, he chortled gleefully over the phone. "Some of my best customers will be at that tea. And I suspect, after seeing you walking among them like a living model, more of the ladies will come flocking to *Maison Joubert*."

She laughed. "Why, Monsieur Joubert, you're beginning to sound like an American."

"One should design like a Frenchman and do business like an American." He chuckled again. "Come this evening. I have exactly the thing for you."

"You can't possibly, unless you're a conjurer."

"On the contrary, I have anticipated this moment. Me, I have been thinking, where are all the places in Paris that my so beautiful muse shall be seen? How shall she not conquer the city with her tragic beauty, her fresh young innocence, and, naturally, my gowns."

She was delighted with him. "I'll see you this evening."

Since she had spent some of her thousand-dollar bonus on

silk stockings and underwear appropriate for designer clothes, she was much less embarrassed to be seen at *Maison Joubert*. When she finished her day's work, she slipped on her coat and gloves and headed out onto Rue de l'Opera. Today's detective was caught off guard, so she nearly bumped into him as he hurriedly pretended to be studying the headlines of today's newspaper.

She took pity on the poor man standing out in the cold. "Good afternoon. I'm headed to *Maison Joubert*. No doubt I'll see you outside." And then she got into a taxi. She felt slightly guilty riding in taxis, but she could not afford to soil her new shoes or her coat.

When she arrived, a little after five, it was Suzanne who opened the door to her. She'd been so ready to dazzle the old crow with sweetness that she was somewhat taken aback. "Where's Madame Lafitte?"

Suzanne rolled her eyes. "She's gone to mass. She's forever down at the local cathedral. No doubt atoning for the sins of how horrible she is to the rest of us."

Abby put up her gloved hand to hide her giggle. Suzanne's eyes danced. "Come along, then. We're all ready for you."

In fact, Paul had been very busy. He led her not to the fitting room, but to the big salon, and there he paraded before her a series of outfits. He sat beside her on the settee and explained the function of each outfit that went by. "For the tea party in the afternoon, this is what I have designed for you." And in paraded models wearing three of the most gorgeous dresses she'd ever seen. She pointed to a teal-colored silk drop-waist. "Is that for tea with the duchess?"

"*Absolument*. With it, you will wear the long string of beads, like so." And he indicated the long string swinging from the model's neck.

"May I wear pearls?" If the duchess were anything like Lady Eleanor, she could value a string of pearls quicker than a jeweler with a loupe. She'd inherited her mother's pearls and knew them to be superb.

He looked slightly perturbed. "Are they those dreadful things made of fish scales?"

"No. They were my mother's. They're real."

He put his head to one side. "You will bring them to me, and I will inspect. If I approve, then yes, you may wear them."

"Thank you," she said meekly. She had learned that where his fashions were concerned, this normally easygoing man was an absolute dictator.

"The other two are for further events of a similar nature." One was in apricot-colored silk and the other pale yellow. Next came a woman wearing trousers and a striped sailor's shirt.

A series of models strolled toward her wearing sporting gear. "For the tennis and the golf."

"But I don't golf."

"Then you must learn."

Two more fabulous evening gowns arrived next, one in black silk and midnight blue silk velvet, embroidered with shimmering crystal beads that made her gasp with pleasure just to look at it. And behind that came another model in a dress and cape that were deep, crimson red. "Stunning," she said.

"But of course."

And finally he presented her with a group of models wearing swimsuits, short casual dresses and trousers and jackets, all in lightweight fabrics. She looked at him with her eyebrows raised in a silent question, and he said, "For when you go to the Riviera."

"I haven't been invited to the Riviera."

He smiled knowingly. "You will be."

He seemed to know her social calendar better than she did herself. Not that she would mind a trip to the south of France. Anything to get out of this cold.

She explained that she would need to take her reporter's

notebook and pen with her to Thursday afternoon's tea and, to her relief, he agreed and even provided her with a black leather geometric bag of his own design.

Gowned in the teal dress and wearing her mother's pearls, graciously approved of by Paul Joubert himself, Abby knew herself to be as well dressed as any woman in Paris—and better than most.

When she arrived at the duchess's Paris townhouse, the door was immediately opened by a British butler. After she'd given him her name, he opened the door and offered to take her coat. A large, bosomy matron with a quantity of tightly curled white hair came fluttering forward. "Miss Dixon, my dear. I'm so very pleased you could come." She looked Abby up and down, her eyes pausing knowledgeably on the pearls, and gave a tiny nod. "I'm Sarah. It's lovely to meet you."

"And please call me Abby."

They kissed, French fashion, so their cheeks barely touched, and the duchess tucked Abby's hand into the crook of her arm. "You must come in and meet everyone. We were all so pleased you could make it."

There were about thirty people in the salon, which was all white and gold, with very high ceilings and highly polished parquet floors. The walls were decorated with mirrors and tasteful paintings. None of the left-bank cubists for the duchess.

While the duchess patted Abby's hand and chattered, her small eyes darted everywhere, inviting the eyes of her assembled guests as though she had brought in a particular and rare delicacy to a banquet.

At Abby's entrance, a kind of rustle went around the room as though the very dresses twitched with excitement. Holding on to her guest quite firmly, so there could be no doubt that Abigail Dixon was her current pet, the duchess led her from group to group to "introduce you to a few people."

She met women who were interchangeable enough that

she'd have trouble telling them apart if ever forced to. They were rich, American or English, and thought themselves a cut above. From the way they looked at her, she surmised that the duchess had made an audacious choice in inviting Abby.

Her decorating style might be soft, but her hostessing mode today was bold indeed. Would they be scandalized? Amused? Thrilled to be in the company of someone involved in a murderous scandal? Or simply bored by her? She wasn't certain, and she didn't think the duchess was, either. They were aristocrats, the wives of industrialists and bankers, with a sprinkling of artists and intellectuals who clearly came for the food and wine and paid for their meals by entertaining the company.

As she was introduced around, she began to feel like a performing bear on a chain being led around by her handler. She certainly felt tall enough, towering over her tiny hostess.

She was led to a group of women who included a thin, elegant woman also wearing a Joubert gown. She had a hungry, pinched look as though on a perpetual diet. When Abby saw her, she gave her a frank smile. "Ah, another lover of Joubert, I see."

The woman nearly choked on her champagne and then said, "Ah, yes, I do like to wear his gowns. They are so very pretty."

"This is Madame Fleuri. Her husband, Claude Fleuri, is the minister of the interior. And a very charming man."

Madame Fleuri said gravely, "I have been reading of your ordeal. I'm very sorry. If there's anything I can do, you've only to ask."

Abby was touched by this kindness from a stranger. Madame Fleuri was an important woman in society and also a customer of *Maison Joubert*. Had she known Lillian? Before she could do more than mutter a quick thanks, she was being ushered to the next group of people.

Abby glanced around the room, wondering how many

people she'd have to meet and which of them might have met Lillian Dixon, when she saw Freddy's mother speaking to a thin, colorless woman who should never have worn black. Larry stood beside her, talking to a well-fed man and looking bored.

Lady Eleanor gave an audible gasp when she saw Abby, and her lips thinned into a hard line. Abby bowed her head slightly and gave Freddy's mother her most gracious smile. With an obvious effort, the woman nodded back.

"But of course, Paris is very thin of company at the moment," the duchess said, as though apologizing to Abby that she wasn't meeting grander people.

A small ensemble of musicians played in another room somewhere, the music a genteel tinkle in the background. Everything seemed to tinkle, from the ladylike laughs to the crystal and teacups served from silver trays.

And then she led Abby to a man in a dark suit with a priest's collar drinking a cup of tea and listening politely to an intense woman with glasses who appeared to be lecturing him. The duchess said, "I must interrupt you, Priscilla, so that I may introduce Abigail Dixon. Abigail, as you know, is that poor young woman who has been falsely and tragically accused of murder in her first week living in this beautiful city." She patted Abby's hand. "We must see what we can do for her."

The intense woman blinked behind thick-lensed glasses and said, "To be sure. How do you do, Miss Dixon?"

"And this is Father O'Sullivan. He's our guest of honor today. We are helping to raise funds for the homeless and destitute, who are always sure of a good meal in his soup kitchen, and, for indigent travelers, there's often a bed in the Presbytery."

Father O'Sullivan had deep-set hazel eyes that twinkled in an otherwise lean and serious face. He said, "And what a great pleasure it is to meet the heroine of Paris."

His voice was as Irish as the rolling hills of County Cork,

and at Abby's gaze of obvious astonishment, he laughed softly. "You're wondering what an Irish priest is doing in Paris. Well, I'd always a pair of itchy feet underneath me, and my da said, 'You'll find the poor and the wretched all over the world, my son.'" He shook his head. "Sadly, he was right. I traveled a great deal but felt called here, in Paris."

"It's very nice to meet you," she said politely.

His eyes twinkled even more. "If you were a Catholic, I'd see you quite regularly. My parish is near the atelier of Paul Joubert. I number some of his seamstresses among my flock."

"Really?" If he ministered to the seamstresses, what did he know of their gossip? Did they ever talk about their customers? No doubt she was clutching at straws, but she'd like to ask him if any of the girls had ever mentioned Lillian. Even as she formed the question, the duchess took hold of her arm. "Ah, good. I want you to meet Lady Eleanor and her son."

Father O'Sullivan said, "You're always welcome. St. Bartholomew's is quite ancient, and we've some lovely art on display, if Christian painting is something that interests you."

Ancient church painting wasn't a big hobby of hers, but it would provide a good excuse for a longer visit with the priest.

By the time they reached Freddy's mother, she'd had time to school her features into an expression of pleasure. Before the duchess could introduce Abby, Lady Eleanor put out her hand and chuckled. "No, no, Sarah, no need to introduce me. Miss Dixon and I had dinner together last week at the Meurice. How are you, my dear?"

Abby had to hand it to her. Talk about taking lemons and making lemonade. She might not like Abby, but she wasn't going to pass up the opportunity to get one over on the duchess.

Sarah smiled. "Isn't that wonderful? And I was worried dear Abigail wouldn't know anyone."

"You remember my son, Lawrence, of course?"

"Yes."

He said, "How de do?"

"And this is Miss Amelia Dayton. Of the Philadelphia Daytons." Miss Dayton was very young, very proper and looked very dull. Larry certainly looked as though there were places he'd rather be and plenty of them. She could imagine that Lillian would have appealed to his jaded palate.

Abby said, "Very nice to meet you, Miss Dayton. I'm Abigail Dixon." She shot a mischievous look at the duchess. "Of the Chicago Dixons."

As they drifted to the next group, the duchess lowered her voice and said, intimately, "Oh, you are too naughty. Eleanor is terrified one of her sons will fall for the wrong girl, of course. She guards them like a mother tiger, but she does push heiresses at her sons with more ruthlessness than flair."

She needn't have told Abby that. She still bore the emotional scratches from their meeting.

"She has high hopes for this one. Miss Dayton's father is in railroads. Or is it lumber?" She shook her head. "Both, I expect. Dreadfully dull, poor thing, but very rich."

While Abby certainly didn't suspect Freddy's mother of murder, it was very convenient that Lillian had died before she could entrap the elder son into marriage, thus depriving the family of Miss Dayton's millions.

Abby was pleased that she'd accepted this invitation. Her reporter's instincts hadn't led her astray. In this room were the very people that Lillian would have wanted to befriend. Her hostess being a prime example. On a hunch, Abby asked whether the duchess had met Lillian.

She was already a fluttery woman, but she became increasingly flighty as the question sank in. Finally, she said, "I believe I did meet her somewhere." She glanced at Abby, then looked away. "I hope you won't mind me being frank with you, but my dear husband, Richard, a keen game hunter, said when he first met your stepmother that she reminded him of an eager young hunter determined to mount the head of the rarest and most prized exotic animal above her fireplace."

Abby allowed herself a very discreet laugh even as she raged inside. That was Lillian all right. Abby's father had been a reasonably good North American prize. A grizzly bear of huge stature. But her ambitions had been much higher. He'd been but a stepping stone in her career. Abby asked, "Is there anyone in particular that she had her gun sights set on?"

Once more, that surprisingly keen glance in a woman who seemed so vacuous. "Certainly she seemed quite keen on Larry, who will, of course, inherit the estate when his father passes away. However, I thought Eleanor had nipped that little affair in the bud. Or Lillian realized the prey wasn't quite as spectacular as she may have hoped."

"You mean she'd moved on?"

A shrug of delicate white shoulders. "If she had, I'm not certain she had quite decided whom she had chosen." The duchess looked around and said, "Ah, I know exactly whom you should meet next. Miss Jean Drummond is an American, like you, and a fellow scribe. She writes a wonderful column for *New York Fortnightly*."

Abby would hardly have put herself in the same category. Jean Drummond had lived in Paris for several years and wrote wonderful, gossipy reports about the goings-on in Paris. She was in her thirties with keen gray eyes and a handshake as strong as a man's. She was nearly as tall as Abby and inspected her frankly.

"I'm a big fan of your work, Miss Drummond," Abby said, feeling she'd met the most interesting person in the room.

"Thanks. I'm a fan of yours, too, though sorry you had to get your big break by sticking your head in a noose."

The duchess smiled and said, "I'll leave you two girls to get to know one another."

When the duchess had fluttered away, Jean leaned closer.

"She means well, but you do rather feel like a performing monkey when she passes you around with the champagne."

Abby laughed. "I did feel a little on display."

"Okay, one American gal to another, what can I do to help you?"

Abby was about to demur, but then she thought better of it. This woman earned her living from Paris gossip. "Did you know Lillian Dixon?"

Jean Drummond leaned past Abby to take a tiny sandwich from a tray in the hands of a passing waiter in black tie. "You're as direct as I am. We're going to get along fine." She popped the sandwich in her mouth and ate it before saying, "I met Lillian a few times, sure. But she wasn't interested in me."

Abby was quite sure of that. "What was she interested in?"

She glanced across the room at Lady Eleanor and her son and Miss Dayton. "Larry. He's the Earl of Lambridge, but that's only a courtesy title on loan until his father dies, when he gets the real goods. He'll be the Marquess of Witney, which comes with an estate and lands. He's a catch, all right, if you go for the self-involved polo-playing type."

Abby nodded. "I've met him through his younger brother, Freddy."

"Freddy's twice the man, frankly. Too bad he's not the eldest. Mother has big plans for her eldest son. She wants to unite him to a princess of some royal family or, if that fails, she's not averse to a nice, fat American fortune."

"Aren't they rich enough already?"

She laughed. "Honey, one thing you need to know about the rich is they're never rich enough. Besides, death duties are crippling the old families in England. A few American millions wouldn't go amiss."

"And Larry? Is he as ambitious?"

"He's not as obsessed as his mother, but he knows his own worth."

"So, marriage with Lillian Dixon?"

Jean Drummond shook her head. "Unless she brought a few million along in her steamer trunk, she was only a diversion." She paused. "I don't get the feeling that you and Lillian were close?"

"No."

"Then I'll be honest. Lillian was determined to climb the social ladder, and she didn't much care how she did it. She wanted Larry. I think she'd have gone to any length to get him."

This was nothing Abby didn't already know from bitter experience.

"But Larry's no fool. I suspect he took what she was offering and didn't plan to reward her with a ring and a title. I hope I'm not being too blunt."

"No." She looked around at the well-heeled crowd and at Larry standing with the rich and respectable Miss Dayton. "Lillian was no fool, either." She'd taken his cigarette case. Had she given herself a farewell gift? "Did she seem interested in anyone else?"

Jean nabbed another sandwich and, while she munched, seemed to be thinking. "The last time I saw them together, she was giving Larry the cold shoulder. She seemed to be flirting with every man in sight, like a butterfly trying to decide which flower to land on. But, if you don't mind me saying so, your stepmother always seemed to be flirting with someone."

Abby glanced around the room as though seeking inspiration. "I'm trying to find out who she saw in the last days of her life. Someone must know something."

Jean Drummond looked at her thoughtfully. "You know, I love a good detective yarn as much as the next girl, but you're in a serious mess. Maybe you should leave the sleuthing to the police?"

Abby snorted her disgust. "You sound like Inspector Deschamps. He also thinks I should keep my nose out of his business, but, you see, my nose is on my head, which I do not want cut off."

"Perfectly understandable. And it is a very nice head." She drained her glass and reached for another from a passing waiter. "So you've met Inspector Deschamps."

"Not by choice. He was the one who came when I—" She tried again, "When Lillian—" She sighed. "That dreadful day. He's been playing cat and mouse with me ever since, trying to unnerve me, I suppose."

"He's a good man," her new friend said. "He doesn't have to work, you know. His family is in wine. They have a massive estate in the Loire. Drives his superiors crazy."

"I can imagine." No wonder she kept bumping into the inspector at social events. He really did live in that world. Much more than she did.

"Of course, half the women of Paris are madly in love with him. Well, he does have those rugged good looks and fierce intelligence, a deadly combination."

She made a face. "I feel for his poor wife. He must be a devilish husband."

Jean raised her head and said, "Ah, there is much you have to learn about your new home. Inspector Deschamps's wife is dead."

"Dead? He keeps her photograph in his office."

"She was killed in the war. She volunteered as a nurse and died at Passchendaele in 1917."

Abby shut her eyes against the sick feeling in her stomach. "Oh, I blundered dreadfully."

Jean's eyes twinkled. "Now I want to help you even more. Shall I write about your plight in the *Fortnightly?* Happy to do it."

"Why not? The more publicity I get, the more difficult it will be to punish me for a crime I didn't commit."

She spent the next two hours drinking tea and chatting, but

Abby was always aware of her borrowed finery. She did her best to stand and move as she'd been taught, showing off this beautiful dress in the most flattering light.

Father O'Sullivan was invited to say a few words, and he kept his talk both short and humorous, inviting anyone who was so moved to leave behind them a small donation with his kind hostess. It was delicately done. Abby had the pleasure of watching women write out checks and slip bills from their purses discreetly.

She made a few notes on her reporter's notebook and quietly popped a ten-dollar bill in the kitty. And then, after thanking her hostess, Abby prepared to leave. The butler helped her into her coat, and as she was slipping on her gloves, Father O'Sullivan joined her in the ornate foyer.

"What a bit of luck for me. I was just leaving."

"I intend to write up a nice piece about this event for my newspaper, including an invitation to our subscribers to support your charitable work."

"Well, that's grand. I'm very obliged to you."

They walked out together, and he turned to her, the twinkle in his eyes gone and a serious expression on his face. "I've read about your case. I would like you to know that if there's anything at all I can do, or if you simply want someone to talk to, you'll find me at St. Bartholomew's."

She was touched by his kindness. "Father O'Sullivan, did you ever hear of Lillian Dixon?"

"Before I read about her murder in the newspaper?"

"Yes. Did any of the women who work at *Maison Joubert* mention her?"

"No." He pulled his coat closer against the cold. "You're a long way from home, and you're going through a terrible ordeal. It's natural that you, being a journalist, would want to look for facts, find the story, but you have to remember that whoever killed Lillian Dixon is still out there."

"You believe I'm innocent?"

"I believe you should be careful where you poke that pencil of yours. You don't know what you might provoke."

"I want to find the truth."

He looked at her with great understanding and some sadness. "At what cost?"

TWENTY-TWO

"I'm getting tired of being that plucky heroine with a guillotine hanging over her head," Abby complained to Vivian when she returned home to their new apartment that night.

Viv shook her head. "Since that head is wearing a divine hat and has just been coiffed by Monsieur Raymond himself, I am not feeling very sympathetic."

Abby threw herself into one of the very comfortable gold-framed armchairs, upholstered in champagne-colored silk, and stretched her feet out in front of the cheerful fire. "I know there is good fortune as well as bad in what's happened to me, but this is so different than what I imagined my life in Paris would be."

Vivian wrinkled her nose. "I think I would trade places with you even with a guillotine hanging over my head. It's so glamorous and exciting."

"Until the drop."

Their telephone rang, startling both of them. Abby went to answer it. The operator informed her it was a transatlantic call, and she immediately grabbed the paper and pencil she kept on the tiny ornate telephone table.

Soon she heard the hearty tones of Charles Abernathy. "Abigail? Is that you?"

"Yes, Uncle Charles. I'm here."

"I've got some information for you. I looked into Lillian's background."

She pressed the earpiece harder against her ear. "Anything interesting?"

"A couple of things. First, your father wasn't the first married man she tried to entrap into marriage. Six months earlier, an oil baron in Texas left his wife for Lillian."

"I knew it. I knew there had to be more. What happened?" Oh, how she wished Lillian had prospered with the oil baron. Then both her parents might still be alive.

"Seems he changed his mind. She was going to sue him for breach of promise, but he bought her off with a sizable sum of money."

"So she's from Texas? I was certain she wasn't from Boston."

"No. Lillian lied about everything."

She felt a niggle of excitement. "Go on."

"In order to marry your father, she had to show her birth certificate. Guess what?"

"Stop toying with me, Uncle Charles. What?"

He waited a beat, and she could hear the rattle and click on the line as though even the transatlantic cables connecting them were quivering with excitement.

"Turns out your wicked stepmother was French."

She nearly dropped the receiver. "French? Are you certain?"

"I don't think her birth certificate was forged. It says she was born in Paris and her birth name was Lillianne Petit. Oh, and she was born in 1886, if you're interested."

She stared at the telephone apparatus as though it was a crystal ball. It told her nothing. Her thoughts were as jumbled as Lillian's lies. "Uncle Charles, can you do something else for me? Find out when Lillianne Pettit arrived in the United States."

"That might not be so easy. She probably came through as a child. She sounded as American as you and me."

"If she came through Ellis Island, there must be records. Especially now that we know her birthdate."

"I'll put a researcher on it and get back to you."

"Thank you, Uncle Charles. Lives could depend on this. My life!"

* * *

Abby found herself facing Inspector Deschamps in his office a second time. She was hoping that by giving him information she might make up for the error of having taken Lillian's handbag away with her.

His brows rose briefly as he took in her chestnut-colored two-piece suit in wool jersey. The skirt was box pleated, and the jacket fastened diagonally at the shoulder, giving a slightly military look, which had seemed a good choice when coming here. With it she wore a brown cloche hat with a black ribbon and brown suede shoes.

His gaze returned to her face, and he said in some amusement, "Another outfit by Paul Joubert?"

"I never let anyone else design my clothes," Abby said, a line she'd delivered so often in the last days and weeks that the words tripped off her tongue.

He laughed—in genuine amusement, she thought—and said, "Bravo, Miss Dixon. You sound exactly like a very rich, very bored Frenchwoman."

She found herself grinning back at him. "I see I have no secrets from you."

He sobered immediately. "Would that were true. I hope you have come today to share some of your secrets, in fact?"

Apparently the small-talk portion of their meeting was over, which suited Abby fine. "In fact, I have. I've discovered something I think you might find interesting." She felt all the discomfort of knowing she had made a dreadful blunder and, in her frank manner, said, "But first, I owe you an apology. I am most dreadfully sorry about the comments I made in your office the other day regarding your wife. I had no idea."

Momentary stillness came over him, and she glimpsed a terrible pain in his gaze, and then his face was unreadable once again. "I see the ladies of Paris have been gossiping."

"I was at the Duchess of Cirencester's afternoon charity event. Gossiping seemed to be the chief occupation."

"My wife died saving lives. She was a heroine, and I am extremely proud of her." His expression shifted to all business. "And now, what information do you have to share?"

She paused for dramatic effect. "Lillian Dixon was French."

If her words had shocked him, he gave no indication of it. "Why do you think she was French?"

Abby smiled. "I'm a journalist. I always try to have proof. I asked our sister newspaper, the *Chicago Post*, to look into Lillian Dixon's background, and it transpires that she was born Lillianne Pettit here in Paris."

"That is, of course, most interesting. May I ask, what is your proof?"

"Her birth certificate. A photographic copy is on its way."

"This Lillianne Pettit moved to America as a child, perhaps?"

She smiled with pure triumph. "Lillianne Pettit is listed on a boat record from February 1919 entering into Ellis Island."

He leaned back, and she thought he was resisting the urge to smoke as he raised his hand and then returned it to his lap. "That is curious. Of course, many young women left Paris after the Great War. Six million French were killed, and of the four million casualties, many of them were the young men that

French girls would have married. She may well have left to find a better life elsewhere. I have heard young French women today called a generation of virgins."

Abby rolled her eyes. "Lillian was no virgin."

He nodded.

Abby straightened her spine and leaned forward. "I would like to think this information might encourage you to share some of your own discoveries in this case."

"Would you?" he said in a bland, questioning tone.

She dropped the prim and proper tone. "Oh, come on, you know I didn't kill Lillian Dixon. I'm a journalist. Where I come from, it's very common for reporters and police to share information with each other." That was only where the police were corrupt, and no cop had ever told her anything useful, but she doubted that the inspector would check up on her story.

He stood up, and when he stood, he was really quite imposing with that boxer's nose and chiseled jaw and certain hardness about his body. She shrank back instinctively in her chair. He said, very slowly and very clearly, "Miss Dixon, where I come from, people who are involved in murder investigations should be very careful how they behave."

Abby rose to her feet, hoping the cool elegance of her outfit would disguise the way her heart was pounding. "Are you threatening me?"

"Certainly not. I am merely suggesting, and not for the first time, that you leave murder investigations to those who are trained for the task."

It was so unfair. "But without me, you never would have known that my father's wife was a French émigrée who left here right after the war."

"On the contrary. You are not the only person with colleagues in America able to do research."

She was deflated, but for all she knew, he was bluffing. She said, airily, "No doubt you even know that she arrived in steerage aboard the *Aquitania*."

The rigid line of his jaw eased, and he shook his head at her. "Miss Pettit arrived on the *Rotterdam,* and she was traveling first-class."

Darn it, he wasn't bluffing. He'd certainly taken the wind out of her sails. She said, "I'm sorry to have wasted your time."

"Not at all," he said politely and walked across the room to open his office door for her.

He nodded to her as she left. She couldn't have felt more dismissed if he'd put a boot to her backside.

* * *

When she arrived home, Vivian said in a tone of awe, "Paul Joubert himself called you on the telephone. He said you were to go down there at once."

Abby groaned. "I had nothing in mind for this evening but a long, luxurious soak in our marble bathtub."

Vivian giggled. "I know. I will never get used to this luxury."

"Well, he's been so good to me, if he whistles, I shall fly."

Vivian squeaked. "Straighten your stockings."

Guiltily, Abby complied. She even put on fresh lipstick without being prodded.

When she arrived at *Maison Joubert*, the lights were all on upstairs. She knew that the seamstresses would all be working late in the run-up to the delayed unveiling of his collection. It would be one of the most exciting events in Paris.

"Good evening, Madame Lafitte," she said. Surreptitiously the doorwoman crossed herself, but Abby was becoming used to that.

She unbent enough to say, "*Monsieur*, he is expecting you. You know the way."

Even though the words were insulting, she felt that being allowed to roam the building unescorted meant that Madame Lafitte grudgingly accepted that Abby was part of all of this.

She walked upstairs and found Monsieur Joubert's door closed. She knocked, and he asked, testily, who was there. When she gave her name, she only had a moment more to stand there before he opened the door to her. "*Imbeciles!* They should have told me you were here, and I would have come down to greet you."

He held her away from him and inspected her thoroughly before kissing her on both cheeks. When they entered the room, she saw there was another man there. He was around forty years old and had the clothing and demeanor of a businessman. He seemed very out of place in this house of fashion.

Paul said, "Miss Abigail Dixon, allow me to introduce to you Monsieur Fleuri, who is here to pick up a dress for his wife, who is one of my treasured clients. She very unfortunately stepped on the hem getting out of her car, and it had to be repaired."

"I am so pleased to meet you," Monsieur Fleuri said with a smile, stepping forward to shake her hand. "I hear of you everywhere, not least because Paul Joubert proclaims your innocence by clothing you so exquisitely."

Abby doubted there were many people with the surname Fleuri in Paris who wore Paul Joubert gowns. "I believe I had the pleasure of meeting your wife at the Duchess of Cirencester's afternoon tea."

He smiled the careful smile of a politician. "No doubt she recognized your frock?"

She chuckled. "As I recognized hers."

Paul tenderly removed a linen dress bag bulky with its contents from a hook on the wall and said, "I myself will carry the dress down and place it into your automobile."

The other man raised his eyebrows. "You do not trust me?"

Paul shook his head. "Not in the slightest."

Both she and the minister laughed, and the two men left the room. Then she settled to wait.

When the designer returned, he said, "I have created for you, my beautiful muse, something a little daring, a little unusual. I would like to see it on you before I continue."

She felt mildly nervous. She already felt that his clothing was daring. She'd bared her back, given up her corset and cut her hair. What more could he ask of her?

As though he felt her trepidation, he reached for the notebook that was never far from his hand and flipped it open so she could see his pencil sketches and the swatches of fabric. The dress was a thin column of silver and black with a headdress featuring upstanding ostrich feathers.

"But I'm already so tall," she said, fearing that with the headdress on top, she would dwarf everyone in the room.

"*Exactement*. You stand above every other woman. This gown merely emphasizes that fact."

She shook her head. "Well, I'm game if you are."

"Excellent. We will have a fitting now, if you are willing, and we labor night and day to have it ready for Saturday."

Abby was puzzled. "Saturday?"

He looked at her, and his eyes widened. "The Champagne Ball?"

She shrugged, mystified. His eyebrows drew together in a frown. "But surely, Lord Ashton has invited you? It is the annual celebration of spring. Everyone will be there."

She felt a momentary pang of hurt pride that, in fact, Freddy hadn't invited her to this ball. She said, "Now, I'm the opposite of Cinderella. I have the beautiful gown and no ball to go to."

He chuckled. "Nonsense. If your Frederick is so foolish as to pass up the opportunity, I shall escort you myself."

"You'd do that for me?"

"Abby, it is you who will be helping me, showcasing one of my so beautiful gowns within weeks of my collection being revealed. Together, we shall be a triumph."

And, privately, she hoped to meet more people who might have known Lillian.

"It will be held at Versailles." She was thrilled to see the palace of Versailles, though she wondered who she'd find on Freddy's arm when she got there.

When she arrived home, she discovered she had wronged Freddy. He had not jilted her for another woman. A bouquet of flowers awaited her with the card telling her he had been called back to London on business. He would ring her when he returned in a week or so.

It seemed odd to think of Freddy having any sort of business. He always appeared so carefree. She wondered if she would miss him and thought she would.

TWENTY-THREE

Being escorted to a party by Paul Joubert was quite different than showing up on the arm of Freddy. There were none of the foolish and extravagant compliments. None of the gaiety and silliness. Paul was still an excellent escort, but she felt he was more concerned with the dress's well-being than her own.

His driver chauffeured them to the palace, and she had to force herself not to gawk like a tourist when she first walked in to the sumptuous former home of the French kings from Louis XIV until the French Revolution.

Mirrors, gold leaf, painted ceilings and statuary—everywhere she looked was opulent décor. After they gave up their coats, Paul Joubert ran a professional eye over her and adjusted her skirt before offering her his arm and escorting her to the hall of mirrors, which reflected the beautiful, the connected, and the wealthy. She bit back a smile, realizing he had designed her gown with this backdrop in mind.

When he offered to fetch her a glass of champagne, she was surprised he didn't beg her not to spill any.

However, he knew all the people Freddy didn't. Actual French people in Paris, not just the expats. It didn't take her long to realize that somewhat like the Duchess of Cirencester had, but with much more subtlety, the couturier was presenting her to potential clients.

They were standing at the head of a great staircase where Paul Joubert had paused to speak to an acquaintance. She felt him stretching out the conversation and realized she might as well be a statue arranged on a pedestal. Anyone looking up the wide staircase would see the gown in all its glory and beside it, the voluble designer himself.

Resisting the urge to chuckle, she tried to recall all the instructions she'd received. How to hold her head, to stretch her spine and place her feet just so.

Still, her position gave her a bird's-eye view of the activity below. There was Larry with the dull Amelia, who was making conversation with his mother while his eye wandered.

The Duke and Duchess of Cirencester walked into the room. He tried to take his wife's hand, and she said something very short and pulled away. He was left standing there, looking foolish. In a ball where gaiety was almost a requirement, they looked to be out of step with the revelers.

A voice at her elbow said, "I see you have the world at your feet."

She started and turned. Inspector Deschamps stood there, impeccable in a black tuxedo.

In a room where she towered above everyone, including her escort, he alone seemed to stand taller than she.

Feeling as bold as her couture gown, she said, "Since you will not oblige the *Post* by arresting me, I must make do with reporting on the society events I attend in the meantime."

"I am sorry to disappoint."

"I wonder," she said, looking down once more at the swirling members of society moving around the floor and stopping to talk to this person and that, as though it were a dance.

"You wonder?"

"What Lillianne Pettit did during the war?"

"I am astonished you don't already know."

Her feathers waved as she turned. "But then I do not have your resources. I've asked around, and you'd think she never existed. If I hadn't seen her birth certificate, I'd wonder if she was real."

"Perhaps you'd be better to leave her past alone," he said softly.

She thought of that letter she'd received and ignored, telling her to go home. Now, here was the inspector telling her to stop asking questions. "Are you telling me to stop doing my job?"

"I don't know why you sound surprised. I've been telling you to stay out of police business since you blundered into it."

She tried not to flinch at his chosen verb. "I'm a reporter. Asking questions is my job. Besides, even Lillian deserves justice. Everyone does."

"May I remind you, Abigail, that Lillian's murderer is still out there."

He left her then, and her gaze followed him. She'd discovered two very interesting things. He didn't believe she was guilty. And he'd used her first name.

* * *

With no more harrowing accounts of her persecution by the police, since the police didn't seem in any hurry to prosecute her, Abby was bored at work. February had eased into March, and all she had to show for her time in Paris was a fabulous wardrobe and a string of front-page articles she was ashamed to have written.

She appealed to Walter Strutt. "Please, give me an assignment. Let me cover the latest shooting by the Apache gang."

Walter Strutt shook his head. "Your French isn't good enough. Anyway, your first-person stories have not only boosted our circulation but also the circulation of the Chicago paper. If I got you writing different pieces now, I'd be putting *my* head under the guillotine." When she flinched, he said, "Metaphorically speaking."

"But I've got nothing new to write about. There's nothing very harrowing about going to parties every night in designer gowns. At least let me write about those poor women slaving away upstairs in black smocks creating designer gowns for the wealthy."

"Are you crazy? You'd lose all those fancy clothes you're getting for free and halve your readers. You can write about this new All Black Revue and this dancer Josephine Baker everybody's going wild about. Here's the background." He handed her a pamphlet and a poster. "Five hundred words. Then you'll attend the revue and interview the key players. Get your picture taken with Josephine." And so she found herself pounding out the very sort of tedious piece she'd hoped never to write again.

Hudson, the cub reporter and errand boy, brought her over a telegram. "This just came for you, Miss Dixon."

Hudson was a nice kid. All of nineteen, he had come to Paris to paint and quickly discovered he had no talent. He was, however, very good at doing little ink sketches when no photographer was available, and he was learning to be a reporter.

He also fetched and carried for the reporters and checked the Reuters machine to see if anything interesting had come across the wire. Ever since the night of the murder, when he'd escorted her home, he seemed to treat her like an older sister.

She was accustomed to receiving invitations, notes and cards, but she'd never received a telegram at the office before. She slit open the envelope, read the telegram, and her boredom immediately lifted.

Miss Dixon. Have vital information regarding Lillian Dixon. Photographs and letters that prove you innocent.

The telegram directed her to an address in the poorer part of Paris and told her to walk in the front door and head to the back of the house, where the telegram writer would be waiting.

I will be there at three in the afternoon, but I cannot wait. If they knew I was writing to you, they would kill me. I am in a wheelchair.

She squeaked, jumped up from her seat and ran across the room to Walter Strutt's desk, waving the telegram at him.

He was on the phone, but when he saw her excitement, he ended the call. She shoved the telegram at him, saying, "I can't finish my article, have to go."

He looked at her from under his brows and then scanned the telegram. "Somebody spent a lot of money on this telegram. That's a lot of words."

"But read them," she said, her feet tapping with impatience. She glanced at the big clock on the wall. "It's after two now. I have to go this instant. Walter, this could be my chance to free myself."

He shook his head. "It's probably a crank. A lunatic or a lonely old person who wants some attention."

He put the paper down on his desk, and she grabbed it back up. "But what if it's not? This could be my chance to clear my name."

He glared at her. "You finish that piece yet?"

She had 237 words of the 500 written. She knew, because she'd just counted them out of boredom. "Almost."

He shook his head. "You get back to your typewriter. Hudson, get a cab and go on over to this address. Make sure you get the person's name and some way to get hold of them, otherwise it's useless. Make sure the taxi waits so if they're a lunatic or an old crackpot, you can get out of there fast." He glared at Abby. "Satisfied, missy?"

She'd have been satisfied if he'd let her go herself but she suspected that if she argued, he might tell Hudson to forget the whole thing, so she nodded, reluctantly.

"And let that be a lesson to you not to dawdle. A reporter never knows when a hot story will hit."

Abby didn't think of herself as a flouncer, but she had to admit, when she made her way back to her desk, there was definite flouncing involved.

Hudson grabbed his jacket, looking excited. He said, "Don't you worry, Miss Dixon. I won't let you down."

"Make sure you ask this person how they came across this information and absolutely, positively make sure there's a way I can contact them."

He glanced up at the clock. "Yes, ma'am. I've got to go."

After he left, going to meet *her* contact, she banged the typewriter keys so hard, she bruised her fingertips. What did she care about revues and exotic new dancers when she could be finally getting her big break in this case? A case of life and death. *Her* life and death.

She wondered what Hudson would bring back. Photographs and letters, the telegram said. Hopefully they were love letters from the man who'd caused her to throw the scent bottle at the wall. With luck, the photographs were of Lillian's killer.

She finished her article and ripped it out of the typewriter with a great screech and passed it to Ruth, who handed it back and made her redo the last paragraph. She said it was shoddy work, which it was. The article finally passed muster at three thirty p.m.

She jumped out of her seat and then she waited, with fevered impatience, for Hudson to return.

MURDER AT THE PARIS FASHION HOUSE

She couldn't settle to anything, kept looking at the clock and then at the door and the clock. Finally, at three forty-five, she said to Walter Strutt, "Hudson should be back by now."

The editor glanced at the clock and went back to his work. "Traffic could be bad. The cab could have got a flat tire. The crazy person could be telling Hudson their life story and the kid's too young and polite to get away."

He was probably right. She sat down and tried to work.

Thirty more minutes crawled by slower than the twenty-five years she'd been alive. She couldn't stand it anymore. She stood up. "I'm going out for some air."

Walter Strutt was not fooled. "You're going to get a cab and go rush over to the crackpot's house. Meanwhile, the kid will be on his way back. You'll pass each other in traffic."

"If he's not there, then I'll come back. Tell him to wait for me."

"You're crazy, Abby, you know that?"

"You're not the first person who ever told me that."

She put on her coat and ran out of the building. After the private cars she'd been driven in lately, the cab seemed to rattle and bump its way through the streets. Her eyes constantly scanned the cabs coming in the opposite direction, but there were few of them, and none contained Hudson.

While the pragmatic Midwestern pessimist part of her tended to agree with Walter Strutt that this was likely a wild goose chase, the part of her that was a young woman desperate to clear her name believed she was about to find out who had killed Lillian Dixon and why.

They drove past two nuns with their heads together and then a sidewalk café where the patrons were huddled near the warmth-giving braziers, drinking wine, cloudy glasses of Pernod or tiny coffees. A young man was sketching, a cigarette forgotten in his left hand, an empty coffee cup pushed to the edge of the table. Paris seemed to accept these young writers and artists who took up their tables eating and drinking the minimum while writing or sketching. No doubt some of them were on their way to fame, but she suspected a lot more of them were mere hopefuls.

The cab took her to an area of Paris she had never been before. To the north, past Montmartre. Baron Haussmann had never designed these streets. They seemed small and mean and much less gracious. A fire truck crossed their path, screeching out a siren and causing her cabdriver to slam on his brakes, jerking her forward. As they grew closer to their destination, she saw some kind of commotion ahead.

Her heart began to beat with a painful sense of dread. It wasn't a riot or a demonstration causing the commotion. There was smoke up ahead and more than one fire truck. It looked to be a house on fire. Maybe that was why Hudson hadn't been able to get back. Perhaps he'd been somehow detained by whatever accident had occurred. The cab driver got as close as he could. Gendarmes had blockaded the road.

She paid the cab driver and let him go.

Please let it be a random house fire.

TWENTY-FOUR

Abby approached the gendarme and pulled her press pass from her handbag. The officer let her through, pointing and gesturing to an area where a group of people was gathered. She hurried over. And, as she grew closer to where the smoke was coming from, she let out a sob that sounded like the word *no*.

"It's like the Great War again," a Frenchwoman moaned and began to cry. Her friend muttered something soothing, and the two of them stood, a couple of French housewives, weeping together in the street.

She looked back at the building and understood why they had mentioned war. The remains of the house looked as though it had been bombed.

The firefighters were busy with hoses and ladder. She looked around. Where was Hudson? He was a young reporter. Surely he'd be hanging around, thrilled to be on the scene for a genuine news story.

She searched for the house numbers, but it was difficult to see through the crowd, the smoke and the water.

"Hudson?" she shouted. And she began to run, searching the crowd. She didn't see Hudson anywhere. In spite of the fact that no civilians were supposed to cross the street, she splashed through dirty puddles of water toward the firefighters. "Please? Does anyone speak English?"

"Get back," a firefighter shouted. "It is not safe."

"But my friend was coming here to visit. He could be inside." She saw the way he glanced at the still-burning house and back at her with pity. But all he said was, "You must move back."

She glanced up and, for once, was relieved to see Inspector Deschamps striding toward her. When he drew close, his lips thinned, and he looked at her coldly. "I did not know you had the newsman's passion for human tragedy and disaster, Miss Dixon."

She grasped his sleeve, glad someone could understand her. "I was sent a telegram to come here. We sent a newsboy. Hudson. He's only nineteen. I can't find him in the crowd. I'm trying to tell the firefighters. He could be in there."

She was trying very hard to keep her voice calm, but it was jumping about like the water off the smoldering wooden beams.

His eyes took on a very different expression now. Intent and very direct. "You are absolutely certain? This was the address?"

"I can't see the address." She reached into her bag and she pulled out the telegram.

She pushed it toward him. "This is the telegram." The paper quivered, so she realized she was shaking. He took it and perused the telegram.

He spoke rapidly to the fire officials and then said to Abby, "Wait in my car. There is nothing you can do here. I will come when I know more." He glanced around. "I will get someone to accompany you."

She shook her head. "I can find it." Then she said, "I think I'd prefer to wait in a café." She gestured to one that was on the corner.

He nodded. "As you wish."

She walked back to where the curious bystanders were gathered, many of them now staring at her curiously. She took her small camera from her handbag and took three photographs of the burning building just in case no photographer got there in time. Then she walked to the café. She went inside and ordered a coffee. She paid and took it to a small table. There was a telephone on the wall at the back of the café.

She put through a call to Walter Strutt. She told him what she had witnessed. Even though her throat was dry and scratchy, at least it was calm.

He swore softly. "No sign at all of Hudson?"

She had to swallow before she could say, "No. No sign. He hasn't returned?" There had been a faint hope that he might have arrived back at the newspaper office before this disaster had happened. But when her editor said he had not returned, she feared the worst.

"I think it was a bomb. That's what one of the witnesses said."

"You sure?"

"No. But it doesn't look like any house fire I've ever seen."

"I'll send one of the newsboys down to cover the explosion. You okay?"

Okay felt like another lifetime. "The police want to question me. I gave them the telegram." The silence hung heavy between them. Almost in a wail, she said, "Hudson was only nineteen."

"We don't know he was there. Stick with the facts."

She knew he was right, but her stomach was in turmoil.

"You need anything? Want somebody to come and hold your hand?"

"No."

"If you need that fancy lawyer, you let me know."

"I don't think I'm a suspect this time. I believe I was the intended victim."

After what seemed like an eternity, but she knew from incessantly checking her watch was only twenty minutes, Inspector Deschamps arrived. He looked very stern and businesslike, and she noticed he was limping slightly.

He spoke to the waiter and then walked toward her, settling himself at the small, round, marble-topped table.

"Are you hurt?" she asked him. When he seemed puzzled by her question, she said, "You're limping."

"A souvenir from the war. My leg bothers me if I'm on my feet too long or walk too far."

She said, "People standing there were saying that it reminded them of the war. It was a bomb, wasn't it? That was no house fire." She played with her spoon on her empty cup. "Could it have been some kind of an explosion of the oven? An accident?"

"No. I suspect the explosion was caused by a German grenade."

Her eyes widened. "A grenade."

"I regret to inform you that the body of a young man was discovered in the house."

She bowed her head. The waiter arrived and with a clatter put another cup of coffee in front of her and a glass of amber liquid. He put the same two drinks in front of the inspector. When she looked up, he said, "Brandy. It helps a little."

"Thank you."

He asked, "Would you happen to know what kind of wristwatch your colleague wore?"

"His wristwatch?" And then, with a sick feeling, she realized it was probably all that was left to identify him. Had she ever seen Hudson's watch? She tried to think back on all the times he'd handed her papers or brought her a page off the wire. She saw bony wrists, pale skin, freckles, a few pale red hairs. A wristwatch emerging beneath slightly frayed shirt cuffs. She held the image and described the watch. "His watch had a round face, Roman numerals for the hours. It was silver-rimmed with a black leather band that was cracked in places. I couldn't tell you the brand."

He sipped his brandy, and she noticed a streak of charcoal on his shirtsleeve. In spite of the danger, he'd gone in. She said, "It's Hudson, isn't it?"

"I cannot confirm, but I would say it's very likely."

She put her head into her hand. She'd cry later for the terrible waste of Hudson, for all the years he'd miss. For the unfairness of his fate. He'd died in her place. The brandy glowed amber in the glass. She drank a little even though it tasted fiery and foul. "It was me they wanted. Me they intended to blow up. Not Hudson."

He nodded gravely. "Again, I suspect you are correct."

She swallowed hard. "You've been right all along. If only I'd listened to you. I should have stopped snooping and let the police do the investigating. If I'd left well enough alone, Hudson would still be alive." She imagined him getting promoted to reporter, finding a girl, getting married, living his life, not being cut off at nineteen.

"In the war, as an officer, it was my job to send young men over the top, knowing many of them would not return."

"But they were soldiers. They knew the danger. Hudson was just a kid at the wrong place at the wrong time."

"Miss Dixon, trust me, if you dwell on this and take the blame, it will destroy you. When we are left alive, all we can do is go on."

TWENTY-FIVE

The next day, still stunned by Hudson's murder, Abby walked past the church of St. Bartholomew. The cathedral looked gray and cool and timeless. The stone façade seemed to look down on the busyness of the streets and buildings that had sprung up around her, with supreme indifference, like a queen barely aware of the rabble of her subjects. Something about the regal old church helped to calm the terrible, churning guilt she felt about Hudson's murder.

Which should have been her murder.

Once more she was being followed by a plainclothes policeman, but this time, she was grateful. She knew it was the inspector's way of trying to protect her.

The officer must be wondering what she was doing, walking back and forth in front of the cathedral's arched entrance. She was wondering herself. What did she hope to accomplish in coming here?

She wasn't Catholic. There would be no relief for her in confession. No penance she could suffer through to bring her forgiveness. She'd been arrogant to think she could snoop around, hoping to discover a killer, and suffer no consequences.

Arrogant and foolish, and Hudson had paid the price.

She crossed the road and pulled open the heavy oak door and stepped inside the cool, hushed interior. The Romanesque arches soared high over her head, meeting like intertwined fingers. She understood why Father O'Sullivan had mentioned the paintings. Images of love and sacrifice covered nearly every surface: martyred saints, stations of the cross, Mary and the angels. She smelled the old stone, something damp and earthy and a hint of incense. St. Bartholomew's wasn't a huge cathedral like Notre Dame, but it was probably as old. After the street noise, she noticed the hush.

A scattering of parishioners sat in the hard pews with heads bowed, praying, and a couple of tourists with a guidebook wandered among the pillars, admiring the paintings. She looked down the long transept at the beautiful blue and red stained-glass window at the end.

She had no idea where she would find Father O'Sullivan at this time of day or if he was here at all, but somehow, being in the space was calming. She walked into the alcoves as the tourists did and looked at the paintings and the effigies of long-dead aristocrats with their calm marble faces, hands clasped piously at their breasts. In one alcove were more recent plaques memorializing those who had died in the Great War. So many young men lost.

Her eye ran down the list of names carved in stone that was all that was left of these soldiers, most of them little more than boys. Her sadness grew as she saw groups of the dead with the same surname and realized that they were brothers, sometimes up to four from one family. She came to Raymonde Lafitte, aged forty-four; Gerard Lafitte, aged twenty-one; and Jerome Lafitte, aged nineteen. No wonder poor Madame Lafitte was so bitter and angry.

As though she had conjured the woman, she glimpsed Madame Lafitte walking past, a black scarf over her head and her eyes downcast. She looked as though she'd been crying. Abby turned to study the icon of a dead saint so as not to intrude on Madame Lafitte's private grief.

She waited a couple of minutes, long enough for Madame Lafitte to leave, and stepped back into the central corridor. Father O'Sullivan was making his way down the transept. She walked forward, and when he heard the footsteps coming toward him, he turned and, recognizing her, smiled. When she had come closer, he said, "I'm very pleased to see you again, Miss Dixon."

"Father," she said, "I'm not Catholic, but I'm in sore need of comfort."

He searched her face and nodded. "I have finished hearing confessions. Come, I have a little study where we won't be disturbed." At the back of the church were several small doors, and he opened one and ushered her in. It was a small office containing a crowded desk, a shelf of books, a couple of comfortable-looking armchairs, a crucifix on the wall. When they were seated, he asked, "How may I help you?"

She told him about yesterday's incident, about the telegram and how poor Hudson had gone in her place. She shook her head. "I feel so guilty. The telegram was addressed to me. I was the one who was meant to die."

His face looked both weary and sad. "I am truly sorry. What was the young man's name? I will pray for him."

He settled back, and there was something so comfortable about him. She felt that he shared her grief. "God works in mysterious ways. You say you were meant to be the one killed, and yet, you weren't. Hudson was meant to be safe at the office, and yet he wasn't. Who could ever say why? But if you lose yourself in guilt and remorse, then you become a second victim of the tragedy."

She leaned forward. They called priests "Father," and she

longed for a father now, someone she trusted who would give her direction. "What should I do?"

"Your life is in danger. Go home. Back to America. You'll be safe there."

The idea was instantly appealing. To go home to her country, where she understood the language and no one was trying to kill her, was momentarily dazzling. She would still feel sad and guilty, but she wouldn't have to return to the newsroom where Hudson had worked, where every person working there knew what had happened to him.

Then a sense of injustice rose in her. Hudson had died in her place. The one thing she could do for him was to discover who had done this terrible thing. She sat straighter. "No. Going home is not a possibility."

He looked sorry at her answer, but she imagined he'd seen every emotion a human could experience and nothing surprised him. "Come," he said. "I want to show you something." He rose, so she followed him. They went out of his office and back into the church.

He led her to a wall where she could see a mural that looked to be from the seventeen hundreds. Madonna and child smiled down, chubby and benevolent. But beneath that painting another, much older fresco emerged. "Because of bombing in the war and damp, something older and very precious was revealed. It seemed to be a disaster until this wonderful medieval wall art began to emerge."

"It's beautiful," she said, amazed at how well preserved the earlier painting was. The saints were ascetic and their crowns of gold still fresh-looking.

He said, "History always informs the present. This wonderful church has withstood time and siege, war and riot, and still she stands, a reminder that there are things bigger than ourselves."

"Like justice."

"Justice is a fine and good quality; just make certain you don't confuse it with revenge."

Abby thanked Father O'Sullivan for his time, and he invited her to come back anytime. "I was a chaplain in the war. I've seen the guilt of those who survive. It appears so random to a surviving soldier that the fellow he was joking with or playing cards with only a few hours ago is now dead and he's alive. I will tell you what I told so many grieving soldiers. You can't bring the dead back by putting yourself in the grave."

She knew he was right, and one day, perhaps, she would cease to feel guilty about Hudson's death.

As she was about to leave, she said, "Father, how long have you been with this church?"

"St. Bartholomew's?" He glanced up at the wooden beams overhead as though the answer might be written there. He said, "It was 1911, I believe."

She doubted very much her stepmother had ever set foot inside a church unless it was to steal from the collection plate, but she wanted to leave no stone unturned, no question unasked. "I don't suppose you ever came across a girl or young woman named Lillianne Pettit?"

He shook his head. "I'm sorry, Abby. I never knew your stepmother."

An electric shock ran from the top of her spine to the bottom. As casually as possible, her eyes intent on his face, she said, "I don't believe I mentioned that Lillianne Pettit was my stepmother."

His face went slack for a moment, and then he said, "You didn't have to. I know your stepmother's Christian name was Lillian. What other Lillian could you be asking about?"

It was a slick answer, but he wouldn't have known that her stepmother was French. After one more searching glance at his face that yielded nothing, she thanked him and left.

Her brain was seething with questions and possibilities as

she strode toward the atelier. Was it possible that Father O'Sullivan had known her stepmother? And if he had, why would he lie about it? Or was she seeing lies and deception where none existed? She had no idea anymore. This web of intrigue was like the church paintings. She felt as though the truth was buried under layers of subterfuge that needed to be stripped and flaked away or perhaps scrubbed with something harsh and unpleasant in order to get to what was behind.

When Madame Lafitte let her in with her usual acid expression, as though she were letting the devil himself into her sanctified space, Abby recalled those three names chiseled into cold stone and was filled with compassion. She said, "Good afternoon, Madame Lafitte," and when the woman sniffed and shut the door behind her with a decided snap, she thanked her anyway.

The woman looked at her suspiciously and then said she could find her own way up to Paul Joubert's office. Abby wasn't expected, but she felt the key to what had happened to Lillian must be here. She walked up the stairs slowly, her usual quickness and lightness of step missing. Her feet felt as heavy as her heart.

Someone had overheard two people arguing in French the day Lillian died. She'd dismissed the news as irrelevant, but now she knew it wasn't. Who had Lillian been arguing with in the fitting room of Paul Joubert's fashion house?

When she got to Paul's closed door, she raised her hand to knock, and before her knuckles connected with the wood, she heard a cry of mingled rage and pain that sounded like it was coming from the very depths of a tortured soul.

She pushed open the door, picturing the couturier on the floor bleeding from a scissors wound. Collapsed over his desk, having suffered a heart attack. Blown into a thousand pieces by a bomb. Instead, when she rushed in, she found Paul with a letter clutched in his hand, his face red with fury and a kind of despair in his eyes. "Abby, I did not expect you."

She felt as though she had pushed her way inappropriately into something private and painful. Her first instinct was to back out of the room and apologize, and then she saw the letter in his hand. The envelope on his desk. He had received one of those before and gone pale. She had also received a letter in a very similar envelope that warned her to leave Paris. Now Hudson was dead. If she had not ignored that letter, would he still be alive?

She conquered her instinct to apologize and leave Paul Joubert to his pain in private. She said, "Paul, I'm sorry to interrupt you, but this letter has obviously upset you. Can I help in any way?"

His hands were shaking, and he blinked rapidly. She could feel him trying to pull the edges of his dignity together as though it had been ripped, like one of his own silk gowns torn down the middle, and now he held the pieces awkwardly together, which only made her more aware of the rent down the front. "*Non, non, non,*" he said with a pathetic attempt at bravado. "Bills, always bills."

"I don't think that is a bill," she said softly. "I received a letter very similar to that. It told me that I was in danger and that I should leave France. I thought it was a crank letter; newspaper reporters get them sometimes. I ignored it. And yesterday, I received a telegram inviting me to go to a house where the writer claimed to have letters and photographs of my stepmother."

Paul Joubert was staring at her, his eyes both incredulous and wary. "Did you obtain these letters and photographs?"

She shook her head. She swallowed. This part was so painful to tell. Obviously, he hadn't heard. In as few words as she could, she told him what had transpired.

The couturier seemed to fold into himself and collapse into

his chair. His previously overheated face now looked gray. "My deepest condolences."

She hated to push a reluctant source—it was one of the things she disliked most about her profession. She especially didn't want to push someone she liked. However, now, added to trying to solve her stepmother's murder and clear her own name was the fresh burden of getting justice for Hudson. She said, "Paul, I wish you would trust me."

He looked up at her and back at the letter still crunched in his hand. "Abigail, you are a journalist. There are some things that a man does not wish to make public."

Quietly, she said, "I give you my word that if you'll tell me what you know of these letters and the writer that I will hold your confidence sacred."

He bowed his head and held out the letter. Believing this to be a gesture of acquiescence, she walked forward and took the page gently from him. She went around to the front of his desk and sat down in her usual chair and smoothed out the crumpled page.

"*Cher Monsieur Joubert,*" the note began. It wasn't long, but the letter was written in French. She understood the word "photograph" and the number "Fr. 5000." At the bottom was a crude pencil drawing of two men with mustaches kissing each other.

She glanced up quickly, but Paul was studying his desk as though it were one of his best gowns. Clearly, he was meant to be one of the men depicted in the crude drawing. She knew of such relationships, obviously. In Paris, she had heard of clubs where men dressed as women to entertain other men who danced together and enjoyed intimate suppers. She wasn't shocked to find that Paul Joubert was such a man. She supposed on some level she had known. She wanted to be absolutely certain that she had guessed correctly. "You're being blackmailed?"

He nodded. "It's been going on for years. That vile blackmailer has photographs. Always, I believe this is the last one. Months will go by and I truly believe it is at an end and then another such letter comes."

While homosexuality was against the law in her own country, the French were more tolerant. "Such a relationship is not illegal, is it?"

He shook his head. "Not illegal, *non*. And if it were only for myself, I would not care. It is the other party who is really the target. It is he whose life would be destroyed if these photographs became public."

"A public figure then?" she guessed at random.

He glanced up at her and then back down to the contemplation of his desktop. He nodded.

He looked so miserable, she wished she could comfort him. "Is he married?"

"Oh, yes."

"And does his wife know?"

"Yes, of course. I do not say she approves, but rather she accepts. She very much enjoys her position in society and the advantages of being married to my friend. But make no mistake, if this became public, she would not stand by him."

She knew he would not tell her who his lover was and she would not ask. But with a gust of intuition, she realized she knew. "How long have you and Monsieur Fleuri been... friends?"

His dejected look vanished, and he stood up looking furious. "I do not tell you who is my friend. And you will not guess."

"Of course. I'm so sorry. Forget I ever mentioned a name."

But, of course, he'd confirmed her guess by his reaction. She completely understood how publicly humiliating it would be if those pictures were circulated or, even worse, made public somehow. Monsieur Fleuri was an important cabinet minister in the government. His wife would divorce him; he'd be forced to resign.

Abby also rose to her feet and leaned forward so she was within inches of Paul. "We will stop this blackmailer. You do not deserve to be made miserable, and Hudson did not deserve to die."

Instead of looking nobly invigorated, as she had hoped, Paul looked panicked. "Abby, I beg you. You must not interfere. I will pay this viper as I have many times before."

She wanted to argue with him, but when she looked into his eyes, she understood that he would do anything to protect the man he loved.

"All right. But, please, tell me everything you know about this blackmailer. Why did they target me? I believe this person who is blackmailing you and the person who killed Hudson and Lillian Dixon are one and the same."

He sat down and again put his hand to his forehead. "*Mon Dieu.*"

In the deep silence, she heard the low buzz of sewing machines from the atelier upstairs.

"*Monsieur,* I have an idea." He did not appear excited at her words. He looked as though he wished she'd never burst in on him this afternoon. Before he could say anything, she kept going. "How do you deliver the money?"

She thought he wouldn't answer. Finally, he said, "There is an alcove in Notre Dame Cathedral. It is not the most popular one. In it is a statue of a penitent dying in the arms of death, who holds an hourglass. Death has a skeleton head and flowing drapery. One slips the money into the stone drapery."

Her eyes widened. "You leave five thousand francs in cash where anyone can pick it up?"

His tired eyes lightened momentarily. "I believe that is the point."

"And you've no idea who picks this money up?"

"*Non.*"

"But you must have tried to see who it was?"

He shrugged. "Once, my friend made the donation, and I hung back and tried to see who came and went. I can only say there was no one I recognized. The assigned times are always busy ones."

Her hands went up, begging for information. "Male? Female? Young? Old?"

He shook his head again. "It is not the most busy of the alcoves, but there are always people coming and going. It could have been one of twenty people, and they were, as you say, young, old, large and small, French and foreign, nun and layperson. I believe that is why the clever blackmailer has chosen that spot."

"And how do you get the photograph?"

"It is always delivered to me by mail after I pay. In that, at least, my blackmailer is a person of honor."

She said briskly, "Well, they won't be expecting me. When do you make this drop?"

"Saturday at eleven o'clock, so it will be filled with tourists and the faithful."

"Very well, I'll take my guidebook to Paris along with me and pretend to be studying the architecture like any good American tourist."

"*Non and non and non.*" He banged his fingertips on the crumpled letter. "Everyone in Paris knows that you and I are friends. You are my muse. This blackmailer is not stupid. If you are there, it will be very bad for me."

She wanted to argue, but she knew that he was correct. "If only you would allow the police to get involved. They could send plainclothes detectives to arrest this person."

Once more, he shook his head vehemently. "This blackmailer does not work alone, Abigail. Of that I am certain. If they were caught and arrested, those pictures would be made public."

She could see that his hands were shaking and he was genuinely frightened. "All right," she said soothingly. "No police."

What would Nellie Bly do?

And then she had her solution. "What about this? My friend Vivian and I will go to the cathedral. She has been asking me for ages to go. She longs to show me the sights of Paris. Two American girls in the cathedral will not cause comment. I will not wear one of your creations. It is those that make me so recognizable."

He looked slightly less horrified. "And what will you tell your friend?"

"I shan't tell her anything at all."

Only when she promised not to startle the blackmailer but only to follow at a discreet distance did he agree to her plan.

TWENTY-SIX

Vivian looked surprised at Abby's suggestion that they go to Notre Dame Cathedral that Saturday morning. "Golly. I thought you'd want to go shopping or sit out in a café or something."

"I do want to do those things. But I want to light a candle for Hudson. I don't know if he was Catholic, but I would like someone to light a candle for me in Notre Dame if I died in Paris." Surprisingly, when she heard her own words, they didn't sound like an excuse. They sounded true. She really did hope that if she were to die here that someone would light a candle for her in that lovely old cathedral.

"Well, you are not going to die," Vivian said, sounding quite fierce. "I am going to keep a better eye on you."

Abby was touched. "And I will treat us to lunch afterward."

When they arrived at Notre Dame, Abby understood why the blackmailer had chosen this particular time. She and Vivian were not the only tourists wandering the lovely ancient cathedral. In fact, it was packed. Tourists, Catholic faithful who, based on the various languages she heard being spoken, had come from near and far, and the local faithful.

Any other time, Abby would've enjoyed staring at the blue rose windows that dated from the year 1300. Even with all the people wandering or praying, the cathedral felt cool and hushed. They had arrived almost half an hour before Paul was due to drop the blackmailer's money. She'd slipped in previously, unbeknownst to Vivian, to study the alcove where the drop would take place. She knew the statue now and the convenient spaces in Death's stone robes where an envelope could be surreptitiously placed and then retrieved.

Vivian had protested when she'd come out of her bedroom dressed for their outing in the old tweed suit she'd brought from home. "Why don't you wear one of your glamorous frocks?"

She'd prepared for this question and answered in some honesty. "I always feel like I have to sit so carefully in one of Paul's creations, and I worry constantly I'll drip coffee or spill food or something. I may not look as glamorous in this old two-piece, but at least I can relax."

She also wore her dull brown woolen coat from home. Only the hat was new, and she chose it for its low-hanging brim. If anyone studied her closely, they might recognize her face, but otherwise she felt she would be indistinguishable from the hundreds of American and British tourists.

She checked her bag to make sure her little Kodak was there, and they set out.

They took the Metro to Île de la Cité and entered the hushed gloom of Notre Dame.

As a group of Italians paused to let three nuns go ahead of them, Vivian whispered, "I didn't realize there would be so many people here."

"It does seem popular," Abby agreed. Her heart began to beat quicker as she surreptitiously studied the other people around them. It was exciting to be part of an undercover operation, though she had to be careful not to arouse Vivian's suspicion or, even worse, alert the blackmailer.

Her friend currently had her nose in the guidebook and was reading out such choice snippets as, "The Emmanuel bell weighs thirteen tons and is located in the south tower house. Goodness, that's a big bell."

She turned the page. "And the two towers are sixty-nine meters tall, or three hundred and eighty-seven steps." She looked up. "That makes me tired just reading it."

Abby said, "We won't climb all the stairs then." She began edging them toward a spot she'd found that would have a good vantage of the blackmailer's alcove.

She wanted to be close but not too close. She managed to maneuver them so that Vivian blocked her view to the door where she knew Paul would be arriving, and this left her with her back to the alcove. By asking Vivian to read a little of the history of Notre Dame, she was able to keep her flighty friend in place. Paul Joubert came in, and, like she had, his gaze scanned his surroundings. He walked past them and not by the slowing of his step or darting of his gaze did he seem to have noticed the two women.

She pointed out the highest of the stained-glass windows to Viv, so her friend was looking up when the couturier went by.

He went into the alcove and very soon came out and walked away.

She waited a minute or two, watching carefully. It was impossible to have a completely clear view of the alcove as tourists ambled in front of her vision. Finally, she said to Vivian, interrupting her in the middle of her reading about the cathedral's many gargoyles, "I'm going to light a candle for Hudson, and maybe for my mother and father, too."

Vivian stopped reading and looked up at her, slightly puzzled. "Your parents weren't Catholic, were they?"

"No, but I don't think God cares. It's a nice way of remembering them."

She dug into her bag for her change purse as a way of keeping her head bowed as she approached the alcove. Her heart was pounding now. Surely, in such a busy church and on such a busy day, the blackmailer wouldn't let all that cash sit there for very long. The pickup had to happen soon.

She was very aware of her promise to Paul that she wouldn't do anything that could make his blackmailer suspicious. This made it difficult for her to be as aggressive as she would have liked to be. It would have been better if she could have taken Vivian into her confidence. Perhaps later, if she could get a photograph of the blackmailer and follow that person, she could explain her odd behavior. She asked Vivian to keep reading so she wasn't required to make any small talk as they walked slowly toward that alcove.

She took her camera out and said, "I want to get a photo of the interior. It's so lovely."

The rows of votive candles loomed before her, flickering and glowing in their red glass holders.

And then she heard words that she had dreaded to hear. "Why, Miss Abigail Dixon. Good morning to you."

At the cheerful Irish-accented words, she glanced up to find Father O'Sullivan smiling down at her. She tried to look around him, but he was taller than she was. Breezily, in a Saturday tourist voice, she said, "Good morning, Father O'Sullivan. This is such a beautiful cathedral. I was telling my friend here that I want to light a candle for my colleague who was killed last week. And for my parents."

Vivian seemed concerned that there might be some theological tomfoolery here, so she said, "Abby's parents were not Catholic. She won't get into any trouble, will she?"

His kind face relaxed, and he gave her one of his benevolent smiles. "No. God will understand."

Could this really be a coincidence? But the thought of this

nice priest as a blackmailer was horrifying. Desperate for a glimpse of the actual blackmailer, she said, "I must go and light a candle."

Father O'Sullivan didn't stop her. He moved out of her way, and the three of them walked forward to the three-tiered stand of flickering votive candles. She dropped her centimes into the offering box. Then she lit one of the provided spills from the flame of a burning candle and lit a fresh candle.

If she'd been truly here for Hudson's soul, she'd have prayed or at least thought about him, but she believed Hudson would rather she find his killer than pray for him. At least, she hoped so.

While she pretended to pray, her eyes were feverishly searching for the blackmailer. There was no one in the alcove. She waited, hoping the pickup would happen soon. Father O'Sullivan had only been in her way for a minute or so.

Could the blackmailer have pocketed the ransom money that quickly? Her nerves stretched with anxiety as she waited for footsteps to approach. Behind her, Father O'Sullivan was explaining to Vivian that she must not miss a view of the Holy Crown of Thorns, believed to be the very one placed on Christ's head during the crucifixion.

She said, with what she hoped sounded like naïve American enthusiasm, "What a fascinating statue." She walked forward into the alcove to make certain the envelope was still there. Father O'Sullivan couldn't have taken the envelope, as he'd been with her right after it was dropped. He couldn't have gone into the alcove without her seeing him.

He followed her into the relative peace and quiet. "This is the tomb of Claude Henri d'Harcourt. It was designed by Pigalle and suggests that the dying man is about to fall into the open coffin while death holds an hourglass over his head," he said, as though he were a tour guide. No doubt he meant well, but she wished Father O'Sullivan would go away. While he was speaking, she walked forward.

She looked closely into every possible spot one could leave an envelope. There was nothing. She'd failed. Paul Joubert's money was gone.

Abby tried not to squeak or swear or stamp her feet in frustration. Instead, she turned and scanned the area behind her. There were so many people.

One of them had five thousand francs in cash. She thought that if she were carrying that much money in ill-gotten gains, she'd be desperate to get out of this house of God.

Most of the people seemed contemplative. Worshipers or tourists, they took their time. She caught sight of a young woman wearing a dark coat and a head scarf. She didn't walk quickly, but what drew Abby's attention was that, unlike most of those gathered, she wasn't looking around but had her head down as though she were counting the tiles. Of course, she could be searching for the gravestone of a famous person or an ancestor, but then wouldn't she stop to study the faded writing on the stones?

The woman headed, without hurry, but also without detour, for a side door.

Abby had an instinct that this was her blackmailer. She wanted to get rid of Father O'Sullivan so she could follow the young woman. He and Viv had begun to talk about various ways of remembering the dead.

The woman had reached the door now. Abby didn't have time for elaborate ruses, so she simply grabbed Vivian's arm and said, "I'm so sorry, Father, we must run. We have another appointment."

She gave Vivian's arm a warning squeeze in case her friend had any qualms about telling an untruth to a priest. Vivian kept her mouth shut, and with a hurried goodbye, Abby walked quickly toward the side door, dragging her friend along with her.

Vivian waited until they were outside in the chilly sunshine before asking her what on earth was going on.

Abby was scanning the crowd around them, the sellers of icons and crucifixes and trinkets of all sorts, tourists who'd paused outside to admire the magnificent edifice. She didn't see the woman. Frustration boiled within her. "I promise I'll tell you. Just come along with me, will you?"

"Sure. But you're acting crazy. Poor Father O'Sullivan—"

Abby hurried across the bridge and looked up and down, but there was no sign of the woman. She caught a glimpse of what she thought might be the young woman, but even as she ran forward, the person got onto a bus. She was about to run across the road, regardless of traffic, when the bus pulled out.

She felt so frustrated that she'd bungled what should have been a simple task of following the blackmailer that she wanted to cry. She'd let down Hudson and Paul Joubert.

"Abigail Dixon, what is going on?" Vivian asked, running up breathless behind her.

Most of the chatter around them was in French. Still, she dropped her voice. Even though she knew all of the reporters at her paper, there were plenty of other English-language reporters and just plain English-language gossips in Paris who'd be only too pleased to overhear what she had to say. She knew she had to tread warily, but Vivian did have a right to know why she'd been rushed through Notre Dame and out again in undignified haste.

"I can't explain why I know, but I believe that young woman might know something about Hudson's death."

Opposite her, Vivian's blue eyes opened as wide as a china doll's. "But that's simply too awful. Someone involved in a murder going into a cathedral?" She shook her head, and her blond bob swung in disbelief. "I'm surprised the cathedral itself didn't fall in and crush her. Who commits an atrocity like that and then goes into a house of worship?"

Privately, Abby suspected that a lot of the souls who worshipped on Sunday morning had plenty to ask forgiveness for. She turned and looked back at Notre Dame, wondering if Father O'Sullivan was one of them.

TWENTY-SEVEN

Tuesday evening, Vivian entered the apartment with a sigh. "Today, I convinced a woman that wearing our new signature perfume for spring—cleverly called Paris Spring—took a decade off her face. I did. I convinced a perfectly sane woman that dabbing a bit of scented oil behind her ears made her look ten years younger. My boss was so terribly impressed, he wants me to start writing some of our ad copy in English."

"That's wonderful," Abby said, looking up from the dining table, spread with blank newspaper and a scatter of grease pencils.

"He was in such a good mood, he sent us both home a sample bottle of the new perfume. I think he's hoping you will make it all the rage, do for perfume what you've done for Paul Joubert gowns."

She took off her gloves, then her coat and hat and carefully put them all away. When she returned, she looked at what Abby was doing at the dining table. "What's that? Is it some kind of craft project?"

She looked down and toyed with a rubber eraser. "I thought if I wrote down all the people who are connected with Lillian and looked at the ways in which they are linked with each other, I might begin to see how it all fits together."

She stepped back and Vivian stood behind her as they both studied her work. Abby had written "Lillian" in the center of the page and then a list of names.

"Well, it looks like a spiderweb to me."

"Exactly." The names connected by lines shooting out from Lillian's name in the middle of the page included Madame Bernard, the *première*; Madame Lafitte; Paul Joubert; Larry (Lord Lambridge); Lady Eleanor; the Duke and Duchess of Cirencester; Father O'Sullivan.

There were lines connecting the various people to Lillian and to each other, so it did rather resemble a spider's web. Except she couldn't decide which of them was the venomous spider in the middle of the web. Vivian contemplated the names. "You really suspect Father O'Sullivan of killing your stepmother?"

"I don't know. I feel that we must consider him at least. He was suspiciously in the cathedral at the same time as the blackmailer."

"But blackmail isn't murder."

"No. However, don't forget I got a letter similar to the one Paul Joubert received, and it said I should go back to America. That suggests to me that whoever is doing the blackmailing could be involved in Lillian's murder."

Though, she argued with herself, he couldn't possibly have picked up the envelope of money between the time Paul Joubert dropped it off and she and Viv had bumped into him.

Unless he had an accomplice. That young woman she had chased and lost. It still rankled that she hadn't been able to catch her.

"But did the priest even know Lillian?"

"I don't know." She pointed to the lines. "But we know he is acquainted with Madame Lafitte because I saw her coming out of confession."

Vivian used her finger to trace the next name. "And I see you have Madame Lafitte as a suspect as well?"

"I suppose she's on the list because she's connected to Father O'Sullivan. Because she is also connected with Paul Joubert." She looked at the page. "I should add Suzanne, too. She knew Lillian slightly."

"And why have you got Madame Bernard on the list?"

"Because the *première* is also one of the people who deals with customers directly. Most of the women working in the atelier would have no reason to interact with Lillian in any other way than making up her dresses. She'd have spoken to Madame Lafitte when she arrived, and Madame Bernard would have helped her during the fittings, exactly as she helped me."

She added Suzanne's name, drawing a line that connected Suzanne with Paul, with Madame Lafitte and with Madame Bernard.

"And you have Paul Joubert as a suspect? Do you really think he killed one of his own clients?"

She'd told Vivian of the blackmail but said it was a private matter, and Vivian hadn't pressed. If the couturier had suspected Lillian of blackmailing him, might he have been driven to desperation? But he was, at best, an unlikely killer. "She died in his couture house. He must at least be considered."

Vivian said, "And you have Lord Larry on the list?"

"Yes. I'm convinced Lillian was trying to get him to marry her. She stole his cigarette case. I knew Lillian. She may have threatened to cause a scandal. I've been watching Lord Larry, and I believe he could be violent if he perceived that person as his enemy. If she threatened to ruin his reputation among mothers with marriageable daughters, who knows what lengths he might've gone to. So yes, he's a suspect."

He was actually her prime suspect, but she didn't say so.

"Also, don't forget the Englishman who bought handkerchiefs the very day that Lillian was killed. I can't prove it, but I believe it was Lord Larry. The handkerchief he offered me when I had dinner with them that night possibly came from Paul Joubert's atelier."

Vivian continued to look at the newsprint with the scribbles on it and said, "Shouldn't you add Hudson to this list? Lillian was not the only murder victim."

"But I was the intended victim. Hudson went in my place."

"Then you need to add your own name," Vivian insisted. "Abby, I read all those true crime articles in the women's magazines and the newspapers. The heart of the story is always the victim."

Of course, as a journalist, Abby was scrupulous about keeping herself out of the story, but in this case, Vivian was right. She took the pencil and added Hudson's name and her own, and then she drew a line connecting Hudson to herself, and then the line stretched from herself to Lillian and through Lillian to every person on her list.

Vivian's pretty face crinkled in a frown. "Lillian had only been in France a few weeks. How could she have made a deadly enemy so quickly?"

Abby felt that she'd been looking at this paper full of names and pencil scrawls for so long that Vivian walking in brought fresh perspective. "Of course, Vivian. You're brilliant."

Vivian did not hear those words very often, so she looked quite surprised. "I am?"

"Yes." She stepped forward and wrote beside Lillian, *Lillianne Pettit*. "Lillian wasn't only in Paris for a few weeks. She'd grown up here, lived here for most of her life."

Their telephone rang, and Vivian went to answer it. She said, "Just a moment," and turned to Abby. "It's your Aunt Ida. She's downstairs. The doorman wants to know if he should send her up?"

Abby had a moment when she wanted to deny that she was home, but she couldn't do it. Aunt Ida had come a long way to help her, and even if she was interfering and a zany, she was her mother's sister and she loved her. "Tell him to send her up."

Aunt Ida enfolded her in a scented embrace and then held her back and looked at her face. "How are you holding up, my dear?"

"As well as can be expected."

"I so enjoy your articles. Your writing is excellent. Your mother would be so proud."

She wasn't sure that her mother would be very proud that her only daughter was suddenly famous for being suspected of murder, but she appreciated the spirit behind Aunt Ida's words.

Her ebullient aunt announced, "I've come to take you girls to dinner. Now, I don't want any arguments. I've made a reservation at *Maison de Prunier*. I hear the oysters are wonderful."

Vivian's eyes went wide. "Gosh, I've always wanted to go there, but it's so expensive."

"We're celebrating. I've got some good news for you."

"I would dearly love some good news."

"I've spoken to the American ambassador and told him in no uncertain terms that I expect him to intervene in this disgraceful treatment of you."

Abby shuddered at the very idea that this was good news. "Aunt Ida, the ambassador can't pervert the course of justice."

"Nonsense. He can when his mother and I were dear friends at school." She smiled graciously. "Even better, the Duchess of Cirencester has promised to do anything she can to help you."

"You know the Duchess of Cirencester?" Aunt Ida often surprised her but rarely for such positive reasons.

"When she read in your excellent newspaper that I had arrived in Paris, the duchess telephoned the hotel and asked if I could help her contact her late husband."

"I wouldn't have thought of her as the sentimental type."

Aunt Ida's blue eyes began to twinkle. "There were some stock certificates that she has been unable to find since her first husband's death." She rearranged several strings of crystal beads that had become tangled. "I was able to direct her to where they were located. She's so grateful, she would do anything for me."

"You found her stock certificates?" Abby couldn't keep the shock from her voice.

"I didn't find anything, dear. Her late husband told me where to find them. He also sent her a very nice message saying he hoped she was as happy with her second husband." She paused to think. "Though I'm not sure he wasn't being sarcastic. People change surprisingly little when they're dead."

She walked deeper into their apartment and noticed the scribbled pencil sketch of names and connections on the dining table. "What's all this?"

Briefly, Abby explained as she had to Vivian who all the people were and why they were connected.

Aunt Ida tapped her gloved finger on the name Lord Lambridge. She said, "I saw that young man with his mother at the opera last night. He was escorting Amelia Dayton."

Abby waited a beat, and when her aunt didn't say anymore, she asked, "Do you think that's relevant to Lillian's death, somehow?"

"Well, my dear, the Daytons would never let their daughter be seen in public with a man until they had investigated him thoroughly and met him privately several times. That would have taken several weeks."

Abby immediately picked up a pencil and wrote Amelia Dayton, and a line from Lawrence to her. "So what you're saying is that Lord Larry was being scrutinized by the Daytons before Lillian was killed."

"Exactly."

"Which gives him a stronger motive to have killed her. What if she threatened to go to the Daytons and tell them what kind of a man their daughter was about to marry?"

Aunt Ida shook her head. "I've been moving in society much longer than you have, my dears. Lillian would no more do that than she would turn up at a social event dressed in rags. She may have railed at him in private, but she would have preserved her reputation in society at all costs. No, however angry she may have been with him in private, Lillian Dixon was a calculating minx. She may have demanded a very expensive parting gift, and no doubt she did, but having lost one fat fish, she'd waste no time baiting her hook and fishing for the next one."

"You're right. Of course, you're right." Taking her pencil up once more, she drew yet another line radiating from Lillian and wrote New Lover. She put down the pencil. Aunt Ida picked it up. She drew another line coming from Lillian to right under where "New Lover" was written and, in her elegant copperplate hand, she wrote "New Lover's Wife."

Vivian gasped. "Did the spirits tell you who it was?"

"Nothing so easy, I'm afraid. No, I'm acting merely on a knowledge of Lillian's character. She may certainly have preferred a single man but, as our own history shows, she wouldn't stop at going after a married man if the prize were worth the scandal."

"Which gives us an unknown suspect. Or two."

Aunt Ida sighed. "Sleuthing is exhausting work. We must refresh ourselves with oysters."

Aunt Ida's driver took them to *Maison de Prunier* on Avenue Victor-Hugo. Vivian was twittering with excitement to be at a place she'd read about and never believed she'd dine in.

The maître d' took one look at Aunt Ida's furs and Abby's Joubert gown and seated them at a lovely table by the window. The décor was very modern with sleek lines and a curved bar, where seafood was displayed in large silver bowls like bouquets of flowers in vases.

Aunt Ida ordered champagne cocktails for all of them, and while she sampled the heady cocktail, Abby continued to puzzle over the list of suspects and their connections.

Aunt Ida and Vivian carried the conversation, and she barely attended until Vivian made a sound like a squeak and said, "Don't look now, but I'm sure that's Valentino, sitting at one of the center tables on the upper level."

Almost as interested as Vivian to catch a glimpse of the famous film star, she surreptitiously glanced around, and sure enough, Rudolph Valentino gazed about him, as imperious as he'd looked in *The Sheik*. He was sitting with an elegant young woman almost as beautiful as he was.

"That woman is not his wife," Vivian whispered. The young woman was trying very hard to pretend she wasn't aware of all the attention they were attracting.

Now that she was looking in that direction, Abby noticed another familiar face. Seated behind Rudolph Valentino was Lord Larry, dressed in an evening jacket, with Amelia Dayton, who looked stiff and as though careful to be on her best behavior. "Aunt Ida, that's Lawrence and Miss Dayton behind the Latin lover."

Aunt Ida put down her drink and searched the room. "Oh my, yes. Poor girl, she'd be much prettier if she could relax."

While they were sitting there, someone else came up to Aunt Ida. "Mrs. Tumulty. I hope you will excuse my intrusion, but it has long been my ambition to attend one of your séances. My name is Winifred Cabot." The woman was about thirty, and her jewels proclaimed her wealth. She said, with a quick, embarrassed glance at Vivian and Abby, "My mother and I have need of your gift for contacting the departed."

Aunt Ida was not above flattery. Her cheeks pinkened with pleasure. She said, "Well, I am only barely getting settled, my dear. But if you'd like to give me your visiting card, I will contact you when I next hold one of my séances."

"I'd be so very grateful."

Aunt Ida took her hand. "Is it a loved one you're trying to reach?"

She blinked rapidly. "It's my brother. He was killed in the war. My parents and I came over to visit his grave. I suppose I only want to know that he's all right. That he's comfortable. And to let him know how much we miss him. Especially Mother."

Aunt Ida's green eyes were grave but calm. "My dear, those who've passed on are always all right. Always comfortable. We suffer much more here on earth."

"Thank you. That's such a comfort."

She pressed her visiting card into Aunt Ida's hand and walked quickly away.

"Well, that was nice. What a sweet young—"

"That's it!" Abby said suddenly, tapping her open palm firmly on the tabletop. "Séance."

"I beg your pardon, dear? Did you want to come to a séance with that young woman?" Aunt Ida looked at her in some confusion.

"No." Abby shook her head with impatience. "You see, there are all these links between people, and I do not understand how they are connected or why, but one or more of them caused Lillian's murder."

She looked up and beamed at the two other women and took a sip of her champagne cocktail, which was delicious, and she said so.

"That's all very well, but what is all this about a séance? You know we didn't have any luck reaching Lillian last time."

"No. I don't want to reach Lillian. I only want to pretend to reach Lillian."

Aunt Ida's expression of interest began to dim. She frowned down her nose. "What are you suggesting, Abby?"

"Here's what I want to do. You said the Duchess of Cirencester offered to do anything for you, didn't you?"

"Yes, I did. And for you. She was quite taken with you when she met you at her afternoon salon."

"Good. I want her to host the séance. No one will turn down one of her invitations. It will be an eclectic group, and the invitation will say so. Once all the suspects are gathered around the table, I want you, dear Aunt Ida, to pretend to be receiving certain messages from beyond the grave."

Aunt Ida's lips thinned, and she shook her head. "Abigail Louise Dixon, I'll have nothing to do with any fakery. As I'm sure you're aware, my profession has been seriously damaged by fakes and quacks. I am an open conduit to the spirits." Here, she opened her hands wide so she looked rather like a Greek urn. "They will cease to trust me and speak to me if I demonstrate any sort of charlatanism." She rearranged her silver tableware. "I wrote a paper on the subject for the Chicago Spiritualist Society."

Abby knew she had to tread carefully if she was going to get Aunt Ida to agree to her plan. "I'm sure the spirits would understand if you let them know it was for a good cause."

"But I don't see how."

"Aunt Ida, don't you want to find Lillian's killer? Don't you want to save my life?"

She took a moment to answer. "Well, yes, of course I do. But I do not want to give up my reputation in the process."

"Only we three will know that the messages you get are not coming from beyond the grave. If my plan works, you'll be more famous than you've ever been before."

Her aunt sniffed. "I don't need any more fame. I'm quite famous enough, thank you."

She realized she'd gone a bit too far. "Of course. And I can understand it would be difficult for you to have even more anxious and bereaved people clamoring to come to your séances. Why, you'll be far more famous than Valentino."

Aunt Ida looked thoughtful. "More famous than Rudolph Valentino." And then she chuckled. "All right, Abigail. You know I'd do anything to help you, if only for your dear mother's sake."

As they dined on oysters and sole meunière, Abby laid out her plan. Vivian grew increasingly round-eyed as she listened. When Abby had finished, she asked, "Do you think it will work?"

Abby speared a mushroom with her fork. "Honestly, I have no idea. But for Hudson's sake, we have to try."

TWENTY-EIGHT

Abby delivered the invitation to Inspector Deschamps herself, wanting to be certain he attended the séance. He seemed quite surprised to see her when she was led up to his office for the third time.

When she revealed the purpose of her visit, she knew her instinct had been right to deliver his invitation in person. She made certain that the officer had left them alone and then leaned forward slightly in her chair. "Inspector Deschamps, this will not be an ordinary séance."

One side of his mouth lifted as though fighting a smile. "Miss Dixon, with you, nothing is ever ordinary."

Having a strong sense that he wasn't complimenting her, she ignored his comment and, instead, explained exactly what she was planning. His amusement vanished, and he looked at her quite sternly—an expression to which she had become accustomed. "Miss Dixon, I believe I have mentioned to you on more than one occasion that I would vastly prefer you to stay out of police business."

She sighed. "And as I believe I have mentioned to you on

more than one occasion, I would very much like to prevent my delicate American neck from being sliced off the rest of my body."

He gave an exclamation of annoyance and muttered something under his breath in French far too rapid for her to understand. He got up and strode across the room and opened the door. "You there, go and see if the commissaire would be available for a few moments."

Having sent the young officer running, he came back and asked her how she was enjoying Paris. With supreme urbanity, he chatted with her about the ballet and the opera. "Have you had an opportunity to visit Miss Beach's new bookshop?"

"Of course I've visited Shakespeare & Company." She recounted a vaguely amusing anecdote of finding Mr. Ezra Pound and Miss Gertrude Stein in the bookshop arguing about an E.E. Cummings poem. Sylvia Beach had sat between them, rather like a referee. "Though I believe it was a friendly match," she ended.

This was the kind of light conversation she might have enjoyed in one of the Duchess of Cirencester's salons, so she found it disconcerting to be sitting in police headquarters talking about American and British writers and poets with the police officer who suspected her of murder.

After some minutes, the same officer who had shown her into the office returned to say that the commissaire was available to see them now. Abby felt unaccountably nervous as he stood and indicated politely that she should do the same thing. She said, "You're not planning to arrest me, are you? A simple 'no, thank you' by way of RSVP would be sufficient."

"Come," he said, ignoring her sarcasm. "We must not keep my superior officer waiting." Though she detected a little sarcasm on his part when he called the commissaire his superior officer.

They went up another level, and the inspector knocked on

MURDER AT THE PARIS FASHION HOUSE 249

the door. A curt voice invited them to enter, and she was ushered in first. The commissaire rose and came around his desk. He was a fussy man of medium height with very tidy whiskers, his hair perfectly brushed, his suit trousers creased perfectly and his shoes so shiny, she could have styled her hair by using them as a mirror.

He looked displeased and said to the inspector, "What is the meaning of this? Who is this young woman?"

Though she suspected he knew, since he spoke in English.

"Commissaire, I wish to present to you Miss Abigail Dixon. She's anxious to have her passport restored to her."

She was surprised as she had made no such request, although naturally, she would like her passport simply to feel less like murder suspect number one on a very short list.

The commissaire immediately shook his head. "Out of the question. Mademoiselle, I regret the inconvenience, but you must understand that the evidence against you is very strong."

She had no idea why she was here. She was completely taken aback and unprepared. It was as though she had been thrown on the witness stand and asked to defend her life before a judge and jury with no preparation, no lawyer. As though they were all waiting for the guilty verdict so they could lead her out to her death.

She opened her hands in mute appeal. "I can assure you, I did not kill Lillian Dixon."

"It would be better that you allow the police to finish their inquiries, mademoiselle."

While she was trying to think of what she should say next, if anything, Inspector Deschamps called her name. "Miss Dixon? I believe you dropped this?"

In his hand was a pencil, and he tossed it in the air to her. Reflexively, she reached for it even though she hadn't brought a pencil with her. What was he up to?

He turned to the commissaire and said, "I hope you noticed, sir, that Miss Dixon caught that pencil with her left hand."

The man did not look impressed. "It could be a trick."

"I understand your concerns, sir. I had them myself. But I asked one of Miss Dixon's colleagues to watch her working, and she writes with her left hand. I have myself observed her on several occasions. She is undoubtedly left-handed."

She wanted to ask how that was relevant, since she was a journalist, after all, but some instinct for self-preservation caused her to keep quiet. The inspector continued. "As you know, the pathologist's report concluded that the murderer was most definitely right-handed. Miss Dixon cannot possibly be the murderer."

The man sniffed, looking very displeased. "Very well, though I did not need a theatrical display. You may restore this young lady's passport. However, I hold you personally responsible if you have made a blunder."

The inspector nodded his head, and without saying a word, Abby preceded him out of the office.

She was so stunned, she couldn't say a word until they were back in Inspector Deschamps's office once again. "How long have you known?" she asked, feeling extremely indignant.

"How odd. I thought you'd be pleased to have your passport restored and your innocence confirmed."

"I am delighted, but I'd have been very pleased to have known I was off the hook as soon as you did." She thought of the hours of wakefulness, the bad dreams she'd endured.

"I had my reasons."

She opened her mouth and shut it again. "You suspect someone else. So long as everyone, including me, assumed I was your prime suspect, you could investigate the real culprit while they believed they were in the clear."

He didn't answer, but he didn't have to. She was certain she was correct.

"Do you know who killed Lillian?"

He sounded angry when he answered. "Knowing isn't enough. We need proof."

"I truly think it would be worth your while to come to this séance, Inspector."

TWENTY-NINE

"Will you stop fidgeting, Abigail," Aunt Ida snapped. They were seated in the Duchess of Cirencester's grand dining room, around a gleaming walnut table where no doubt every head of state and royalty from every country had dined. The only thing that was going to be carved and served up here tonight, however, was the truth. Or at least Abby desperately hoped so.

The table seated twenty and was lit by a massive chandelier dripping with crystals that were reflected in the huge, gilt-framed mirror. Marble-topped tables held priceless treasures from the duke and duchess's travels: ivory carvings from India, porcelain from China, and marble statues that looked Italian. Among these treasures, Aunt Ida had placed fat beeswax candles.

Abby asked, "How can I be calm? What if they don't all come? What if my plan doesn't work?" Or the worst possibility of all. "What if I'm wrong?" She was putting everything on the line tonight: her reputation, her standing in the city, possibly even her life. Abby didn't like making a fool of herself, and she had a terrible suspicion she might be about to do just that.

Aunt Ida looked spectacular. She had decided, in honor of

her exalted hosts, to go whole hog in looking the part of a séance-leading psychic. Her turban was purple and black, shot with silver threads; her gown black and lacy; and her excessive jewelry bordering on vulgar, from the enormous diamond drops at her ears to the fat pearls at her neck and the many rings on her fingers—diamond, ruby, emerald, sapphire and even jet.

Abby had also dressed for the part. She wore a chic black and silver dress with a beaded hem. Around her throat were her mother's pearls, which she wore for comfort as well as a reminder of the damage Lillian had done. She also had a woolen scarf that had belonged to Hudson, which he'd left hanging on the office coat tree.

Vivian wore a pale blue drop-waist and seemed as nervous as Abby, though she suspected her friend was more nervous about the possibility of communing with the dead than she was about trapping a killer. She fussed with the candles Aunt Ida had asked her to light.

The electric lights were dimmed and candles flickered from a heavy, silver candelabra in the center of the table and from every surface.

Abby got up and went to the window and pushed aside the heavy gold silk drapes to peer onto the street. "What if they don't all come?"

"They'll come, my dear. The duchess herself invited them. No one in Paris says no to an invitation from the duchess."

She fluttered the curtains back into place. "And you haven't forgotten your lines? Should we practice again?"

"Much as it pains me to pretend that I don't have a gift, I will do this for you and your dearly departed mother. And I do not need further rehearsal," she said in injured tones.

"Thank you."

The duchess and the duke walked in at that moment. Sarah Barncastle greeted Abby warmly, kissing her cheeks French fashion. "This is very exciting. And Mrs. Tumulty, we're so pleased to have you among us again."

Aunt Ida nodded her head regally. An outsider would have thought that Aunt Ida was the duchess.

Abby had been at pains to arrange the table strategically, and as a result, there were tiny name cards set out. The duchess found her place, and directly across from her, her husband settled himself in his chair.

He was a jovial man who'd clearly been handsome in his youth, but years of good living had caught up with him, and he was portly and slightly dissipated-looking. "I would have said there was nothing in all this séance business. I'm a practical man, a man of business, and if you'd said to me that I would believe that there truly were mediums who could converse with the dead, I wouldn't have believed you. Not until your aunt helped my wife find her missing property."

Aunt Ida waved her hand in a gracious manner. "As I told your wife, I am merely a conduit, an open channel through which the dearly departed may choose to speak to their loved ones still in the earthly realm."

Lawrence, Lord Lambridge, arrived next, accompanied by his mother and his brother, Freddy. Abby had struggled with inviting all three of them, but as Aunt Ida had reminded her, Lawrence was unlikely to come here by himself. It was his mother who was the scheming social climber, and if she were invited to an event hosted by the duchess, she would make absolutely certain that her son came too.

They'd decided that it would look odd not to invite Freddy, and besides, Abby was happy to have someone in the room whom she knew to be innocent of any crime and moreover one who was friendly toward her.

Not everyone in this room would be, and by the time she was finished, she expected hostility. Freddy would be a great comfort. As was the Browning pistol in the evening bag hanging from her chair.

Lady Eleanor checked slightly at the sight of Abby, and her rather protuberant eyes looked as though they might fall out and roll into the middle of the table like a couple of suspicious marbles. Still, she collected herself and rushed with sycophantic haste to the duchess. The duchess then presented her to Aunt Ida and invited her to sit at the place that had been set for her lower down the table, close to where Abby was sitting.

Her son Larry sat beside his mother while Freddy sat beside Abby. He leaned close and said, "I'm looking forward to this. Not my usual cup of tea, but in Paris, one is always trying something new."

They made careful small talk until Abby's straining ears picked up the sound of a motorcar outside. Soon the maid ushered in Paul Joubert, and with the couturier were Madame Bernard, the *première*, and Madame Lafitte, the woman who opened the door. If Abby hadn't been such a nervous wreck, she'd have thoroughly enjoyed the discomfort on Lord Larry's mother's face as she realized she was going to be spending an evening with women who earned their living sewing.

The duchess, however, was made of kinder stuff. She greeted the two black-clad women as though they were honored guests. Madame Bernard was seated between the duchess and Lord Larry. Directly across from her was Madame Lafitte, who found herself beside the Duke of Cirencester. The two women looked as though they had not enjoyed the trip over. Paul Joubert, resplendent in one of his brightest waistcoats, whispered to Abby, "*Mon Dieu*, I did not think I would survive a trip between those two women."

She introduced him to the duchess, who beamed at him. "No need to introduce us, my dear. We're old friends. My dear Paul, it is a pleasure to have you in my house. Please, sit beside me and tell me all the gossip."

That put him between the duchess and Aunt Ida at the head of the table. The Duke of Cirencester, clearly a man accustomed to entertaining the lower orders, began a painful conversation with Madame Lafitte. Lord Lambridge, not as well bred, talked to his mother. Abby got the feeling he was suggesting they should leave, but his mother was having none of it.

Freddy leaned closer and said, "Interesting mix of people you've got here, Abigail. You up to something?"

He was too smart for his own good. She was reminded once more how that foppish exterior hid a sharp mind. She admitted, "I am, and I rely on you to keep your eyes open and your wits about you. I may need your help."

"Anything for you, old girl."

They were interrupted once more by the maid, who brought in Father O'Sullivan. He stepped in and glanced around, looking somewhat surprised. Madame Lafitte got halfway out of her chair and said, "*Mon père!*"

He smiled graciously to all. "Good evening." The duchess rose and went to him. "I'm so pleased you could come, Father O'Sullivan."

"Anything for you, my dear patroness." Then he looked around, somewhat confused. "I wasn't entirely sure what tonight's activities were. You were a tad obscure, Sarah."

She placed a hand fleetingly on his wrist. "I confess, I was worried you might not approve of our little séance tonight, but it's all for a good cause."

Father O'Sullivan did not look as humorously benevolent as he normally did. He shot a quick, sharp glance at Abby and then allowed himself to be led to his seat between Aunt Ida and Lord Cirencester.

Abby began to despair of her last guest but, just as she was thinking they would have to start without him, the maid came in with Inspector Deschamps.

MURDER AT THE PARIS FASHION HOUSE 257

He paused in the doorway, a rugged, handsome man whose sharp eyes took in everything and everyone.

When the duchess went to rise, he stopped her. "No, no, Your Grace, don't get up. I was honored by your invitation." He went over and took her hand and kissed it with old-fashioned gallantry that clearly tickled her to her toes. She said to the assembled company, "Monsieur Deschamps is a dear family friend. His mother and mine were great friends. We are distant cousins of some sort."

Abby never ceased to be amazed at the connections between people who seemed worlds apart and yet were closely knitted together by fate, or history, or family connection.

He sat beside Madame Lafitte, which put him beside Vivian. Beside her was Freddy, and then there was Abby. When the greetings were done and everyone was looking at Aunt Ida expectantly, she said, in her gracious way, "Thank you all for coming this evening. As you all know, I am an open conduit for the spirits. But there is one spirit who is uneasy and unable to rest. She has begged for our help in finding justice for her untimely and brutal end."

There was absolute silence around the room. Aunt Ida said, "Her name was Lillianne Pettit."

As Abby watched, Madame Bernard jumped as though a pin had been stuck into her. Madame Lafitte glared at the woman directly across from her, and then Aunt Ida continued, "Lillianne left Paris in 1919 and sailed to New York. She married a man named Dixon and began a life in Chicago, where she could bury her French roots and pretend to be an American. She had an American mother, so she learned our language from her infancy."

She gazed around the table as though reciting a history lesson. Such was her command of the table, her dramatic presence, that no one uttered a word.

"Lillian returned to this country six years later, now a

widow, in order to buy fashion and, at *Maison Joubert*, she met her brutal and untimely end. In short, my niece by marriage was murdered."

The "niece by marriage" line had been Abby's idea, and she thought it was a good one. It appeared as though this was somehow a personal investigation by Aunt Ida herself.

Lady Eleanor said peevishly, "That's all very sad, but I don't understand why you've invited me and my sons. We had nothing to do with that young woman's unfortunate death. I find this rather unseemly." She waved a pale hand toward the duchess and the duke. "Surely, this sordid business cannot be of interest to the Duke and Duchess of Cirencester."

The duchess answered with a smile. "On the contrary, my dear. I dearly love to see justice done. As Father O'Sullivan can tell you, I am always anxious to help in a good cause. Helping to solve the murder of a poor unfortunate widow would be an honor."

Larry's mother said no more, but two bright spots of color burned high on her cheekbones, and she pinched her lips together with annoyance.

Aunt Ida said, "May I continue?"

"Of course," said the duchess. "Please do."

"I will now attempt to contact the spirits. I must ask for complete silence. Empty your minds of all but a willingness to seek the truth. And join hands."

She began to breathe in and breathe out and breathe in and breathe out, and then her eyelids fluttered shut. As many times as Abby had seen her aunt do this, it was always a grand theatrical moment. A kind of flutter went around the table. Then she said in a deeper, slower, voice, "Lillian, dear, are you with us?"

A light flared and went out, and someone gasped.

"Lillian, is that you?"

In a lighter voice, she said, "Yes, Aunt Ida. It is me."

"Tell me, my dear, is your murderer among us this evening?"

A few seconds of strained silence felt like a physical pull around the table.

Aunt Ida said, "Lillian's not certain. It's not uncommon for the recently departed to be a bit fuzzy about the details of their passing. What do you remember, dear?

"I am but an open conduit," Aunt Ida said again. "Lillian, dear, speak through me and tell the assembled guests what you want them to hear." Aunt Ida seemed to fall into a trance, and her eyelids fluttered. Then, in that entirely different voice, lighter and higher, she said, "I am Lillianne. I cannot move on until I have finished my business on earth. I did not always act as I should have in life. Before I can reach the next realm, I must make reparation. First, I must return things I took. Larry, darling, if you will look in your pocket, there is a message from me."

Aunt Ida remained relaxed with her eyes closed, but everyone else looked at Lord Lambridge. He seemed less bored than previously. He patted his suit jacket pockets and said, with relief, "There's nothing there."

Vivian asked, "Did you have an overcoat?"

"This is ridiculous. I'm not going digging through my clothes on a fool's errand. This is nonsense."

His brother jumped up from the table. "No trouble at all. I'll fetch it." Before Larry could stop him, Freddy had stepped out of the dining room with his light tread. Everyone waited, and no one dared utter a syllable. In a very short space of time, Freddy returned, holding his brother's overcoat.

"I don't want it," Larry said irritably. "Put it back."

Freddy shook his head. "If a young woman comes back from the dead to return something, it would be good manners to let her know you received it." Larry made a lunge for the coat, but Freddy was too quick for him and plunged his hand into the pocket. He pulled out a silver cigarette case with a crest embossed on it and placed it in the middle of the table. The room was so quiet, the metal clicked as it hit the glowing mahogany table. The candlelight gleamed on the coat of arms.

His mother gasped. "Larry, you said you'd left your cigarette case in London."

Even in the lamplight, Abby could see his countenance go a deep shade of red. "I lent it to Lillian, and she forgot to give it back."

Aunt Ida spoke up in that strange light voice that sounded oddly like Lillian's would have, had she grown into a much older woman. "No. I stole it from you. And I must return it. You were in my hotel room, and we—"

"Yes, all right," Lawrence said, sounding harassed. "Perhaps I did leave it there."

The inspector spoke up. "And you were intimate with Mrs. Lillian Dixon?"

His eyes darted furtively toward his mother, then back to the cigarette case in the middle of the table. "Really, Inspector. Not in front of my mother."

"Larry," his mother said with alarming coldness. "Answer the question."

He looked utterly harassed. "All right. Yes. There's no crime in that, is there?"

"Not at all," Inspector Deschamps said. "But there is certainly a crime of murder."

THIRTY

"I didn't kill her. We enjoyed each other, that's all. I suppose she believed my intentions were more serious than they were. When I realized that, naturally, I ended things." He made a face as though in remembered pain. "She threw things at my head. I must have left my cigarette case behind."

"When you were running away?" Freddy asked.

Abby said, "It would have been very inconvenient for you had Lillian made a scene in public, especially as you were attempting to woo a strictly brought up young woman. No doubt her parents would have disapproved of your suit had they known you'd been linked with such a scandalous woman."

He scratched his neck, and Abby was almost certain she saw hives rising on his skin. "I didn't kill her, I tell you."

"And yet, you were there, at *Maison Joubert* the day she was killed."

He turned to Abby as though he'd like to throttle her. "How do you know that?"

"The serving man remembered you." In fact, Eugene remembered selling handkerchiefs to an Englishman, but she didn't feel guilty stretching the truth.

And it seemed she was right. He glared at her. "A man can buy handkerchiefs, can't he?"

Lillian's voice came again, "I also apologize to the duchess. I am sorry I caused her such anguish."

And then to the shock of everyone, the normally mild-tempered, placid Duchess of Cirencester burst into tears. "I can't forgive you. How can I? I know it's the Christian thing to do, and I will try, but you nearly destroyed everything I hold dear."

Once more, it was Freddy's mother who gasped. "What can this mean? How did that dreadful young woman hurt you, Duchess?"

The duke suddenly rose and puffed out his chest. "I'm sorry, I cannot be a party to this. I will not see my wife made upset. I am leaving this gathering." He pushed back his chair. "Come, Sarah. I think it's time we retired."

Before he'd gone more than a step, Aunt Ida spoke again in Lillian's voice. "I would have made you happy, you know, Dickie. Maybe you weren't as rich as I was hoping you'd be, but I liked the idea of being a duchess."

He put his hands over his eyes. "Stop it. You're an impostor."

His wife shook her head, still crying. "She did call him Dickie. I intercepted one of her notes."

Abby doubted that was by accident. Lillian would have made sure the duchess knew what her husband was up to. She'd have wanted the duchess to throw her husband out of their home or act in a way that would make beautiful, easygoing Lillian seem even more desirable.

Abby was content to let this séance continue, though so far, it wasn't going quite as she had planned. She hoped that the revelations tonight would make this muddy picture clear.

Her vision was like one of Mr. Picasso's pictures. Pieces

MURDER AT THE PARIS FASHION HOUSE 263

were distorted and out of place, but the general shape was there if one had the right vision.

Over the sounds of Sarah Barncastle's painful sobs, Lillian's voice came again, "I wish I could remember that last dreadful day better. I was lured into the dressing room while I was at *Maison Joubert*. I don't remember why or who sent me there. Was it you, Dickie? Or you, Sarah, who plunged the cold, hard scissors into my neck?"

The duke sat back down and said, in a shaking voice, "No, Lillian, my dear, I'd never hurt you."

His wife cried harder now.

Abby put her hand to her mother's pearls, reminding herself that causing Sarah Barncastle pain was an important part of her plan. "Lady Cirencester, why did you need those stock certificates now? Your first husband has been gone for some years."

She was certain that under normal circumstances, the duchess would have given her a well-deserved set-down for her nosiness, but she was still crying and her emotions were raw. "Richard was being blackmailed."

She glanced over at Paul Joubert and saw his eyes widen. The duchess said, "Wasn't it you, Lillian, blackmailing my husband? I can't believe, Richard, you'd be so stupid as to fall in love with a blackmailer."

Aunt Ida spoke again in Lillian's voice. "I was never a blackmailer. My crimes did not extend that far."

Abby said, "But someone was. Who knew about you and my stepmother?"

The duke shook her head. "No one. I was the soul of discretion." She looked at the duchess. "Lady Cirencester? Did you confide in anyone?"

"No one. Only Father O'Sullivan. He could see that I was in distress, the dear man. My mother was Catholic, you know, and I was brought up in that faith. It felt natural to confess my troubles. I suffered greatly from the sin of anger."

This was Aunt Ida's cue. Would she remember?

She did. In her Lillian voice, Aunt Ida said, "Father O'Sullivan knew a lot of secrets."

Abby spoke up now, "Lillian is right. Madame Lafitte, you also went to confession, didn't you? And you told the father certain things about your employer, Paul Joubert, that he might not have wanted made public."

Madame Lafitte looked up for the first time, and her eyes were wide and pleading as she turned to Father O'Sullivan. "*Mon père*, I unburdened my soul to the priest, as is natural, to ask God's forgiveness."

Father O'Sullivan suddenly banged his fist on the table. "What is it that you would accuse me of?" he asked the room in general. "As a man of the cloth, I cannot condone such nonsense as this. Séances are the work of the devil. I will not allow myself to be part of such foolishness any longer."

He stood, inviting Madame Lafitte to go with him. Inspector Deschamps spoke up and said courteously, "Please sit down, Father. I believe that Lillian Dixon's murderer is in this room. No one may leave until I'm satisfied."

"But that's preposterous. I'm a priest. I wouldn't murder anyone."

"But you would blackmail them, wouldn't you, Father?" Abby said. She looked around the table. "Lady Cirencester, you aren't the only one being blackmailed. I bumped into Father O'Sullivan at Notre Dame, where he was picking up a payment."

Father O'Sullivan laughed unconvincingly. "Notre Dame is a very busy place, Miss Dixon. If this is your only proof, I suggest you stick to writing about fashion in your newspaper and leave investigating murders to the police."

Madame Lafitte began to moan. "Monsieur Joubert, I ask your forgiveness. I believed I spoke in the sanctity of the confession. I would never harm you."

Abby spoke up again. "No, you wouldn't. That's why you allowed Madame Bernard to continue to work at the atelier, didn't you? How it must have hurt you to see her day after day, knowing what you did about her."

"I wasn't certain," Madame Lafitte began haltingly. "If I had told the police what I suspected and she'd been arrested, then Monsieur Joubert would have lost his *première*. I would not see him hurt."

"So instead, you punished her in your own way, with petty cruelties, and she never knew the source of them."

Madame Bernard had been staring at Madame Lafitte. Now she pointed a finger at her, making stabbing motions. "You? That was you?"

Madame Lafitte raised her voice. "Do not point your bony finger at me, you traitor."

Abby's heart began to pound. This was what she had hoped for. Tears were rolling down Madame Lafitte's cheeks. "My husband, my boys, sacrificed in the war, what if it was your information that caused them to be killed? They died, and my future, all my hopes, died with them."

Madame Bernard shrieked, "How dare you tell these lies? I am a good Frenchwoman."

"No. You ran a notorious spy ring in the war."

"Such terrible lies. I scraped by, taking in sewing and helping the rich ladies refresh their dresses, since we had no fabric. The couture houses were closed."

Abby said, "It was a brilliant front. No one would question why attractive young women were coming and going at all hours. You were a seamstress, refreshing their gowns, remaking them."

The *première* said, "All the warehouses were closed during the war. I helped women keep their wardrobes looking well. I did them a service."

"At your house, a woman could have a dress refashioned,

the trimming refreshed. Perhaps you even had some bolts of silk and velvet tucked away for your special customers. Those young women who were spies for the Germans delivered their information to you."

Aunt Ida spoke up again in Lillian's voice. "That is true. I was one of those women. I, Lillianne Pettit, was a German spy, and Madame Bernard was my spymaster. It was easy work, and I was paid well. I would become friendly with French officers, once or twice a British officer, and seduce them. Some men like to whisper secrets in the dark, or I would search their uniforms and bags while they were sleeping. Any information I gathered, I took to Madame Bernard."

"It isn't true."

"Once, I even planted a cigar bomb in a naval officer's kitbag after he spent his entire leave with me. I waved him off from the dock, knowing his ship would blow up when the timer ran out."

Madame Lafitte groaned loudly.

Aunt Ida had gone off-script. Where had she come up with this tangent about bombs? Abby took back the floor. "When Lillian returned to Paris, she gave you a terrible fright, didn't she, Madame Bernard? You thought, after six years, that you were safe from prosecution. But Lillian was American now. She could turn you in at any time. She used her knowledge of your past against you, didn't she? She wanted Paul Joubert creations, preferably without having to pay for them."

Abby looked at Paul. "I thought it was strange that she'd be in a fitting room that day when Monsieur Joubert said she had no dress to be fitted, but she did. She was supposed to have a secret fitting, with you, madame. What did she do? Buy one dress, and you'd secretly make her two or three?"

"*Non.* You lie." She glanced nervously at Paul, who seemed more shocked that she would steal from him than that she'd run a German spy ring.

"You knew that so long as Lilliane Pettit was alive, you'd always feel the sharp shadow of the guillotine hanging over you."

Madame Bernard jumped to her feet and cried, "No. This is nonsense. This woman is a fake. Everyone knows Abigail Dixon murdered her stepmother. She's concocted this ridiculous séance to try and throw suspicion on someone else. Where is your proof?"

And that was the problem. Abby had no proof.

She continued on, hoping against hope that Madame Bernard would crack, but it was a faint hope. As much as anything, she needed to say the words aloud, so the dirty secrets of the past would be out in the open.

"Either her demands became too great or your fear too strong, but you murdered Lillian. What a convenient way to shift blame. Who would connect the dead American widow with the French girl who spied for you? Everyone accepted that she was Lillian Dixon, an American widow. And there was I, the stepdaughter, so horrified to see her at *Maison Joubert* that I couldn't go into the showroom. You took your chance and killed her, then let me take the blame."

"*Non.*"

"One of the seamstresses overheard the two of you arguing in French." The woman hadn't been able to identify the voices, but she didn't share that fact. "Were Lillian's demands getting too much for you?"

"Monsieur Joubert, I beg of you to stop this persecution of one who has been your loyal employee for so many years."

The couturier looked helplessly from his *première* to his muse and clearly wasn't certain which of them to believe.

Abby felt her throat going dry and swallowed. "But I kept coming back, kept asking questions. You knew it was only a matter of time until I worked out who Lillian Dixon had been in the war. You sent me a letter, telling me to go home. When I didn't, you decided to kill me. But a young copy boy went in my place. He's the one you blew up."

Did the woman's eyes flicker?

"But you wouldn't care about causing one more innocent young man's death, would you? Not when you've already caused so many."

Paul Joubert stared at his *première*. "Madame Bernard?" he asked, as though willing her to deny the charges.

"It is not true, *Monsieur*. The girl is lying." But there was a note of fear, now.

For a long minute, Abby felt the tension build. If only she had even a shred of evidence, but Madame Bernard was right. All she had was a theory, though she was certain she was correct. Madame Bernard's chest was heaving and there was sweat on her brow, but as she glared at Abby and Abby remained silent, her expression changed to one of sly triumph.

Aunt Ida opened her eyes wide and looked at Abby down the length of the table, hoping for a sign or some direction, but Abby had nothing else to offer. She'd played all her cards now, and her opponent was holding fast, bluffing no doubt, but she was going to win this round.

But not the next, Abby promised herself. Somehow, somewhere, she'd find evidence to convict this traitorous woman.

Then, in a shaky voice, Father O'Sullivan spoke up. "You are wrong in one thing, Abigail. It was I who sent you that letter telling you to go home. I meant it for the best. I pray that God will have leniency on me. I have papers and a signed confession from one of the spies confirming that Madame Bernard was the notorious spymaster, Fraulein Stücknadel."

His head bowed, he continued. "Lillianne Pettit was part of her spy ring. You are quite right, Miss Dixon. The girls would bring whatever they discovered from their lovers, sometimes a rumor, or a report of troop movements, which they would copy down. Then they would go to Madame Bernard to have some dressmaking done. Who would raise an eyebrow at lovely young women going to a dressmaker?"

"No one," Abby said.

"Madame Bernard kept pigeons."

"For food!" the *première* shrieked.

"Carrier pigeons who flew the messages to her home in the Alsace." He clasped his hands in front of him and stared down at the table, looking like a penitent at prayer. "One of the young ladies came to me after the war was over. She was filled with guilt as she watched the broken young soldiers returning home. She confessed all to me. I gave her absolution but also asked her to give me all her proof."

He dipped his chin, and the white of his clerical collar was obscured. "She believed I would go to the authorities. But, God help me, I didn't do that. I was in great need of money. And so I told myself I was punishing Madame Bernard in my own way. Forcing her to pay for her crimes." He looked at the stunned *première*, who had moved back from the table so she stood in partial shadow. "I believe you thought it was Lillianne Pettit who'd been blackmailing you all along, Madame Bernard. But it wasn't. It was me."

"You were the blackmailer?" It was Paul Joubert who spoke up, shock making his voice sound hoarse.

"Yes. Madame Lafitte was my unwitting informant. She came to confession regularly, and from her, I learned much that was useful."

"*Mon Dieu,*" Madame Lafitte cried, then began to sob.

He turned to Inspector Deschamps and said, "Naturally, I will give you all of the evidence I have against Madame Bernard. It is time for Fraulein Stücknadel to face justice." He sighed sadly. "And for me."

Madame Bernard screamed, "You!" And then, from her pocket, she pulled a pistol. Amid gasps of shock, she launched herself at Father O'Sullivan.

The inspector reacted quickly, but before he could reach her, a gunshot blasted. Father O'Sullivan made a sound as though he'd been punched and slumped forward.

Lady Eleanor screamed. The duchess put her lace handkerchief to her mouth.

The *première* turned her gun toward the inspector and backed toward the door. "Stay back," she warned.

Her chest rose and fell, and her round cheeks were flushed. "I am glad I killed all those filthy Frenchmen," she spat. "They took my homeland." She glared at Madame Lafitte. "And I am overjoyed that Lillianne planted that cigar bomb. It was a triumph. He was a British naval officer. The explosion blew such a hole in the bow that the ship went down and all those aboard were prevented from killing *my* people." She dragged in a breath and shouted, "Gott strafe England."

Abby saw Freddy shift in his seat—it didn't seem like anything more—and then, like a snake going after prey, he moved from stillness to lethal attack in the time it took her to bite her lip against a cry of surprise.

He threw himself at the *première*, his head hitting her side like a battering ram. She'd been so intent on the inspector, she was thrown against the sideboard before she had time to react.

Dishes crashed and the candles jumped. Freddy wrapped his arms around the struggling woman while the inspector grabbed her gun hand and twisted the weapon from her grasp.

A uniformed police officer came running in and placed her in handcuffs. She cursed them as they led her out. In German.

Abby and Madame Lafitte both ran to Father O'Sullivan. He was alive, though the bullet had penetrated his chest. He lifted up his good arm and said, with his kind smile, "Forgive me, madame, as I pray God will forgive me."

"But why?" she asked him in a broken voice. "Why would you betray me? Betray all of us?"

"I am afraid the stipend from the church is enough for a

single man to live a simple life, but not enough for his mistress and child."

Madame Lafitte recoiled from him and bowed her head over her crucifix, crying and praying.

"That's who picked up the money that day," Abby said. "Your woman friend." As she spoke, she took her handkerchief and pressed it against the bleeding wound in Father O'Sullivan's chest. He tried to wave her away, but it was a feeble attempt. The blood was flowing. She glanced up. "Cloth. I must have more cloth."

Freddy came to her side. "Best if we lay him on the floor," he said gently. She nodded, and together they lifted the priest down to the floor.

The duke gave her his handkerchief, and the duchess jumped to her feet and, with great speed, reached under her long skirt and removed her petticoat. Lawrence was at her elbow, passing her his handkerchief, so Abby bundled all of it together into a pad and pressed as hard as she dared on the wound.

The priest groaned.

"My Sabine has a habit which is very expensive." Speaking in painful gasps, he said, "It is how I met her, ministering to addicts, never understanding that her downfall would lead to mine."

"Addicts?"

He nodded. "I met her in an opium den. I was ministering to the other poor souls when I met my own lovely, damaged angel. She has a child, you see. My child." His breath began to grow labored. He reached out and took Abby's hand. His skin was gray. "In my little office in the church, you will find a strongbox under a loose stone beneath my desk. In it is everything you will need to prosecute Madame Bernard. Also, there is the information about my child. Gerard is safe and being brought up in the country.

There is money in that strongbox, ill-gotten though it is, to provide for him."

He seemed to be growing paler. "Vivian, someone, bring some water," Abby called.

Freddy rose. "If you will direct me to your telephone, Lady Cirencester, I will telephone for an ambulance."

The priest gripped her wrist with his good hand. "My Gerard will need a benefactress. He is a good boy. Perhaps you can find such a one."

"Yes, of course. But you mustn't talk any more. It's taxing your strength."

He smiled at her. "I believe my time has come."

Then, looking at Madame Lafitte once more, he whispered, "Forgive me, my daughter, for I have sinned."

THIRTY-ONE

Before the still-cursing Madame Bernard was taken away, another man entered the dining room. She recognized him as the commissaire and Inspector Deschamps's superior officer.

He ignored the wounded man and rushed up to the duchess, all graciousness and fawning. "Your Grace, I cannot sufficiently express my sorrow that you should be subject to this sordid occurrence. I am Commissaire LaFevre, and your bravery will be forever in my mind." He took her hand and kissed it. "Through your efforts, you have aided me and my men in bringing to justice a vicious spy."

Abby looked up, shocked. What had he done? She looked for Inspector Deschamps, but he must be outside with the prisoner.

The commissaire continued. "I will formally charge Madame Bernard and take her away. I hope you will permit me to call on you in a few days to ensure you have not suffered any ill consequences?"

"Why, certainly," the duchess said, at her most regal.

He bowed and headed back out.

"When will the ambulance get here?" she asked Freddy,

who was back at her side. "He's losing blood faster than I can stanch it."

"Steady on, old girl. I think I hear them now."

Sure enough, a doctor and nurse arrived. While the doctor examined the priest, who'd lost consciousness, a nurse, carrying a stack of thick bandages, took over from Abby and kept pressure on the wound. As Father O'Sullivan was lifted onto a stretcher, he regained consciousness and looked about him. "I do not want a doctor," he said, "but a priest to administer last rites."

She and Freddy watched them load the priest into the ambulance. "Will he live?" she asked.

"Sorry, old girl," Freddy said gently. "I've seen that look too often on the battlefield. He's mortally wounded."

"Will he at least get his last rites?" Somehow it seemed important to her. Even though Father O'Sullivan had done wrong, she wanted him to die in a state of grace.

"If the padre gets there before morning, I should think so."

"I must wash my hands," she said, noticing the bloodstains.

The duchess came to her. "Oh, my dear, come with me. I'll show you to the bathroom."

"Thank you, Your Grace."

The older woman chuckled. "I believe you may call me Sarah after tonight's events." Then she raised her voice, sounding like the society hostess she was. "And you must all go into the front parlor. Richard, dear. Ring the bell and order hot tea and get out the brandy."

Abby washed and tidied herself in the duchess's bathroom, but, once again, she found herself with blood on her skirt. Her kind hostess lent her a shapeless house dress and helped her into it. She laughed when she looked at Abby. "Well, it's not couture and far too big, but at least it's clean."

When she and Sarah returned to the parlor, the duke had followed instructions. He'd poured liberal doses of brandy for all his guests. The butler came in with a tray of tea and plates of cake and biscuits.

Sarah, the society hostess, looked uncertain. "I wasn't certain whether tea and cake were quite right after violence. It was all I could think of to do."

"You did right," Freddy said. "Tea is very good for shock." Sarah poured tea, and Freddy handed the cups around. To Abby's surprise, Inspector Deschamps had remained. She went up to him. "You aren't needed at police headquarters?"

He looked at her with sardonic amusement. "On the contrary. My esteemed superior, Monsieur LaFevre, the commissaire, is quite happy to take over."

She shook her head. "And take all the credit for the arrest, no doubt."

"He is, after all, heading this investigation."

She wasn't fooled. "But, Inspector Deschamps, it was you who led the investigation. Why, I'll write an article saying how it was you."

"Please don't. And I think after all we've been through, you may call me Henri." He didn't look downcast to be left out of the final act of this drama. Perhaps he was accustomed to having a lesser man take the credit for his work.

Abby took her tea and found a seat beside Vivian. She sipped hot tea and accepted a small glass of brandy from her host, which she placed on a handy marble side table.

She looked around the room. Larry opened his newly returned cigarette case and looked at the two remaining cigarettes. Before his mother could protest, Freddy said, "Here, have one of mine."

The two brothers spoke quietly in the corner while their mother looked on, first as though she'd be required to step in and break up a fight, and then fondly, as it seemed they were chatting in a friendly manner.

Aunt Ida settled back in a red velvet armchair, looking exhausted.

Madame Lafitte sipped brandy. She looked as she must have done when she learned of her sons' and her husband's deaths. Stunned and bereft.

In the sudden lull, Vivian asked, "Abby, how did you know it was Madame Bernard?"

"I think it was when Hudson was killed with that German grenade. Everything since Lillian's death has been leading back to the Great War and old secrets."

She thought back on her mental process. "I kept wondering why Lillian had lied about her past. What was so shameful about being French? And when she came to Paris, she was so careful never to speak French. On the day she was killed, one of the seamstresses overheard two women arguing in French.

"It didn't occur to me that one of them was Lillian until later. The other Frenchwoman had to be someone who was accustomed to moving in and out of the fitting rooms. Like the *première*."

"And then she nearly killed you, Abby." Vivian reached out a hand and placed it on Abby's wrist. "I'm awfully glad she didn't succeed."

Henri said, "That was also fear. She'd been living all these years worried that someday her secret would come out. Her spies were all gone, scattered or dead. There were three unsolved murders of young women at the end of the war, women who had gone to Madame Bernard for dressmaking."

Abby was shocked. Even knowing the woman was a killer, she still shuddered. "She killed her own spies?"

"It would fit with her ruthlessness. She protected herself and her secrets at all costs."

"What a terrifying woman."

He nodded. "And someone was blackmailing her. It must

have kept her frightened and on edge, making her a very dangerous enemy."

Then he turned to her. "I regret I found it—" Here he paused, and she felt he was searching for the right word. "—convenient to let you believe the police had no suspects in the murder of your stepmother but you."

She nodded. "You were gathering evidence against Madame Bernard."

"Yes. When I discovered Lillianne Pettit had been in Paris during the war and dug into her background, I began to hope that we might finally gather enough evidence to arrest Fraulein Stücknadel."

"And you had detectives following me in order to lull Madame Bernard into a false sense of security."

He lifted his hands in a very Gallic gesture. "Also to protect you." His gaze met hers, and she saw not only a man dedicated to justice but one who cared. "We did not want you to suffer an unfortunate accident."

Sadness stabbed her suddenly, and she half-closed her eyelids. "If I'd gone that day when the telegram came for me, your men would have followed. They might have stopped me from walking into that trap. But poor Hudson—"

He cut her off. "They would not have stopped you, Abby. Their orders were to report your movements to me. Had you been attacked on the street, yes, they would have protected you." He walked forward and took her hand. "But had you gone into that building, you would have died. Regret is a pointless emotion."

She felt that he was speaking from experience and hoped that one day this terrible sense of guilt over Hudson would diminish.

Into the sudden, painful silence, Sarah said, "I do think Ida is to be congratulated. You were wonderful."

That perked Aunt Ida up, and she sat straight in her chair, looking pleased with the compliment.

"That was an inspired guess about the cigar grenade," Abby said. "I knew you were pretending, but that seemed so real."

"What cigar grenade?" Aunt Ida asked, looking puzzled. Then she sighed. "When they take over me, I often don't remember what was said." She opened her arms in a familiar gesture. "I am but an open conduit."

Abby stared at her aunt. *Surely not.*

THIRTY-TWO

Two invitations to the launch of his fall collection arrived from the atelier of Paul Joubert. The delivery man brought them up himself, handling the embossed envelopes as though they were the rarest treasures, which, in Paris, they were.

He handed Abby her card and looked at Vivian. "Miss Vivian O'Connell?"

"Yes."

He handed her the second card. She nearly fainted.

"Monsieur Joubert asks that you attend his atelier at two o'clock tomorrow for the fitting of your gowns."

"Gowns?" Vivian asked, breathless.

"Oui, madame. One for each of you."

Vivian's squeal of delight was answer enough, but still Abby said, "Please tell Monsieur Joubert that we will be delighted to attend."

Vivian, still dizzy with excitement, opened the precious invitation with infinite care, and Abby suspected it would find its way into her scrapbook. "Oh, Abby, I shall die, I shall absolutely die." She sighed. "Of bliss."

Vivian hugged her friend. "How far you've come since you

arrived in Paris. I don't have to chide you about makeup or hair. Now you dress beautifully. You're a credit to me."

Then she tilted her head to one side and said, in fairness, "And to Paul."

The following day, Abby spent the morning in the *Post* newsroom, where she wrote another in a series of front-page articles that was truly worthy of its placement. She was digging deeper every day into the story of spying, betrayal and, finally, arrest. She stuck to facts, having had enough of writing her own sob stories.

Father O'Sullivan had received his last rites and then died before dawn, the night of the séance, as Freddy had predicted. Madame Bernard had been formally charged, not only with the murders of Lillianne Pettit and Hudson, but with treason.

When she'd finished her latest article, Abby left the *Post* building and took a taxi to St. Bartholomew's Cathedral. It was odd not having detectives following her. Still, she was glad to have no witnesses as she entered the dim, cool church.

Inspector Deschamps didn't know she was here. He didn't know that Father O'Sullivan had told her where to find his secret stash.

A young priest was speaking to a couple with a baby standing near the baptismal font, and she made her way as quietly as she could to the back of the church where Father O'Sullivan's office had been.

Fortunately, it was unlocked. She slipped in and, pushing a wooden chair from in front of his desk, dropped to her knees. The flagstones were uneven and wobbly, but she found one near the wall that lifted when she tugged it. Underneath was a hole, and as she put her hands into it, she felt the rough edges of a box. The scraping sound seemed horribly loud as she pulled it into the light, but no one came through the thick door.

She opened the box and removed the contents, which she

put into her handbag. Then, heart pounding, she returned the box to its hiding place.

She slipped back out and, holding her bag close to her side, made her way slowly to the entrance to the cathedral. She couldn't leave, though, without paying her respects to Madame Lafitte's husband and sons. She was moved to light a candle in their honor, and in Hudson's, who was a delayed casualty of the Great War.

She arrived an hour before her fitting at *Maison Joubert*. Madame Lafitte was red-eyed and seemed older. She showed no friendliness, but at least the animosity was absent, though Abby thought she'd have welcomed that much energy in the woman.

She ran upstairs and knocked on the couturier's door. Paul Joubert opened the door, and his brows rose. "But, Abby, you are early."

"I've come on another errand. May I come in?"

"But of course. I'm delighted to see you."

"You'll be even more delighted when I show you what I have with me."

She shut the door behind her and, reaching into her bag, brought out a dusty envelope. She handed it to him.

He snatched the creased envelope, which smelled of earth, and said, "Is this...?"

"Yes. It's all the photographs and the negatives. You'll want to burn them."

He held the musty envelope against his chest. "Finally My torment is at an end."

"I'm so glad."

He locked the envelope in the drawer, explaining that he wanted to burn them together with Monsieur Fleuri.

"There's something else I want to ask you about," she said. And she told him what she'd been thinking.

"Yes. It's a very good idea," he said when she was finished.

"I'll need your help."

"Very well." He opened the door and said, "Ah, Suzanne. *Bon*. Will you request Madame Lafitte to come to me, please? And in her absence, you will watch the door."

"Certainly."

Madame Lafitte entered, looking nervous and gray. Her eyes darted from Abby to Paul, and she clasped shaking hands in front of her. "I expect to be dismissed, of course. But please let me tell you how deeply sorry—"

"But *non*," Paul interrupted her. "I shall not dismiss you."

"But I betrayed you."

"Madame Bernard betrayed me. Father O'Sullivan betrayed you. You will, in future, perhaps not discuss my private life?"

"Oh, *Monsieur*. I only ever told the priest. And I'll never do such a thing again."

"Please, sit down."

She did, pressing her knees together and still looking anxious. Abby said, "You heard Father O'Sullivan say that he'd fathered a child."

She nodded.

"A boy. Gerard."

Paul said, gently, "The same name as your own dear son."

"*Oui*."

"That boy is now fatherless, and the mother cannot care for him."

Madame Lafitte glanced up, her eyes narrowed. "I cannot have another child. I have no husband. I'm too old."

"No," Abby said. "The boy lives in the country and is being raised by good people. What he needs is a godmother. Someone who will take an interest in him and make sure he is raised properly. You could spend as much time with him as you were able."

Her eyes gleamed suddenly, and then she shook her head. "I do not know."

"That boy is all that's left of Father O'Sullivan," Paul reminded her. "And in spite of his terrible errors, he did a great deal of good in the parish."

"I do not know," she repeated and rose. "I must return to my post."

"Wait," Abby said. "Here is a photograph."

The boy was six. Already tall with an earnest face. "He has Father O'Sullivan's eyes."

Madame Lafitte took the photograph. "I do not know," she said for the third time, but she took the picture with her when she left.

THIRTY-THREE

Walking into the Paris Opera House was like walking into a fantasy. Ornate columns of gold reached to a painted sky where cherubs cavorted. Ornately carved arches held up golden galleries that seemed to rise forever, all of it lit by more chandeliers than Abby could count. She felt as though she were part of the fantasy; she'd arrived in Paris with a suitcase of books and no clothing sense, and now she was muse to a couturier, wearing a gown so exquisite she hardly dared breathe in case she caused a wrinkle.

This fantastic building was at the end of the street where her newspaper turned out stories that dealt in cold, hard facts, and she'd faced some difficult truths in the past months. Tonight, however, she was ready to celebrate the debut of Paul Joubert's fall collection. Paul had asked her to arrive early, and so she was able to witness the excitement of final preparations.

The staff ran up and down stairways with pins, irons, and gowns. Hired photographers were on hand, even a news camera.

Still, Paul found time to greet her and Vivian and spend some time with them. After having their hair styled by

Monsieur Raymond and makeup professionally applied, she felt that she and Vivian would not let him down. He complimented them both, and then he sent them to a private dressing room, where Suzanne, buzzing with excitement and overwork, helped them into their gowns.

"You look beautiful," she said. "But I must run. There's so much to do."

Abby felt all the excitement and pleasure of knowing she looked her best as she headed down to the main foyer. Her gown was white, embroidered on the bodice in silver and gold and beaded with tiny crystals. The back plunged, so cool air wafted on her naked skin. The gown featured trailing panels and a tiered skirt.

When he caught sight of her, Paul kissed his fingers to her and immediately called a photographer over. He wanted photographs of Abby posing at the first landing on the Grand Staircase. He turned her so her back was to the camera, and she faced the statue of a Greek goddess, so her face was in profile. As she studied the goddess, she noted the similarity of the stone drapery to the way her own dress draped.

She burst out laughing. "Why, Paul, you've gowned me to look like a proper Greek muse."

"But, *non*. You are a goddess."

"I got a promotion," she said to Viv, who looked radiant in a blue drop-waist with a dazzling beaded fringe.

Then he wanted photographs of himself with Abby. She noted that his waistcoat was gold and silver and matched the bodice of her gown.

He ordered photographs of her and Viv and promised them copies. Then Paul rushed off as his guests began to arrive. Her stomach was jumpy with nerves as she hoped her friend's collection would be a success. In the time they'd spent together, she had grown to care for him greatly. He was a good man, a talented artist and, she hoped, a friend.

The show would be held in the Grand Foyer, a massive space with gilt columns, painted ceilings and sparkling chandeliers. Chairs were set up in rows, and the models would walk down the center of the aisle, showing off the new collection.

Abby found herself being hailed once more by reporters. At least this time, they weren't asking her about a murder. One called out, "How does it feel to be the muse of such a great man?"

She turned and posed as Madame Bernard had taught her to. "It is a great honor. Paris is the most beautiful city in the world, and Paul Joubert creates the most beautiful clothes in the world. They belong together."

She and Vivian walked into the grand foyer, and as she looked around the glittering throng of people, she realized with a start that she knew many of them. She, who had arrived in Paris dreaming of becoming a hard news reporter, had not imagined what was ahead of her.

Instead of reporting news, she'd become newsworthy and for the worst of reasons.

Jean Drummond from *New York Fortnightly* complimented her on her gown, and before she could say more, Paul rushed up. "My muse, my beautiful Abby. When you came to me, you were a worm."

She was slightly taken aback, and Jean said, laughing, "A worm?"

He nodded. "Yes. The worm who wraps herself in a cocoon and emerges resplendent—a glorious butterfly floating through the society of Paris."

"I think you mean a caterpillar," Abby said.

"Yes, yes." He was impatient of correction and much more interested in letting both her and Jean know that not one invitation had been spurned. Every important woman in Paris and a number of men were here tonight to celebrate the launch of this collection.

The *Post* photographer saw them together, and he immediately rushed over and posed them and took a photograph that would, no doubt, run on the front page.

Among the milling crowd of beautiful people stood a man who looked far too shabby for his surroundings, and with a shock, Abby recognized Ernest Hemingway. She went to him with her hand outstretched. "Mr. Hemingway. I've never thanked you for your excellent advice."

He held on to her hand in his much larger one. "You did well. Prose is a little flowery for my taste, but you lived your story and then you told it."

"I hear you've got some very exciting news, too."

He tried to look casual but didn't quite manage it. "You have good sources. My book's coming out next year. *The Sun Also Rises*. It's about running with the bulls in Spain."

"You lived your story and then you told it."

A woman named Pauline, who was a fashion journalist at *Vogue*, walked up and asked if she could interview Paul's muse. Abby was amused to find that instead of being the woman with the pencil and notebook, she'd somehow become a story. "You must feel like Cinderella," Pauline said to her.

Before she knew how to reply, Hemingway said, "Cinderella with a sharp mind and a nose for the truth."

She couldn't imagine anyone saying anything nicer about her.

In her turn, she gushed about Paul, about his talent and how if a woman put herself into his hands, she, too, would be transformed.

The woman laughed. "Cinderella, I'll let you get to your ball."

She'd expected a seat somewhere in the back, but to her amazement, Paul himself walked her and Vivian to their seats. Many of the guests were already seated. She nodded to

Lawrence and Miss Dayton, as well as to his mother, who sent her a cool nod in return.

Freddy had been called back to London but had sent flowers every day and exacted a promise that she would have dinner with him when he returned.

Paul swept his two young American guests to two of the prized seats in the first row. She tried to protest. "Paul, you should put your big-spending clients here."

He shook his head. "Abigail, you bring me more business than any of my clients. Besides, every great artist needs his muse near him."

Also in the front row were Monsieur and Madame Fleuri and the Duke and Duchess of Cirencester. Clara Bow was working a powder compact like a movie prop, and near her was a beautiful but restless young blond woman sitting with a handsome man. It was F. Scott Fitzgerald and his wife, Zelda. Abby pointed them out to Viv. "Everyone's talking about his new novel, *The Great Gatsby*. It's coming out in April. I can hardly wait."

Viv whispered back, "I tried to read *This Side of Paradise*, but I didn't see what all the fuss was about."

The last guests were being seated, and she started when she recognized Inspector Deschamps with a beautiful woman on his arm. He caught her gaze and nodded. She mirrored the gesture.

Vivian claimed her attention. "Would it be rude of me to ask for Clara Bow's autograph?"

"Maybe just tell her how much you enjoy her pictures." She put a hand to her heart. "It's about to begin. I'm so nervous."

Within moments of the show beginning, she knew she need not have worried. Not his personal struggles, the blackmail, the recent murder in his atelier—none of that showed in Paul Joubert's work. The collection was glorious. She heard gasps from the women behind her and even gasped herself once or twice as model after model walked by showcasing everything from silk gowns to trouser suits. He had outdone himself. As the last model walked past, spontaneous clapping erupted.

Paul Joubert himself came out surrounded by his models. Abby jumped to her feet, clapping wildly, and noticed that nearly everyone else was on their feet too. The launch was a resounding success.

Afterward, when they were sipping champagne and discussing the collection, Inspector Deschamps walked by with his very elegant escort. Abby never got used to how different he was when he wasn't on duty. His evening clothes were impeccable, and he seemed as at home in society as he did chasing criminals. He paused in front of Abby. "What a triumph."

She wasn't entirely sure whether he meant the couturier or her, but she chose to believe the former and said, "It's an amazing night for Paul. His collection was outstanding."

"And now that this adventure has ended, I imagine your editor will be only too pleased to give you your heart's desire and put you on the hard news beat."

As he said the words, she realized her ambition had changed. "You know, when I arrived here, that was my heart's desire. But I no longer wish for that. I am very happy to be working on the women's pages of my newspaper. I'm proud to be writing about Paris fashion and fine perfume and hats and food."

He bowed his head in acknowledgment. "Then I imagine our paths will not cross quite so often in the future."

Vivian was standing at Abby's side. She looked from one to the other and said softly, "I wonder."

A LETTER FROM THE AUTHOR

Dear Reader,

Thanks again for reading *Murder at the Paris Fashion House*. I had a lot of fun writing the first in this 1920's series and I have plenty more adventures in store for Abigail!

If you'd like to join other readers in keeping in touch, here are two options. Stay in the loop with my new releases by clicking on the link below. Or sign up to my personal email newsletter on the link at the bottom of this note. I'd be delighted if you choose to sign up to either – or both!

www.stormpublishing.co/nancy-warren

If you enjoyed reading *Murder at the Paris Fashion House* and could spare a few moments to leave a review, that would be hugely appreciated. Even a short review can make all the difference in encouraging a reader to discover my books for the first time. Thank you so much!

Join other readers in hearing about my writing (and life) experiences, and other bonus content.

www.nancywarren.com/newsletter

You can also connect with me via my private Facebook Group. It's a lot of fun.

www.facebook.com/groups/NancyWarrenKnitwits

Until next time, Happy Reading,

Nancy

www.nancywarrenauthor.com

facebook.com/AuthorNancyWarren
x.com/nancywarren1
instagram.com/nancywarrenauthor

Printed in Great Britain
by Amazon